PARADISE VALLEY
THE WILD AUSTRALIA STORIES 8

JENNIFER SCOULLAR

PILYARA PRESS

Version 1.0
Print: ISBN 978-0-6483089-6-6

Pilyara Press
Melbourne

ALSO BY JENNIFER SCOULLAR

THE WILD AUSTRALIA STORIES

Brumby's Run

Currawong Creek

Billabong Bend

Turtle Reef

Journey's End

Wasp Season

The Mallee Girl

THE TASMANIAN TALES

Fortune's Son

The Lost Valley

The Memory Tree

To the Australian Conservation Foundation

CHAPTER 1

Del Fisher sipped champagne and waited. And the longer she waited, the more her hope slipped away. She pushed aside the bowl of half-eaten chocolate-dipped strawberries. When Nick had invited her over for a special dinner, she'd been so sure. Everything pointed to him popping the question tonight: a bottle of Moët & Chandon, her favourite lobster salad, the soft strains of Beethoven's 'Moonlight Sonata' sounding from inside the cottage. Stars in the night sky shone so large and low she might have touched them. Had there ever been a more romantic evening?

But so far, she'd been mistaken. Over dinner Nick hadn't talked of love. He'd talked of a looming union dispute and his father's plans to expand the Mount Morton mine. He'd asked about the article coming out the next day in the local paper – the last in a series Del was writing on prominent local families.

'Have you unearthed some scandalous skeleton in our family closet?' Nick had teased. 'Is that why you're shooting through on me?'

'Honey, I'm not shooting through,' she said. 'Sydney is only three hours away.'

'More like four. And when you're on the trail of a juicy story, will you still have time for me?'

That wasn't fair. Nick frequently spent time away on family business and she'd never complained. The twinkle in Nick's green eyes said he wasn't serious, but Del was in no mood for jokes. Soon she'd be taking up a position on the investigative reporting staff at the *Sydney Morning Herald*. It was a fabulous opportunity, but it would mean a long-distance romance. Del would miss Nick terribly. She'd feel much better, much more secure in their relationship, if they became engaged before she left.

Del caught her reflection in the crystal bowl on the table filled with floating tea light candles. Her normally straight blonde hair framed her face in soft curls. Hazel eyes gazed from behind dark mascara-tipped lashes, and sapphire earrings flashed against her olive skin. She'd even worn lipstick, which she hardly ever did outside of work. But it seemed Nick hadn't noticed her extra effort to look good.

He finished the last lobster tail and wiped his chin with a linen napkin. 'That was delicious, if I do say so myself.'

Del had managed a tight smile as he served her a bowl of chocolate-dipped strawberries with mascarpone cream. She was too tense to enjoy the dessert.

'It's not like you to leave chocky strawberries,' said Nick, now noticing her unfinished bowl.

'I don't seem to have much appetite,' she said. 'Tired, that's all.'

'Well then, sweetheart, you just sit back, relax and let me clear the table.'

Del reached for his arm. 'Can't that wait?'

But Nick was already collecting plates and crockery, balancing dessert bowls in the crook of his elbow like an expert waiter. He disappeared inside the cottage.

Del topped up her glass and sagged back in the chair. Perhaps she should make some excuse and go home.

As Nick emerged from the house, an owl hooted from a nearby tree. He went to the porch rail and peered into the moonlit gardens, looking suddenly mysterious – a shadowy silhouette of a man. Tall, lean and straight-backed. Sandy-red hair luminous in the pale porch lights. His chiselled profile sent a familiar shiver of desire through her. Nick had no right to be so handsome.

Of course, that wasn't the main reason why she loved him. She loved him for his intelligence and kindness and integrity. For his respect and his commitment to his family, even when they made things hard for him. Although she did wish that he'd stand up to his father more. Nick had put Carson on a pedestal that she wasn't sure the man deserved. But Nick's good qualities far outweighed his few faults. They were a perfect match. She was serious and he made her laugh. She obsessed over her career, and he reminded her that there was more to life than work. He rang her every day, made the best coffee ever and had perfect timing when it came to thoughtful gestures. Nick had a way of always making her feel special. Well, almost always. Not tonight.

What on earth was he doing now? Fussing about the antique jardinières ranged along the slate verandah. Pulling the odd weed from the rainbow plantings of hyacinths, anemones and early daffodils.

'Have a look,' he called. 'A triple bloom. Very rare.'

'I'll pass,' said Del.

'Oh, come on, sweetheart. You'll be impressed, I promise.'

Del breathed a small sigh, put down her champagne flute and joined him. A giant tulip grew in the centre of the pot, holding its head high above its modest companions, putting them all to shame. She had to admit it. The flower was spectacular.

Del took a closer look. The bright blue tulip, shaded with orange, seemed to glow with an inner fire. The colours reminded her of an azure kingfisher, her favourite bird. And then she recalled something her mother had once told her. There's no such thing as a blue tulip.

Nick lightly stroked her hair, his touch electric. 'Pick it.'

Del brushed the smooth flower with her fingertips, then plucked it from the pot by its crystal stem. Nestled within the translucent petals was a ring.

Nick extracted the jewelled band and went down on one knee. 'Marry me,' he said, his voice thick with emotion.

3

Del didn't – couldn't – speak. She didn't have to. Her eyes said yes. Nick slipped the ring on her finger, and they sealed their betrothal with a kiss. She closed her eyes and relaxed into Nick's arms. This was, without doubt, the happiest moment she'd ever known. A bright future lay ahead of them, a future filled with joy and love. Life didn't get any better than this.

CHAPTER 2

Del climbed from Nick's bed, basking in the warm afterglow of dawn lovemaking. He reached out and murmured her name, eyes still closed. Del kissed him, whispering for him to go back to sleep. She wanted to get home – to shower and change. To properly process the events of last night. She couldn't do that here. Nick was way too much of a distraction. After work she'd head straight back to Westbrook so they could announce their engagement to his parents. It would be a magical Saturday night – a true celebration.

Del dressed and tiptoed from the cottage, relieved to have a reasonably clear head after all the celebratory glasses of champagne. *Don't count your chickens*, she told herself. Hangovers could kick in later. She glanced skywards as she hurried to her car. The day should be brightening, but a cold front had moved in overnight, bringing dark clouds and driving rain. Del turned on her car's headlights, crossing the Red River bridge and splashing through occasional patches of water lying over the road. Hard to believe that last night's clear skies had changed so quickly.

Del yawned, feeling wearier than she'd realised. She should have taken the day off. She should have fallen back to sleep with Nick, cradled in the protective circle of his arms. So what if she hadn't written the 'Dear Daisy' agony aunt answers for Monday's edition of the *Winga Gazette*? So what if she hadn't checked the Shaw family feature for typos that might have crept in? Del switched the windscreen wipers to high and dodged an overflowing pothole. She yawned again, her eyes growing heavy. When she got home she'd catch a few winks.

During the week Del stayed at the historic Vines Guesthouse on Main Street. She parked and ran through the rain to her private door behind the rose arbour. Del had been drawn to the place by its name. She'd helped her father plant a small vineyard back at the farm, before he became too ill to tend to it.

Del rented a sitting room cum office, a little galley kitchen, and a light-filled bedroom complete with an ensuite and a huge four-poster bed. The arrangement suited her well. She didn't have to cook or clean; Vera Bennett, the proprietor, was generally on hand to provide meals when Del wasn't at Nick's. Unfortunately, she was also on hand to offer opinions and advice about Del's journalistic choices: 'You should've interviewed Joan Hammond for that piece on the flower show. She knows what goes on behind the scenes, my word she does,' or 'You shouldn't have been so hard on Harry Blunt. He's a top mechanic and didn't know those parts were stolen, I'm sure of it,' and 'Why not do an article on my sister? Mary's making a go of selling her pottery online. I'm sure your readers would be interested.'

At least Vera's scrumptious cooking made up for her interfering ways. Nobody, except perhaps Del's own mother, could rival Vera's prowess in the kitchen. Her eggs Benedict with homemade sourdough muffins were to die for.

Del tossed her overnight bag in a corner of the room, flopped down on the bed and took out her earrings. Dammit; she'd lost one of them. No matter – it was probably at Nick's. She'd find it tonight.

She wanted to call her best friend, Kim Khan, and tell her the exciting news, but it was still too early in the day. A kaleidoscope of questions tumbled round her head. When would she and Nick marry? Where would they marry? What would her mother say when she knew? How would they stop Nick's father from taking over the wedding plans? What did their future hold? And as Del pondered these unanswerable questions, she fell asleep.

Del shook water from her umbrella as she entered the *Winga Gazette* office. She'd woken without enough time to shower, change and get to work by nine. Del hated being late. And despite the umbrella, she'd been soaked through during the short walk from the Vines at the other end of Main Street. Wild winds drove the rain sideways. She should have taken the car.

Del dumped the dripping brolly in the stand by the door and smoothed her hair a little self-consciously. She hadn't expected that being engaged would make her feel very different, but it did. It was a rite of passage after all, and she felt more sophisticated, more mature – as if at twenty-eight years old she'd finally grown up.

Del couldn't resist extending her left arm a fraction and spreading her long, slim fingers to make the ring more noticeable. An unnecessary ploy, surely. The antique engagement band shone like a tiny sunrise on her finger, radiating a luminous fire in every direction. A halo of sapphires framed the brilliant centre diamond, gathering and mirroring the light, all set in 22 carat gold. How could anyone fail to notice it?

So, it was both surprising and disappointing when her entrance didn't receive the anticipated response. Debbie, the receptionist, ignored Del's cheery 'Good morning' and turned her attention to answering the phone. Not even a nod of acknowledgement. How odd!

Del passed through to the newsroom. Celia Bloom, her boss and the *Gazette*'s editor-in-chief, always swore that country newspapers were the beating heart of their communities. She was right, and for three years Del had thrived on the warmth and energy of this place.

But recently, she'd found that it wasn't enough. She longed for the larger stage that Sydney would offer. No more covering local council meetings and agricultural shows. No more inventing horoscopes and doling out romantic advice in the 'Dear Daisy' column. She was an investigative journalist, not a hack, and she'd proved it by breaking some important stories. Maybe she'd stepped on some toes along the way, ruffled some feathers, but that couldn't be helped. You had to be tough to reach the top in this game. And when the inevitable complaints rolled in, Celia always backed her, often saying, 'So you hurt a few feelings. It was worth it to get the scoop.'

And Del had plenty of scoops under her belt – not an easy thing considering the limited circulation and resources of the *Winga Gazette*, a paper that only published four days a week. She'd followed up on rumours of cannabis plantations in Yenga National Park and her investigation had led to a major drug bust. A reader tip-off helped her expose a native bird smuggling ring. And after a spate of unexplained fish deaths, Del had uncovered the widespread, illegal dumping of chemicals along local waterways. This last story had garnered national media attention, led to a NSW government inquiry and resulted in some high-profile convictions. It's also what had led to an offer from the *Sydney Morning Herald* for Del to join their reporting team. She couldn't wait.

In the meantime, she had another two months left at the *Gazette* to fulfil her contract. Del planned to enjoy these last weeks, marking time with safe stories and, yes, arousing a little jealousy by her engagement to the most eligible bachelor in the district. Well, why not? There was nothing wrong with savouring some well-earned envy.

That was how Del had thought it would go. But looking around the small newsroom, she knew something was up. As a rule, it was always a hive of activity – a dozen people typing away at their desks, talking into headsets and waving sheafs of paper. People heading to the tearoom for coffee, stopping on the way to bounce ideas around with colleagues or to share a funny story – there was never any shortage of those in a small town.

But today was different. Nobody was roaming around the newsroom, chatting or laughing. All were diligently glued to their desks; the usual buzz of voices reduced to a steady murmur. Many of the staff seemed to be fielding phone calls, which usually happened when the *Gazette* had published something controversial. What might that be, she wondered? Del hadn't read the latest edition yet. She hadn't even had time to check out her feature article on the Shaw family. Nick's father, Carson Shaw, was the popular mayor of Central Ranges. He was also its most prominent businessman, being the CEO of Westcorp Mining and Pastoral, a multi-million-dollar corporation.

The council district encompassed towns from Winga in the south, right up to the rugged forests and national parks of the Great Escarpment. Del's article focused on the Shaws' historic ties to the region and their development of coal mines that had provided families with jobs and prosperity for more than a hundred years. There was some local opposition brewing regarding Westcorp's planned mine expansion in the northwest. Del hoped that her article might help to resolve it, as it emphasised the valuable contribution that Carson Shaw had made to the district.

She wandered around the dozen or so desks, flashing her ring, trying to catch someone's eye, but everyone's heads remained firmly down. It was almost like people were deliberately ignoring her. Perplexed, Del headed for Celia's glass-partitioned office, grabbing a copy of the latest *Gazette* from a pile as she passed.

She breezed into her boss's office. Celia was a slim, dark-haired woman of about fifty, although she didn't look or act her age. As usual, she was overdressed: cream linen pants, a satin camisole, a leopard print jacket and a necklace of chunky wooden beads. Somehow she pulled it off.

Celia was on the phone, talking low and fast, and looking grim as she sat behind her large oak desk She didn't even seem to notice Del come in. What was wrong with people today? Del waited impatiently, staring through the window. A sudden squall tossed the old camelia tree outside, stripping its pink petals. Rain drummed louder on the tin roof, causing Celia to raise her voice.

'Marty, you're the lawyer. Truth is a defence. The woman's on the record.' Celia looked up, saw Del and offered a strained smile. 'Marty, I'll call you back.'

'Trouble?' Del asked, not really interested. With only a few weeks left at the paper, she did not intend to get involved with one of Celia's dramas. She extended her left hand. This time she was determined not to be ignored.

Celia saw the ring and went white. 'Nick's?'

Del rolled her eyes. 'It's an engagement ring. Who else would I be marrying?'

Celia stared at the ring and ran her tongue over her crimson lips. She always wore such outrageous lipstick. Bright colours didn't suit middle-aged women, even ones like Celia who'd been born with natural style.

Del pulled her hand back, more puzzled than irritated now. 'Are you going to congratulate me or not?'

Celia heaved a big sigh and pointed to the newspaper tucked under Del's arm. 'Have you read your feature?'

'Not yet.' Del tossed the *Gazette* onto Celia's desk. 'I had a late night, you know, getting engaged to the man I love? Drinking French champagne and planning our future? Activities that were a tad more important than proofreading.' She'd run out of patience. 'Why aren't you happy for me? I thought we were friends.'

'Sit down,' said Celia, indicating a chair across from her. 'Read the article.'

'Why?' Del asked in confusion. 'I wrote it. I know what's in it.'

'Do you?' Celia's expression was almost tender as she delivered that cryptic remark. 'Humour me, Del. Read the article.'

CHAPTER 3

D el sat in the chair, unfolded the newspaper, and turned to the double-page centrespread where Celia ran the main features. *What the hell?* Her original headline had been replaced by the outrageous 'Coal King has Feet of Clay'. Celia often made alterations to copy, but this was ridiculous. Del had gone out of her way to put a positive spin on everything to do with Nick's family. It wasn't hard; Carson Shaw was a paragon of virtue. He gave generously to charity. He ran apprenticeship programs for disadvantaged young people. He knew half of his constituents by name. Del had duly reported these things. Nothing in her article justified such a salacious header.

There were the photos she'd picked. The poignant Shaw family snap of Carson as a young man standing alongside his older brother, Bobby, and their parents. Those three had died in a shocking car accident a month after the photograph was taken, leaving Carson as the only survivor. There was the recent shot of Carson looking regal in the mayoral robe and chains, and there was an aerial shot of the Mount Morton mine – and a photo that Del didn't recognise, the picture of a pretty blonde woman, late twenties or thereabouts, with huge hoop earrings and sad eyes. The caption read, 'Stacey Turner, former Central Ranges Environment Officer'. Del had never heard of her. So, why did her picture accompany the article? She shot her boss a questioning glance.

'Read,' said a stony-faced Celia.

Del scanned the familiar text. An introduction to the Shaws' one-hundred-and-fifty-year connection to the area and the phenomenal growth of their mining and pastoral holdings, just as she'd written it. The article continued with the tragic accident that had left Carson sole heir to a fortune, and it recounted his marriage to Natalie Astor, Nick's mother and daughter of a former NSW premier. So far all was in order.

But when Del read the paragraph about Carson's mayoral achievements, alarm bells sounded. She *had* written that Carson was elected to his current term with over eighty per cent of the popular vote. She *had not* written that the woman in the photograph, Stacey Turner, had an intimate relationship with Carson when she worked at the council last year – a relationship initiated by Carson, who was more than thirty years her senior.

Worse was to come as Del read on. When Carson ended the affair, Stacey alleged that he made life so difficult for her that she had to resign. 'Our relationship was defined by a significant power imbalance and was, at times, abusive,' Stacey was quoted. 'Mayor Shaw took advantage of me in every way and derailed my career. It's time I spoke up. He's not the saint he's made out to be.'

Del felt sick. Blood rushed in her ears and her heart pounded out of control. 'I didn't write this,' she stammered, thrusting the paper forward to show her boss and pointing to the offending paragraphs.

'No,' said Celia, her tone almost apologetic – almost. 'I did.'

'You?' Del tried to make sense of what she was hearing. 'But it's my article, my by-line. What do you think Nick will say when he reads it? You have to ring him right now and tell him it wasn't me.' Del took her phone from her pocket and found Nick's number.

Celia got up, locked her office door, and sat back down. 'You must admit, it's quite a story. And the credit's all yours.'

Del pushed her phone across the desk, adamant. 'Ring him.'

'No.' Celia pushed the phone away.

'What do you mean, no?' said Del, beginning to panic How could her boss betray her like this? 'I can't let this stand. It will devastate Nick and his whole family.' She frowned and flicked her fingers at the article. 'And besides, I'm engaged to Carson's son. No one in their right mind would believe that I wrote this.'

'Are you sure?' Celia leaned back in her chair and steepled her fingers. 'You're famous for chasing headlines and riding roughshod over reputations. The golden girl who always gets the scoop, right? It's why the *Sydney Morning Herald* wants you. How often have you said that getting the story is all that matters?' She gestured to the newsroom beyond her office's glass walls, to Del's colleagues who were wisely keeping their heads down. 'They've all heard you.'

'Who cares what they've heard? I didn't write this.'

'That might be hard to prove. Your reporting has doubled our circulation and advertising dollars, but we've also never had so many complaints.'

Del pursed her lips. True – she'd made some enemies along the way, attracted a few trolls. It was why she'd closed her Twitter account, and why she took a steadying breath before diving into her other social media accounts each morning.

Celia gave her a searching look. 'You've been variously described as heartless, insensitive, duplicitous, pushy . . .'

'Shut up!' yelled Del, confusion turning to outrage. 'Why are you doing this?'

'Suffice to say it's an important story – one that I knew you'd never agree to write.'

Del stood, speechless, twisting the engagement ring around and around her finger.

Celia seemed to mistake Del's silence for a change of heart. 'Think about it,' she said in a wheedling tone. 'Taking down the King of Coal is right up your alley. Your new employer will be super impressed.'

The hard-headed newshound in Del had to admit that Celia was right about one thing; this was exactly the sort of story she'd usually be itching to write. *If* Carson wasn't soon to become her father-in-law. *If* it wouldn't break Nick's heart. He was devoted to his father, and it would take more than some allegations from a disgruntled former employee to sway his loyalty – or hers.

Del paced the room. She had to pull herself together, exercise some damage control and try to understand why Celia had acted in such an extraordinary way.

'Is this woman genuine?' asked Del as she stopped pacing.

'There's a short phone video of her having sex with Carson. I've seen it for myself. Only twenty seconds long, but it proves she's not lying. Stacey's since got cold feet and doesn't want to show it to anyone else.'

'Well, without another source, it's just her word against his.' Although Del knew full well that such allegations, true or not, could prompt more women to come forward. 'What does Carson have to say about it?'

Celia shrugged. 'I didn't ask. First thing our mayor will know of this breaking scandal is when he reads the paper today.'

'What!' It was standard practice to seek statements from people prior to publishing allegations against them – not to blindside them like this. Celia had thrown every convention of ethical journalism out the window.

'Carson should be grateful the article didn't go further,' said Celia. 'A government spokesperson has confirmed that Carson is a person of interest in a confidential NSW crime and corruption investigation. That's all we have so far.'

'We?' Del gave an angry snort. 'There is no *we*. For some reason, you decided to publish this half-baked story and make me the fall guy. Well, it ends now.' She shoved her phone back across the desk. 'Ring Nick and tell him you got it wrong. Tell him this was all your idea, and that the paper will issue an apology and a full retraction.'

Celia glanced at the phone, then took a packet of cigarettes from her desk drawer, lighting up with shaky fingers. In the three years that Del had worked for the *Gazette*, she'd never seen her boss smoke.

Celia took a drag deep into her lungs as the rain on the roof hammered. 'I've been in this game for two decades, Del, and you're the finest investigative journalist I've ever seen. Try to set Nick aside for a moment and tell me – what does your instinct tell you about this story?'

Del stared at Celia, thrown by the question. It sneaked beneath her anger and outrage, causing her to momentarily take an objective view. What did her instinct say? It said that this could be a very big story indeed.

CHAPTER 4

Nick raised the kitchen blind, surprised to see the gardens shrouded in sheets of rain. He opened the fridge and poured himself a pineapple juice, thinking of the previous evening, thinking of Del's delight when she found the ring in the crystal tulip, and of his own delight when she let him slip it on her finger. This was the start of an exciting new chapter in their lives, a consolidation and strengthening of their love. He'd been debating when to pop the question for a while, and last night had been the perfect time. They'd weather the challenge of a long-distance relationship best with this commitment in place

He sculled the glass of juice and turned on the espresso machine, wishing he hadn't drunk quite so much bubbly the previous night. The kernel of a headache was germinating in his skull. Nick sat at the kitchen bench, waited for the coffee to brew and turned on his laptop to read Del's feature.

He logged on to the *Gazette*'s latest online edition and started reading. He read the lengthy piece twice, and then a third time. Shaking his head. Disbelieving. The article accused his father of being a philanderer. There'd clearly been some sort of mistake. The offending paragraphs must relate to somebody else and, due to some colossal editing error, they'd found their way into the Shaw family feature. It couldn't be Del's fault. He knew how she worked – she was meticulous, researching stories with the rigorous eye of a scholar crossed with an ace private detective. Checking and rechecking her facts and sources. Agonising over each word she wrote. She'd be absolutely mortified when she read it.

The ache in his temple increased a few notches. Heads must roll over this cock-up. He needed to talk to Del, and fast. Nick snatched his mobile just as it rang. Dammit – Dad. He answered, holding the phone away from his ear as the tirade began.

'Your girlfriend's really done it this time! First, she pries into everyone's lives with that ridiculous chemical-dumping story. A storm in a teacup that led to charges against Scotty next door. Remember? Caused him and a lot of other decent people a truckload of trouble, but apparently it wasn't enough. She needed more publicity, wanted to make a bigger splash. So she goes after me. And to think I cooperated with an interview. Sweet as pie she was, too. Well, at least you discovered what a snake in the grass she was before you took things any further. She won't have her job or two cents to rub together by the time I've finished with her.'

Nick cleared his throat. This did not seem to be the best time to announce their engagement. 'Dad, calm down. It's some sort of mistake. I'll talk to Del and sort it out.'

'You'll do no such thing,' Carson's voice dripped with fury. 'My lawyer's already on the job. Heaven knows how Celia let such an outrage slip through. She's usually a competent enough newspaper editor. No doubt your girlfriend went out of her way to conceal her treacherous plan.'

'Why would Del want to damage our family?'

'I already told you – for the publicity. Don't be naive, son. That woman saw an opportunity to raise her profile as a reporter, so she took it. And to hell with you and the rest of us.'

'That makes no sense. Del wouldn't just make stuff up … ' said Nick, battling confusion.

Carson sputtered into the phone, too angry at first to string words together. 'Are you saying you believe her filthy lies?'

'No … No, of course not.' The phone beeped. Call waiting showed a second incoming call – Del.

Carson must have guessed. 'Don't you dare answer that!'

Nick took Del's call. She sounded frantic, barely making any sense.

'Yes, of course I've read it,' said Nick. 'Along with half the population of the Central Ranges, including my father. No, don't come here —' he began, but Del had already hung up.

Nick lived in Westbrook's historic farm manager's cottage, lovingly renovated and extended by his mother, Natalie. His parents lived in the property's main house. Built circa 1840, that magnificent homestead stood on a rise, five hundred metres to the north of the cottage, overlooking Nick's place. They shared a driveway, so there was every chance that Carson would see Del's car arrive and come storming over before Nick had a chance to clarify things.

He tried calling Del back. She didn't pick up. He texted her. No response. She must already be on her way. Nick swore, fixed himself a double-shot espresso and gulped it down. The scalding coffee burned his throat, but he was in too much of a hurry to care. He pulled on jeans and a T-shirt, grateful for the caffeine hit that was chasing away his hangover. Then he grabbed a coat and ran to his car. It would take twenty minutes for Del to drive to Westbrook from Winga. He had time to head her off.

Del almost skittled a pedestrian as she tore out of town, windscreen wipers working overtime. She accelerated past a stop sign, jets of water streaming under the tyres. A car beeped at her. *Bloody idiot.* Del beeped back, nerves stretched tight as a drum. If she didn't speak to Nick in person soon, she'd burst.

What was it with this rain? It pelted down so hard that she could barely see the road ahead of her. Del almost missed the Westbrook turn-off. Water no longer lay across the way in shallow puddles; it inundated broad stretches of the narrow road. Despite the urgency of her mission to see Nick, she had the sense to slow down.

A fire-engine-red ute sped up behind her, just as a large dog loomed out of the rain to cross the road ahead. Del braked, causing the ute to honk loudly and make a reckless attempt to overtake. She pressed the horn, trying to warn the other driver of the animal in the middle of the road. Too late – the ute raced past. The front-seat passenger gave her the finger, then the ute's tail-lights vanished into the gloom.

Where was the dog? She told herself it was probably fine, that it had probably leaped out of the way in time. But as her car gathered speed, Del saw a dark, sodden heap on the verge of the road. She stopped the car. What to do? She desperately wanted to keep going. After all, she hadn't hit the dog. This wasn't her problem. For all she knew, it was dead already.

Just as she'd convinced herself to continue on her way to West-brook, the dog moved. It struggled to its feet, standing briefly on three legs before collapsing. Dammit, she couldn't leave it like that. Swearing beneath her breath, Del got out of the car and ran to the injured animal. The dog trembled and briefly raised its head as she approached. Good grief, it was even larger than she'd thought. At least it had a collar; maybe the owner's phone number was on a tag or something.

She gingerly reached out to check, but not only was the collar bare, but it also seemed too small for the dog's neck. It dug into the skin, as if it had been put on the dog as a small puppy and hadn't been adjusted as it grew. And she couldn't help noticing how thin the dog was – hollow-flanked, with each rib showing. Blood streaked its shaggy grey coat, mixing with the rain in pink puddles on the road-side gravel. One front leg lay at an impossible angle. Fuck. She'd have to get it into the car somehow. God knows how. It was wounded and in pain. Probably in shock, too. She'd be lucky not to be bitten.

The rain redoubled its efforts to drown her as Del ran back to fetch the car. She parked it close beside the dog, then pulled a picnic rug from the boot. 'Easy, boy.' The dog cocked an ear towards her and managed a few weak thumps of its straggly tail. She tossed the blanket over it, tucking it as firmly around the dog's head as she could. Then she took a deep breath and clumsily scooped the animal into her arms.

It uttered an agonised, ear-splitting shriek. Del screamed too, in fright, almost dropping her sodden, blood-stained burden. With a grunt she shoved the dog onto the back seat and slammed the door shut.

Now to ring Nick and explain why she'd been held up. Heaven knows what he was thinking. Del got behind the wheel, relieved to be out of the deluge. In her haste to make the call, she fumbled and dropped the phone between the driver's seat and the centre console. It rang, but she couldn't quite reach it to answer. It took a few precious minutes and the tip of her umbrella to finally retrieve the phone.

The missed call was from Nick. But when she tried to call him back, her phone had no service. It had lost its last bar. Reception was notoriously bad along this stretch of road. She'd just have to keep driving to Westbrook and go to the vet in Winga after talking to Nick. If the dog died in the meantime, too bad. After all, it wasn't her responsibility. She hadn't hit the bloody thing.

Del started the car, trying to ignore the pitiful whimpers coming from the back seat. After driving a few hundred metres, she pulled over. It was no use. Damn that dog! Uttering a string of curses, she swung the wheel hard and headed back towards town.

CHAPTER 5

E ven with the windscreen wipers on full blast, Nick could barely
see five metres ahead of him. Lashing rain hemmed him in.
Water flooded the way in low sections, and he couldn't judge its
depth. But Nick powered through, feeling reckless, his adrenaline up.

The words of Del's article burned in his brain. He couldn't imagine
the sort of damage such a vile public slur would do to his father's
reputation. And not just to his father. The reputation of the entire
Shaw family was tainted. Their business would inevitably suffer. *Mud
sticks*, he thought, *however unfair that is*. And what about his mother,
Natalie? She was a fragile person at the best of times, having lived
with depression for many years. An incident like this was more than
enough to worsen her mental health.

One of Nick's most vivid childhood memories was of her being
taken from the house by paramedics. She'd called for him as they led
her away. Dad had held his shoulder. 'Mummy's not feeling well. She
needs a rest – somewhere quiet,' he'd said, trying to comfort his
sobbing eight-year-old son. 'She'll be home soon.'

Nick had squirmed from his arms and climbed after his mother
into the back of the ambulance. She'd clung to him, weeping into his
hair, saying over and over that she didn't want to leave him. As a child,

he couldn't understand. Mum didn't look sick, and for a long time he blamed his father for sending her away.

As he grew older, Nick came to realise that Natalie was indeed ill. At times she seemed happy – an engaged mother and supportive wife. But at other times she'd lock herself away in the guest suite, barely eating and silent for weeks on end. A string of doctors would arrive, each – according to Carson – more useless than the previous one. Their ministrations seemed to accomplish nothing more than giving Natalie an addiction to prescription drugs.

The one treatment that seemed to help was admission to the Mayfair Clinic, an exclusive private hospital on Sydney's North Shore. Carson was so grateful for the fine work they did there that he donated millions to the facility. Although often away for weeks at a time, Nick's mother would be more like her old self when she returned. Nick and Carson never knew how long her recovery would last, so they always savoured that special time with her. Mum had only recently returned from the hospital again and was in better spirits than she'd been in years. Nick dreaded to think what effect that disgusting article would have on his mother's mental health. Hopefully, Dad would be able to hide it from her until they had a satisfactory explanation.

Nick tried to keep a growing kernel of anger at bay. He hadn't yet heard Del's side of the story, but could she be wholly innocent? It was up to her to double and triple check her copy. And to let such a catastrophic editorial error slip through? It was unforgivable. Nick powered through low-lying water that came up to his wheel rims, too distracted to notice. He was struggling with his feelings – torn between loyalty to his family and faith in Del. He mustn't rush to judgement. Carson would do enough of that for both of them.

Ted Barlow's shearing sheds appeared through the rain on Nick's right. Ted produced award-winning ultrafine fleece. Some said his Merinos grew the best wool clip in Australia. A crew had shorn his whole mob last week, all three thousand of them. Bad timing. With a cold snap and this deluge, Ted would lose more than a few head to hypothermia.

The road curved down towards the fertile flats. Red River would be running high, maybe overflowing its banks, but Nick knew the road. He'd get through, he had to. What about Del? He sped up, hoping to waylay her before she hit the worst of the water. His need to see her was like a physical pain in his chest.

Damn this weather! It was hard to get his bearings in a world turned to featureless grey. The car skidded. Had he reached the bridge? Nick wrestled with the wheel for a moment before the tyres found traction. A worm of worry squirmed in his stomach – and then it happened. The Jeep stalled. He tried the key again and again, but the engine wouldn't turn over. Nick fought rising panic as he felt the car being buoyed by rising water – inexorably slipping sideways.

What a fool. Carson had drilled the dangers of flooded roads into Nick from childhood. 'Never drive through water, son. A 4WD can be moved by water only forty-five centimetres deep. If it's flooded, forget it. Deciding to keep going could be the last decision you ever make.'

Carson should know. Twenty-five years ago, his father, mining magnate Hugo Shaw, had attempted to drive through a flash flood at Manning with his wife and two sons in the car. Carson alone had survived, although his older brother, Bobby, hung on in a coma for months. It was the tragedy that had defined their family.

A wave of shame hit Nick as the car slid faster and he realised where he was – on the bridge and skating towards the edge. He'd seen Red River in flood; plunging into that surging torrent was a terrifying prospect, and the bridge had no safety rail. He tried to get out of the car, but the water was much deeper than he thought. Its weight against the vehicle made opening the door impossible. His breath came in ragged spurts. Had he learned nothing from the grief his father had endured all these years? Was he bound to repeat his grand-father's folly?

Think, Nick told himself. He wished he'd listened more carefully to Carson. His advice had extended further than telling his son to never drive through water – although that was always the main gist of the lectures. Too late now. What else? Carson's words came rushing back, 'If you do get caught in the water, take off your seatbelt and roll down your windows fast. They'll work after the car stalls, but not once water reaches the bottom of them. Its pressure forces the window against the frame, making it impossible to move, even with a manual crank.'

Nick opened the window.

'Then grab your phone and get the hell out of there!'

Nick was a big man. It took a terrifying few minutes for him to drag himself through the narrow opening.

And the Jeep slid over the edge.

A rush of freezing water grabbed him, stealing the air from his lungs and trying to wash him away. Yet Carson's voice in his head helped Nick keep his cool. 'Get to the roof.'

Pain erupted in his left shoulder as a passing tree branch smashed into it, tearing his shirt to shreds and leaving the arm useless. He saved himself by clutching the roof rack with his right hand and clinging on for grim death. Centimetre by agonising centimetre, Nick hauled himself higher until at last he could clamber on top of the car.

He sat and wedged his legs beneath the rails. The storm could not drown out the sound of his pounding heart. Nick shivered and gulped deep lungfuls of air. That was a close call. And he wasn't out of the woods yet. The force of the flood had pinned the Jeep against the bridge, preventing it from being flipped or carried away – for now. But as he watched, a timber stanchion buckled and cracked. If the bridge failed, he'd be lost.

Nick groped for the phone in his pocket, thankful it still worked after its icy dip. Shit – no reception. His frozen fingers fumbled. He lost his grip, and the phone plunged into the murky river below. Great. Just great. A lull in the rain allowed Nick a clearer view of his surroundings. Amazing, how swiftly the waters had risen. The two-metre flood-marker post was almost submerged. And then he saw something else – something that turned his stomach. Another vehicle had fallen victim to the flood. Thank God it wasn't blue. Del's car was blue.

The red ute lay almost fully submerged in the swollen river only metres away. Its bonnet faced his own car, which meant the ute had probably been travelling in the opposite direction when it was swept off the road. The direction Del would be taking. Nick tried to gulp down air, but his throat seemed to have closed up. The driver's window of the ute was shattered, and a blue-sleeved arm had snaked through the jagged hole. It moved with the current in a semblance of life, looking eerily like it was waving. That could have been Del.

A shaft of shame hit him. A person had drowned, yet the first thing he'd felt was relief that it wasn't Del. He averted his eyes from the dead man and kept watch for her car instead. He'd have to warn her. Where was she, anyway? If she'd left Winga when she'd called, she should have reached the bridge by now.

Maybe the road was already impassable. He hoped so. She could easily miss him shouting and waving in this filthy weather. And what would a girl bred in the mountains know about driving on floodplains during a rainstorm? *Maybe more than I did*, Nick thought ruefully. Del wasn't the one stranded in the river.

He settled down to wait, gritting his teeth against the throbbing pain in his shoulder. Wondering how long it would be before someone found him. Thinking about the drowned car and the dead driver. Hoping that the bridge would hold.

CHAPTER 6

Del stood at the front counter of the Winga Veterinary Surgery, remonstrating with Dr Stringer, drawing curious glances from others in the waiting room.

'You don't *need* my details.' Del was sick of repeating herself. 'It's not my dog.'

'Yes, I understand that,' said the vet. 'He's emaciated – probably a long-term stray. But he does need urgent surgery.'

'So?'

'So, I've given him pain relief, but I can't operate without someone taking responsibility for him. It's a little unorthodox, but I was wondering . . . Would you be willing to?'

'Would I be willing to what?'

'Take responsibility for the dog.'

'Can't you just ring the council ranger?'

'He's too badly injured for the pound, and no RSPCA inspectors are available to collect him.'

'That's not my problem.' Del wasn't really listening. Nick must be wondering where the hell she was. She rang him again. Why did it keep going to voicemail? She left a fourth message.

Dr Stringer gave an impatient shake of his head. 'If you don't make a decision, I'll have to put the dog down. Such a shame. He's just a half-grown pup.'

Del turned the full force of her anger and frustration on the man. 'I didn't rescue that mangy mutt, at tremendous personal cost I might add, just for you to kill it less than an hour later. If I wanted it dead, I'd have left it by the side of the road. It would have saved time.'

'So, you're saying—'

'I'm saying treat the bloody thing. You're a vet, aren't you? Then do your job.'

The man gave the young nurse a nod and she rushed off. 'I'll ring you,' he called as Del disappeared out the door.

Del slowed the car. An ancient man wearing a State Emergency Service uniform waved her over. She wound down her window.

'Road's closed,' he said. 'The river's burst its banks.'

'But I have to get through,' said Del. 'I absolutely must get to Westbrook.'

'The Shaw place?' He rubbed his chin thoughtfully while rain poured off his orange jacket and hood. 'Head back into town, take Nine Mile Road and cut across at the Blairgowan turn-off. It'll take you round the back way.'

'But that will take ages. Can't you let me through? Please, it's terribly important.'

'No can do, love. Some bloke's trapped in the floodwater between the bridge and his sinking car. He's in a bad way, apparently. There's a rescue underway. We keep telling folks not to drive through water, but do they listen?'

Del peered down the road through the rain. She'd reported on plenty of flood rescues. There seemed to be more than the usual number of emergency vehicles up ahead. And was that a police cordon?

'Why's there such a big turnout?' she asked, professional curiosity getting the better of her.

The man leaned in close and whispered in a conspiratorial way.

'Two cars went off that bridge. The other poor buggers didn't make it.' His eyes narrowed. 'Are you okay, love? Is that blood?'

Del looked down. The dog's blood was smeared all over her cream shirt. 'I'm fine,' she said, although she didn't feel fine.

The man looked doubtful.

'Don't worry. It's not my blood.' She was in too much of a hurry to explain.

'Well, if you're sure ... ' He straightened his back. 'Now, turn around, and thank your lucky stars I was here, or it might have been you in that river.'

Disappointed tears ran down her cheeks, mingling with the rain angling in through the open window. She tried one futile, final text to Nick, then reversed around and headed back towards Winga. She'd take the old man's advice and drive to Westbrook the long way.

Del wiped her eyes. The delay couldn't be helped, and she needed to calm down. But the shocking headline kept flashing in neon lights before her mind's eye. 'Coal King has Feet of Clay'. Del's foot grew heavier on the accelerator. The longer she delayed talking to Nick, the harder it might be to convince him that she didn't write that hateful story.

Del tried to put her fears aside and concentrate on the road ahead. Nick loved her. Once she had a chance to explain Celia's treachery, he'd understand.

When she returned to Winga, Del dropped by the guesthouse to change. She could hardly show up at Westbrook covered in blood, even if she was in a hurry to get there. The phone rang, making her heart leap with hope. But it wasn't Nick after all. It was Kim.

'Oh, it's only you,' Del said to her friend, unable to hide her disappointment.

'Good to hear your voice too.' But Kim's sarcasm was lost on Del, who simply told her what Celia had done.

'That bitch!' said Kim. 'Why on earth would she do that? Can't you sue or something?'

'Probably. But my immediate problem is damage control. I have to convince Nick that I'm not responsible for the allegations against his father. Look, I have to go. I'll keep you posted.'

Del put the phone down beside her laptop. She should check her work emails; there might be something from Celia. Del logged in, scrolled through the unimportant stuff, and then sucked in a quick breath. Not an email from Celia. An email from Frank Walker, the *Sydney Morning Herald*'s editor-in-chief himself, praising Del's feature article. In part, it read, *I presume this is the tip of the iceberg concerning the good Mayor Shaw? I'm tempted to put an investigative crew on it right now, but this is your story, Del. When you start here in a few weeks' time, I want you to head up the team and bring it home. BTW I love how you led with the positive stuff. Lulled the reader into a false sense of security and then – bam! Very effective writing.*

Good grief – what a vote of confidence! Utterly misguided, of course, but Del still felt an absurd burst of pride at such high praise from one of her journalistic heroes. She'd have to revise her plan to post immediate denials about the article all over social media. It would make Frank feel like a fool. First, she'd talk to Nick, and then she'd approach Frank privately and tell him the truth.

As she pulled on a clean shirt, she made the decision to call Carson. Up until now, she'd been too apprehensive to ring him. He had read the article and would understandably be furious. Del never knew quite what to make of Carson Shaw. He was polite and coolly friendly towards her, but always remote, as if he didn't want her to get close. After a two-hour, one-on-one interview with him for the feature, she still hadn't been able to get a handle on the man.

Did he like her? Del's gut told her no. He seemed suspicious of her, although she didn't know why. As far as she knew, Del had never done anything to offend him. *Until now*, she thought grimly as she washed and dried her hands. It would be hard to convince Carson in a brief phone call, but she needed to protest her innocence to somebody. And she might discover why Nick wasn't answering his phone. Del ran a comb through her wet hair, and dashed through the rain to her car.

Carson didn't take her call. He sent a text instead.

You treacherous bitch! Don't contact me or my son again. The next time I see you will be in court.

Del stood in the pouring rain, gazing longingly in the direction of Nick's cottage. She couldn't even see it through the downpour. The storm continued unabated as broad rivulets washed away the groomed gravel drive. Westbrook's imposing cast-iron gates were closed and when she keyed in the code, they didn't swing wide as usual. She tried three times, four times. It still wouldn't work. The gates were too tall to climb, and the high bluestone walls that flanked them were equally impregnable. The place was like a fortress. She rattled the metal bars and screamed at the storm.

'Nick . . . Nick, are you there? Let me in!'

The wind whipped the words away. Del closed her eyes, feeling dizzy and sick. Only that morning she'd driven out through those same gates, feeling on top of the world. Secure in Nick's love and commitment. And yet, by lunchtime?

Maybe Nick had rung Celia. No doubt she'd tell him that the hatchet job was Del's own work. Is that why Nick wasn't returning her calls? But he hadn't even heard her side of the story. If their love meant anything, it meant that she deserved a fair hearing.

'Don't take the good times for granted,' her mother had often said after Dad fell ill. 'Life can change in the blink of an eye.'

No, she refused to believe that her dream-come-true future could be ruined by the deranged actions of one malicious woman. Del gave the gates a final shake. The ding-dong of a text message caused her heart to surge with hope. But it wasn't Nick. It was the vet, reporting that the dog's operation had gone well.

Del hurled her mobile to the ground. Damn that dog! If she hadn't stopped for it, she'd have crossed the bridge before Red River over-flowed its banks. She'd have talked to Nick hours ago. As she bent to retrieve her phone, a flash of iridescent colour caught her eye. A tiny blue bird was being swept along the flooded gutter. She caught it just before it disappeared down the yawning stormwater drain. Oh no!

The tiny, drowned body of an azure kingfisher lay cradled in the palm of her hand.

Del had often looked for kingfishers around Winga but had never found one – until now.

'I used to see them in the bush along the river when I was a boy,' Nick had told her. 'But not any more. Not since they cleared the banks of snags and put the levees in upstream.'

The kingfishers were common around Berrimilla where she grew up. Her father had called them his lucky bluebirds. 'They know the best fishing holes. When I spot a bluebird, that's where I drop my line.' He loved to photograph them, and she kept a small album of those photos in her bedside drawer. As she gazed down at the bird, a wave of missing her father crashed in.

Fighting back tears, Del carried the little body to the car and gently wrapped it in some tissues. She'd bury it in the guesthouse garden, by the fishpond, so the kingfisher would always have food and water. Del took one last look at the locked gates, overwhelmed by a sense of loss. She wasn't generally a superstitious person, but finding the dead kingfisher seemed like a very, very bad omen.

CHAPTER 7

Nick opened his eyes and blinked at the brightly lit room. He was in a hospital. That much was clear from the stark white sheets, the gently beeping machines and the antiseptic smell. *Why* he was in a hospital was not so clear. He had the headache from hell, an aching shoulder and his left arm was in a cast. He racked his brain, trying to remember what had laid him so low, but his mind was blank. The last thing he could remember was driving back from the Mount Morton mine, where he'd been conducting an audit.

He tried sitting up, surprised at how weak and woozy he was. A dark-haired young nurse came in. She smiled brightly when she saw him.

'So, Nick, you decided to wake up. I'm Nurse Abi, and I'll be looking after you today.'

He found it hard to hear her through the ringing in his ears. She checked the chart at the end of the bed, then took his vitals.

'I'm thirsty.' His tongue seemed to be made of sandpaper. The nurse held up a cup and he sipped some water through a straw. 'What happened to me?'

'You broke your arm, fractured your collarbone and sustained a serious head trauma.'

He took a little while to process the information. 'How?'

Nurse Abi glanced at the door. 'Are you up for a visitor?'

So, Del had come. She'd be able to tell him what happened. How he longed to see her lovely face, longed to feel her slim tanned arms around him.

But it wasn't Del after all. It was his father, with a box of chocolates in one hand and a newspaper under his arm. Nick looked behind him, but he was on his own.

'Where's Mum?' Natalie was such a worrywart. It defied belief that she'd let Carson come visit him alone. Unless … 'Is she okay?' Carson's grim face was answer enough, and Nick countered, 'But Mum's been so well lately.'

'Yes, but we both know it doesn't take much to push her over the edge. And after Del published her wicked lies … '

Nick held up his hand. 'Whoa. What lies?'

Carson gave him a shrewd look. 'You don't remember?'

'I don't remember anything after I left Mount Morton. Did I have a car accident on the way home?'

'Mount Morton?' said Carson. 'You finished the audit there three weeks ago.'

'That makes no sense.' His head hurt and his brain was a mishmash of confusing thoughts.

'Looks like you've lost some time, son. Dr Chen warned that was possible after an injury like yours.'

'What happened?'

'Your car was washed off Red River bridge during the storm two days ago.' His father didn't hide the note of censure in his voice. 'You copped a nasty knock to the head and almost drowned.'

What! Nick burned with humiliation. How often had Carson told him not to drive through floodwater? And then there was Del. What did his father mean about her wicked lies? He racked his brain but came up with nothing.

Carson seemed to read his mind. He passed over the newspaper. 'See for yourself. The Shaw family feature article. Centrespread.'

It was a copy of the *Winga Gazette*. Nick turned to the middle pages. 'Coal King has Feet of Clay'. A strange headline. She'd promised the article would be little more than a puff piece. He read the first few paragraphs. Nothing problematic so far. He glanced at his father.

'Keep reading,' said Carson.

Nick went back to the article, words swimming before his eyes. That knock on the head must have been a doozy. He tried to focus. Hold on ... No, this wasn't possible. Nick ran his tongue over dry lips, reading and rereading the offending text. In a few short lines Del had destroyed his father's reputation. Carson's good name and everything he'd worked for, all torn down by a vicious libel.

Nick's head throbbed and he felt faint. 'Del didn't write this.'

'Oh, I assure you, she did.' Carson hit the paper with the back of his hand. 'It's right there in black and white. I've spoken to Celia at the *Gazette*, and she confirmed it. Del wrote that pack of lies to promote herself with the *Sydney Morning Herald*'s bigwigs. A nice juicy scandal to raise her profile. No matter that there's not a grain of truth in it.'

'Where's my phone?' said Nick. 'I have to speak to her.'

'I did one better than that,' said Carson. 'I confronted her. That bitch fessed up, bold as brass. Thought it was funny, the way she'd tricked us all. Well, she'll be laughing on the other side of her face once my lawyers are through with her.'

A tide of dizziness washed in, muddling Nick's mind and scattering his thoughts. He struggled to concentrate. 'If it's all the same, Dad, I need to speak to Del myself.'

Carson tried and failed to mask the anger on his face. 'That might be a problem, son. Your phone is at the bottom of the river.'

Damn it. Nick winced as he sat up higher in the bed. Each inch of his body hurt. It felt like he'd been run over by a truck.

'Then I'll use your phone.' Nick held out a shaky hand.

Carson stepped away from the bed. 'It's never a good idea to make important calls when you're upset.'

Nick had started to argue when Nurse Abi returned and moved the *Gazette* to the bedside table. 'I'm sorry, Mr Shaw, but your son is scheduled for an X-ray and after that he needs to rest.'

Carson held up his palm. 'Understood. See you later, Nick.' And with that, he backed out of the room.

Nurse Abi took Nick's blood pressure and frowned. 'It's a bit high.' She checked her watch. 'Do you need more pain relief? Are you hurting anywhere?'

What a question. He was hurting everywhere, his mind and heart as battered as his body. He glanced at the newspaper. It looked so innocuous sitting there beside a jug of water and Dad's chocolates. Nothing to betray the bombshell contained within. How could Del have done this? To his father, to his family? Nick loved her and believed that she loved him. He planned to propose and had bought a ring. But after that despicable article?

According to Carson, she'd taken full responsibility for every rotten word. Was that the kind of person he'd fallen for? Had he really misjudged Del so badly? Nick ached with his need to talk with her, and he cursed himself for not having asked Carson for a phone. Perhaps he should simply check himself out. If this was Winga Hospital, it meant that he wasn't far from the main street. He could be with Del in ten minutes and get the answers he so desperately craved.

Nick replayed the conversation over and over in his head. What had Dad said about Mum? It doesn't take much to push her over the edge. A bolt of fear for his mother hit hard. She cared so much about public opinion. Some years ago, a mildly critical television interview with Carson had sent her into a massive downward spiral. It had taken months of medication and therapy to pull her out of it.

But that TV interview had been a walk in the park compared to the savagery of Del's article. His mother would be mortified. Carson may have been the target, but Mum would find a way to take the blame. She viewed any attack on the family name as a personal attack upon herself. And in this case, she wasn't far wrong. If Carson was cheating, then by implication she was a betrayed spouse, an abandoned wife. Carson's loyal but foolish partner who'd been traded in for a younger model. That would hit any woman hard, especially one as fragile and insecure as his mother.

'Time for your X-ray.' A male nurse came in with a strapping orderly who adjusted the bed and began wheeling it from the room.

Nick caught a glimpse out the window as he went past – a city skyscape of tall buildings and manicured parklands. 'Where am I?'

'The Mayfair Clinic,' said the orderly.

'In Sydney?'

'That's right, mate.'

So, Dad had squirreled him away, far from Winga. There'd be no popping out to see Del after all. Nick lay back with a pounding headache, suddenly weary. Maybe he'd shut his eyes for a while. Then later, when he opened them again, he might wake from this nightmare.

CHAPTER 8

Del spread a queen-sized sheet out on the tiled floor of her galley kitchen. The big dog clumsily lay down on it.

'Now stay.' Del turned to go. Her phone had best reception out in the courtyard.

The dog uttered a mournful howl.

Del frowned at the animal. 'Shut up, will you? You've already cost me a small fortune, and now you want to get me evicted as well?'

It patted its shaggy tail on the floor. Del tried to sneak off, but the dog howled even louder.

Del swore and returned to the kitchen. 'I said, shut up!'

The dog wagged its tail again. It tried to stand but lost its balance and tumbled to the floor with a painful yelp.

'Stop that,' she growled. 'The vet said you should rest.' Del slapped her forehead. What the hell was she doing talking to a dog?

Del left the kitchen, ignoring the dog's mounting protests. She'd picked him up from the vet earlier that morning and needed to ring the local council to have him collected. But as she headed for the back door, someone knocked on it.

Nick? Del almost tripped over her own feet in her haste to open it.

But it wasn't Nick after all. It was Vera, her landlady, and it wasn't hard to guess why she'd come. The dog had redoubled its efforts to howl the house down.

Vera looked stern. 'You do know there's a strict *no pets* policy here at the Vines.' She peered past Del. 'Whatever's the matter with that animal?'

Del scrubbed her palm over her face. There was no point denying it. She stepped aside to allow Vera past.

'Oh, the poor wee mite,' said Vera when she saw the dog.

Wee mite? It was as a big as a pony.

'What happened to him?' Vera stared at the plaster cast on his foreleg and the bandage round its neck where the ingrown collar had been surgically removed.

'A car hit it,' said Del.

Vera glared at her accusingly.

'Don't look at me,' said Del. 'I was the one who found it on the side of the road and took it to the vet.'

Vera's face softened. 'That was mighty decent of you, lass.' She patted the dog's head and was rewarded with a toothy grin. 'He looks half-starved. I've a nice ham bone he might like. Let me go fetch it.'

Ten minutes later the dog was happily chewing on a meaty bone, while Del poured them both a coffee.

'What's his name?' asked Vera.

Del shrugged. 'How should I know?'

'No microchip?' Vera tut-tutted. 'Look at his paws. They're huge. He'll be a big boy when he grows up.'

Del stared at her, astonished. Surely the dog couldn't get any bigger. Then she remembered the vet's words. *He's just a half-grown pup.*

Vera topped up her coffee. She seemed to be enjoying herself. Del glanced at the door, anxious for her landlady to leave. She had to organise somewhere for the dog to stay before she could start searching for Nick. It was forty-eight hours since the article came out and they still hadn't spoken after that one brief call. Del had spent yesterday at home, drinking all the wine in her fridge and ringing Nick every few minutes. Too humiliated to go to work. Too heartbroken to face the world. When her friend Kim called to see how she was, Del asked her to get off the phone in case Nick rang. She'd become an emotional wreck. Well, that would stop today. She'd pull herself together and fix this mess.

'Do you know who that pup reminds me of?' said Vera. 'One we had when I was a girl. A terrific dog. Tiny, that was his name, because he was—'

'Let me guess,' interrupted Del, impatient. 'Because he was big?'

She hadn't meant to sound so sarcastic.

Vera, her feathers ruffled, put down her mug. 'I'm sorry, lass, but Tiny can't stay here.'

'I know.' Del tried to put a lid on her frustration. 'I was about to ring the council when you knocked.'

Vera looked horrified. 'The pound doesn't have space or time to care for injured animals. And Barry's a lazy so-and-so. He'll put him down, nothing surer.'

Much to Del's surprise, she felt tears track down her cheeks. She rubbed her eyes but couldn't stop the flow. What had been the point of rescuing Tiny, when everyone seemed determined to kill him?

'Tell me what to do, then,' she sobbed. 'He can't stay here. The vet won't keep him. And now you say the pound will put him down.'

'The pound will, yes. But there are some wonderful no-kill shelters around.' Vera put a sympathetic hand on Del's arm. 'My niece, Brooke, helps run a place at Gosford. How about I give her a ring?'

Del sniffed and nodded, embarrassed by her show of emotions. Following the death of her father, she'd wrapped a shield around her heart. It had served her well for eight long years, protecting her from further hurt. It had also allowed her to write stories that other reporters might baulk at. Public opinion didn't matter to Del. Insults and criticisms couldn't touch her. Nobody, apart from Nick, had penetrated her defences in all that time. And now she'd gone to pieces over a mangy stray. It made no sense. Del didn't even like dogs. They reminded her too much of life back on the farm where she'd grown up.

Vera gazed fondly at the pup. 'A beautiful boy like you should find a new home easily.'

Del looked askance at her landlady. Were they even seeing the same animal? Tiny was as ugly as sin. Rake thin, with legs like stilts. When he lay down, he never knew what to do with them and ended up collapsing in an ungainly tangle of limbs. His tail was whip-like and scruffy, with the odd bald patch, and his rough grey coat still bore clods of dried mud. He resembled an overgrown, shaggy greyhound – and he stank. *The only beautiful thing about him is his eyes*, thought Del. Soft hazel pools, brimming with gentleness and love.

'So, he can stay?'

'For now. In the meantime, let's try to fatten him up,' said Vera. 'But no howling, mind. The gentleman in the front room is writing his science thesis. Something about the diseases humans can catch from animals. He came here for peace and quiet. So, if the pup cries, you'll both have to go.'

Del looked down helplessly at Tiny. 'I'll do my best, but he cries whenever I'm out of his sight. I'll show you.' She went into the bedroom and Tiny began a loud, strangled howl.

'You'll have to figure that problem out for yourself, lass,' said Vera when Del returned. 'Perhaps you can take him with you.'

'What – everywhere?'

'Just for a few days, until the Gosford shelter has a place for him.' Vera gave Tiny's head a final stroke and headed for the door. 'Good luck, lass.' She smiled encouragingly at Del, 'And you might want to give Tiny a bath. He's a bit ... well—'

'On the nose?'

Vera patted Del's hand. 'And, lass?'

'Yes?'

'I want to thank you.'

'What for?'

Vera moved close and said in a conspiratorial whisper, 'Carson Shaw molested my Brooke at last year's mayoral garden party. Shoved his hand between her legs and his tongue down her throat. It's about time someone outed the dirty old bastard.'

Del sat at the kitchen bench after Vera left and poured herself another coffee. That made two women now: Stacey Turner and now Vera's niece. How many more were there? Of course, stories of sexual predators could flush out false accusers; Vera's niece could have made the whole thing up. Del certainly hoped so

Yet she was getting that telltale tingle – the tingle telling her she was on to an important story. Celia may be an unethical, back-stabbing snake but she was also a top-notch journo. Del had the feeling she'd got her facts straight before she wrote that hit piece on Carson. If so, it was a fine example of investigative reporting. Heaven knows why she'd attributed it to Del. If the allegations could be proven, Celia could have simply published it under her own by-line and claimed the credit.

Del groaned. She needed to gather her thoughts and replan her day – factoring in Tiny this time. First, have a shower. Then, of course, ring Nick at regular intervals. There was no point in calling Carson; it always went to voicemail. She guessed that he'd blocked her. A nasty, nagging voice whispered that Nick had blocked her too.

No, she refused to believe such a thing. The article had come as a shock, that's all. He probably just needed time to cool down. Nick was a principled, fair-minded man who loved her. They were engaged to be married. He'd want to hear her side of the story. She'd drive to Westbrook again and try to get in. If that didn't work, she'd visit Celia. And this time she'd get some answers.

Del checked the time. Ten o'clock. Half the morning gone, thanks to picking up that bloody dog from the vet. She went to the bedroom and began to undress. Oh no. Tiny was tuning up. She rushed to the kitchen. 'Shut up.'

The dog struggled to his feet and limped closer, the cast on his foreleg skidding on the tiled floor. His legs slipped out from under him, but he didn't give up. He crawled to Del on his belly and grinned up at her.

Del groaned. 'Oh, for pity's sake.' She manoeuvred the dog back onto the queen sheet. 'Come on, Tiny. We both need a wash.' She grabbed the edge of the sheet with both hands and dragged the dog out of the kitchen and across the floorboards towards the bathroom.

CHAPTER 9

Nick had been at the Mayfair Clinic for nine days now, and still no word from Del. He imagined her walking in the door a thousand times a day, practised what he'd say to her, vowed that he'd give her a fair hearing. People thought of Del as the hard-nosed newshound, relentless in her quest for a story regardless of who got in her way, but Nick knew better. He'd seen behind the curtain. She did a good job of hiding it, but, underneath, Del was as loyal and sentimental as could be – and he loved her for it.

God, how he missed her. Sometimes, when he closed his eyes, he felt her breath on his neck or her soft lips on his. He heard her voice or the lilt of her laughter. It was unbearable. Once he'd asked his nurse if she could smell perfume. Del's signature scent of jasmine hung heavy in the air, replacing the hospital's antiseptic stink.

The nurse had shaken her head. 'Concussion can cause a person to see, hear, smell or feel things that aren't real,' she'd said. 'They're figments of the mind. Don't worry; they'll pass soon enough.'

Nick didn't want them to pass. Such delusions were his only connection to Del. Carson had brought him a new phone, but when he called her, it rang twice before a message said his call could not be connected.

'She's blocked you,' was Carson's explanation.

Nick couldn't bear to hear his father say it. Del loved him. He refused to believe that she was deliberately avoiding him. But the longer it took to hear from her, the harder it was to keep the faith.

'You did let her know that I was here, right?'

'Against my better judgement.'

He could hear the scowl in his father's voice. Nick hated being out of the loop. Back in Winga, the debate over Del's article was in full swing, but the only way he could follow it was online. Celia had doubled down on the story. The *Gazette* stood behind it and would not retract. Unsurprisingly, the *Sydney Morning Herald* had also picked it up, hailing Del as a bright new star and boasting that her laser-focused investigative reporting would soon be coming their way. He could find nothing from Del addressing the article, not even a tweet denying that it was her piece. She'd taken down her Twitter, Facebook and Instagram accounts. But the story had grown legs of its own, with a storm of comments for and against Del on social media.

His father rang each day without fail, but he refused to discuss the allegations against him. When questioned, he simply swore and changed the subject. Nick's mother had suffered a minor breakdown and was too distraught to talk. Nick was desperate to contact Del and hungry for news from home. He had to get out of the damned clinic, but it was taking longer to recover than he'd expected. Even if he'd been in the local Winga hospital, there'd have been no popping out whenever it suited him. He couldn't drive, for one thing, not until his arm was out of its cast. And not until the bouts of double vision and dizziness abated.

Those weren't the only lingering after-effects of his run-in with the Red River bridge. He lay in bed most of the day, yet he was still fatigued and slept more than usual. He suffered periods of confusion when he couldn't think straight or make sense of what people were saying to him. He sometimes imagined that he was back in Winga, and when he glanced out the window, the Sydney skyscape came as a fresh shock.

'How long will these symptoms last?' It was a question he asked his neurologist every day. Dr Kelly Chen was a short pale woman with a noncommittal manner, which did not inspire confidence.

'Not long,' she assured him. 'You should soon be back to normal.'

'Should?'

'Well, such predictions are never a hundred per cent reliable.'

She was fiddling with the stethoscope draped round her neck and looked bored. What on earth did a neurologist need a stethoscope for anyway?

'The human body is not a machine, Nick. You suffered a serious concussion and still have a minor cerebral oedema. But your oxygen therapy is dealing most effectively with that. Another two weeks should be sufficient.'

'Surely I could continue my treatment back home on an outpatient basis.'

'In the country? I don't believe that Winga Community Hospital has a hyperbaric chamber.' Dr Chen failed to smother a derisive titter. 'Most people would be pleased to recuperate in such a nice place.'

The Mayfair Clinic was more than a *nice place*. Nick's private room was essentially a luxury hotel suite. Floor-to-ceiling windows offered stunning views of the Harbour Bridge. Fine linen on the bed. Fresh flowers on the table. Master chefs prepared gourmet meals and his ensuite boasted a spa bath.

Even so, he couldn't bear to be stuck in Sydney for two more weeks. It felt like being stuck at the end of the earth. It had taken Carson three days to arrange the new iPhone for him, and even longer to send his laptop. And due to some IT glitch, he'd lost all his phone and email contacts. When Nick tried recovering them from the cloud, they'd mysteriously vanished. He was reduced to requesting contacts one by one from others, mainly from his father – an exercise in total frustration, partly because Carson took it upon himself to censor the list, and partly because Nick still couldn't remember large chunks of the last month.

'You don't need Peter Lang's number,' Carson told him over the phone one evening.

'Dad, he'll need the new production projections for Mount Morton.'

'He already has them. I put young Geoff Tyler on the job. He's brilliant by the way, and ambitious to boot. Oh, and you don't need Mike Holt's number either.'

'He'll need my report for the board meeting next week.'

'You've already finished that report. Don't you remember?'

'Of course I don't bloody well remember,' Nick said. 'Otherwise I wouldn't have asked.'

'No need to snap my head off.'

Nick struggled to keep a lid on his irritation. 'Dad, this isn't working. You can't expect me to go through you for every little thing. Put me through to my office. Let me speak to John.'

'Not on your life. I've reassigned all your projects until you're well.'

Talk about making him feel completely dispensable. Nick seethed with impotent anger. Working for Westcorp was all he'd ever wanted to do. As a boy he'd idolised his father, and as a young man he'd been proud to carry on the family business. But it was becoming more and more difficult to deal with Carson's controlling ways. Nick hoped to marry and have a family of his own one day. He couldn't live in his father's shadow forever.

'How's Mum?' he asked. 'How's she coping?'

It took a long time for Carson to answer. 'How do you think?' His voice brimmed with pain. 'She's shut herself away again. The only time she talks is to ask about you.'

'Bring her to Sydney,' said Nick. 'Seeing me might help.'

'I've tried,' said Carson. 'She won't come. She's ashamed to leave the house.'

'Then get me out of this bloody clinic and home to Winga. I don't know why you sent me here in the first place.'

'Mayfair has the finest neurologists in—'

'Who cares? Mum needs me, and so do you. I swear, Dad, hyperbaric chamber or not, tomorrow I'm checking myself out and coming home. Before you hand my entire job over to the young and brilliant Geoff Tyler. Before you completely ruin my relationship with Del.' He took a big breath before voicing his fear. 'You didn't tell her where I was, did you? You lied to me.'

Nick sensed the coming explosion of rage before Carson said a word. He ended the call. For all he knew, Del didn't even know about his accident. Nick had wondered why his near drowning hadn't made the headlines in the *Gazette*, which he'd been keeping up with online since the return of his laptop. Carson had kept the whole thing quiet. It was time to spring himself from this gilded hospital cage and go home to get some answers.

CHAPTER 10

Nick scowled and searched the drawers of his bedside table. 'Where are my clothes?' He'd been for an MRI before the phone call with Carson and was still wearing a hospital gown.

'You mustn't upset yourself like this,' said the nurse. 'Get back into bed. Please, Nick. It's nine o'clock at night.' She closed the drawers that he'd left open, and followed him to the wardrobe where he was rifling through shelves with his one good arm.

'Nothing but bloody pyjamas.'

She seemed frantic with worry. 'Why don't I call Dr Chen so you can talk to her?'

'I don't want to talk to her. I want to leave.' He held up a set of navy-blue chequered PJs with the tags still attached. These will do. Help me put them on, will you?'

The nurse shook her head. 'I wouldn't dare. I'll get into trouble.'

Nick threw the pyjamas on the floor. 'Don't worry about it.' He picked up his laptop and marched from the room.

The young taxi driver leaned out the window, grinning like he couldn't believe his luck. 'My GPS says it's a four-hour drive to

Winga.' He looked his potential customer up and down: bandaged head, slippers, hospital gown and an arm in a cast, carrying nothing but a laptop. 'Staging a breakout, are we, mate?'

Nick laughed for the first time since he'd woken up at the clinic. 'Got it in one.'

'Good for you. It'll cost, though.' The driver pressed something on the dash. 'I calculate the ride will be . . . six hundred dollars or thereabouts.'

'Okay.'

'Are you good for it? I can't go traipsing all over—'

Nick opened his phone and gave the driver his credit card details. 'And there's a two-hundred-dollar tip in it for you on top of the cab charge. Now, do we have a deal?'

The driver grinned. 'Hop in, mate. But do me a favour and keep that bloody gown well tucked in.'

It was almost two o'clock in the morning when Nick's cab arrived at the gates of Westbrook. They were shut, and for some reason the code wouldn't work.

'Can you get in?' asked the driver. 'Should I wait while you call someone?'

'Nah, mate. It's fine.' Nick didn't want to alert Carson to his arrival. There'd be plenty of time for an argument in the morning.

Nick gave the departing taxi a wave. Using the torch on his phone to guide him, he edged his way along the wall until he reached an overgrown private gate. As a kid he'd called it his secret passage, but nobody had used the entrance in years. It took a minute for the rusty latch to give. He walked up through the dark garden to his cottage, not needing a key; he never locked up.

Nick let himself in and put down his laptop. After being away for more than a week, he'd half-expected that his mother would have sent over Mrs Marlow, their housekeeper, to clean up. It was a relief to find that nobody had been in. A bunch of receipts and hand-scribbled notes lay strewn over the corner desk. An untidy stack of gardening magazines spilled onto the floor beside the couch. Perhaps being here among the familiar bits and pieces of his life would jog his memory. He turned and locked the door behind him.

Nick went into the kitchen. He'd had a good night, apparently, when he was last home. Empty champagne bottles stood by the door, and a pile of dirty dishes lay stacked on the bench beside the dishwasher. He opened the fridge: a half-eaten fruit platter, stale garlic bread, a drooping bowl of salad. The pedal bin stank of fish, and Nick peered inside. Yuck – mouldy lobster shells. He tied up the rubbish bag, dumped it in the big bin outside the laundry and locked the back door when he came in. After being public property at the Mayfair Clinic, where people barged into his room at all hours, he needed some privacy.

Two champagne flutes sat on the coffee table. Nick went to his room. Jeans, a shirt and socks were on the floor. The bed was a mess, blankets and pillows awry with the telltale signs of lovemaking. Did Del's perfume still linger, or was that another delusion? Nick swore softly. Why couldn't he remember?

Something glinted among the bedclothes; one of the sapphire earrings he'd given Del for her birthday. Blue was her favourite colour – the colour of kingfishers. He picked it up and her lovely face swam before him. He imagined her naked under the satin sheet, imagined that the night lay ahead of them – a night of lust and love and shared hopes. And as he ached for her, a wave of weariness washed in. Nick lay down on the bed, pulled the sheet up and was asleep by the time his head hit the pillow.

Next morning he woke with an unbearable itch beneath his cast and a headache grinding into his skull. He reached for the nurse call button to summon some pain relief, before realising where he was. Oh, well. Panadol would be a poor substitute for morphine, but it would have to do. A loud scratching noise came at the front door. Was that what had woken him? He recognised the sound – Dad's labrador. Trust Winston to be the first to welcome him home.

Early light crept through the casement windows as he climbed stiffly from the bed. He blinked and shut the curtains, shrugged off his hospital gown and went to the wardrobe. The problem was that he couldn't dress himself one-handed, certainly not in his usual garb of buttoned shirts and moleskin trousers. Another sound, a knock this time, soft and insistent. Not Carson's style. Del? The possibility sent Nick rushing to find some loose-fitting track pants. He pulled them on awkwardly and opened the front door.

His mother, Natalie, stood on the porch, barefoot and dressed only in a nightgown. She was tall and statuesque – still a beauty at fifty. No silver showed in the gold of her hair, and her skin remained smooth and mostly unlined. Yet her face was a pallid shade of grey, as if her lifeblood had drained away. The corners of her mouth turned up at the sight of him, but it was a hollow smile. Seeing her like this brought home the full reality of the damage Del had caused. He couldn't help a surge of anger. The longer it took to get the explanation he needed, the harder it was to believe in her innocence.

Winston followed Natalie inside. Normally, she'd shoo him out again, but not today. He began licking a bleeding cut on her big toe, but she didn't seem to notice. Nick called the dog away. He hated seeing his mother like this. It brought back some very painful memories.

Dark circles ringed her bloodshot eyes – eyes that brimmed with tears. 'My poor boy,' she whispered.

He must have looked a sight, with his bandaged head, and his arm in a cast, not to mention the mottled bruises covering his bare torso. That's what happened when you came off second best against a bridge. Nick hugged his mother as well as he could, feeling her stiff frailty beneath his arm. If he squeezed too hard, she'd snap.

'I was so worried,' she sobbed, her rigid body giving a little, leaning into him. 'But I couldn't come to Sydney. Not with reporters parked outside the gate. I couldn't run the gauntlet, I simply couldn't.'

'I'm sorry, Mum.' Nick smoothed her tangled hair. 'I should have been here for you.'

She gradually pulled away from him. 'It's not true, what they're saying about—'

'Of course it's not. It's some kind of terrible mistake. Don't worry. Now that I'm home, I'll sort it out.'

But his mother wasn't listening. Her eyes flickered nervously about, not focusing on anything. She seemed very far away. He'd seen it too many times before. Mum stood right there, but she might as well have been on the moon.

'How could Del write such filth?' she said. 'And to think I welcomed her into our home.'

Nick wished he had something comforting to say. 'Sit down, Mum. I'll make us some coffee.'

It was no use. She'd moved beyond his reach, mumbling something about not being good enough.

She suddenly gave an anguished cry. 'I want to see Bobby. He'll know what to do.'

Where did that come from? Carson's brother had been dead for twenty-five years. Nick took her hand. 'Mum, Uncle Bobby's passed.'

She looked at him uncomprehendingly, smiled and touched his cheek. 'I do love you, Nicky.' Then she shook her head and limped into the kitchen with Winston at her heels.

Nick gulped hard, his mouth dry as sandpaper. He recognised what was happening. Mum was beginning to break with reality. How to get her safely back to the homestead? They couldn't walk there, not with her bare feet.

He found her opening and closing cupboards. 'Mum, what are you doing?'

'Where's that letter? Do you know? I can't remember where I put it.'

'Mum, stop.'

She began rummaging behind jars in the pantry. 'There's next to no food here. Someone must do a shop for you.' His mother knocked over an empty champagne bottle with her foot. 'And look at this mess. I'd better send in Mrs Marlow to clean.' She began stacking dirty plates in the dishwasher.

'Don't worry about that now. Let's drive up to the main house.' He could manage the short trip one-handed. 'I haven't seen Dad since I've been home.'

Natalie turned to him, a look of horror on her face. 'I know what will happen once I'm in the car … ' Her voice became a strangled sob. 'Don't send me back to that place, Nicky. I'd rather die.'

'It's all right, Mum. I want to take you up to the homestead. That's all.'

Natalie escaped out to the rear porch just as a loud knock came at the front door.

Carson barged in. 'What the hell are you doing here?'

'I live here,' said Nick.

Carson glared at him. 'Where's your mother?'

Nick pointed to the back door and Carson stormed over to it. Soon the rise and fall of voices outside indicated an argument in full swing. Nick stayed where he was. Carson had a way with his wife, even when her mental health was at its worst.

Before long, they reappeared. His mother seemed calmer, stroking Winston's soft ears and smiling. She linked arms with her husband who whispered some reassuring words.

'Come with me, my dear. Our boy needs his rest.'

'Take the Jeep,' said Nick. 'The keys should be on a hook by the door.'

'The Jeep?' Carson shot him a withering look. 'Your Jeep is some-where downstream of the Red River bridge.'

Oh. He'd forgotten.

Carson scooped Natalie into his arms. She clung to him, nestling her head against his shoulder. 'Nick, get the door. My car's out front.'

He followed them, watching as Carson gently placed his wife in the front seat. Tenderness showed in each line of his straining body. Nick thought back to Del's article and its absurd allegations. Carson had steadfastly loved and supported his wife through decades of mental illness. How could anybody doubt his love and commitment?

Carson shut the car door and turned to Nick. 'Get some more sleep, son. Then come up to the house for lunch. We'll talk then.'

Sleep. Now there was an idea. The thought made his limbs grow heavy and his eyelids drift shut of their own accord. For a few moments Nick looked ruefully at the empty carport. He'd miss his Jeep.

Maybe he would grab forty winks. Then he'd find Del and get some answers.

CHAPTER 11

Ten days had passed since the bombshell article, and Del was living in limbo. Celia was avoiding her – working from home. Her husband, Greg, had Huntington's disease and used a wheelchair. Apparently, he'd taken a turn for the worse and needed his wife. Even though she knew it was cynical of her Del didn't believe it; Celia was refusing to take Del's calls.

Nick had vanished off the face of the earth. Del remained paralysed with confusion and grief, barely sleeping, comfort eating Vera's home-made apple slice and drinking too much wine. She'd almost been tempted to ring her mother. It would have meant a lot to hear Mum's voice. But Del had cut off all communication when her father died and, even in an inebriated state, reaching out was a bridge too far.

So, she contented herself with long, sometimes tearful, phone calls with Kim. These calls covered the full gamut of human emotions. One moment Del was wailing that her life was over and she wanted to die. Next moment she was threatening to kill Celia. Her friend let Del talk, murmuring consoling words when needed, but mainly just listening. Without Kim's quiet support, Del didn't know how she could have got through this terrible time.

She was officially working from home, though 'working' was too grand a term for it. Celia had relieved her of most duties and Del was now responsible for little more than horoscopes, the 'What's On' community page and junior sport results. To be fair, that was about all she was capable of at the moment. Trying, and failing, to make sense of Celia's betrayal took up most of her time and energy.

Staying home suited her well enough, partly because she could avoid her colleagues and their inevitable barrage of awkward questions, and partly because she and Tiny were now joined at the hip. She had to take the dog with her everywhere; it was the only way to keep him quiet. And though she was loath to admit it, he was company in what would otherwise have been a very lonely time. Nevertheless, Del was desperate for her state of uncertainty to end.

So, when Celia texted on Tuesday morning and asked to see her in the office at 10 am, Del couldn't get there quickly enough. She arrived forty minutes early. Celia wasn't in yet, but that was okay – it gave Del more time to think things through, to decide what questions to ask and to figure out how to maintain her righteous rage without putting Celia offside. Appeasing her boss, however intolerable, might be the only way to get the answers she needed.

Del parked under a spreading lilly pilly tree, wound her windows partway down and told Tiny to stay. The dog sat on the front seat, staring at her with pleading eyes. 'Don't look at me like that,' she scolded, then gathered her courage and slinked in to the *Gazette* office.

How different this entrance was to her last one. No marching about with the air of a conquering hero. No thrusting her left hand under everyone's noses. Del wasn't even wearing Nick's ring. How could she when they hadn't resolved anything between them? So, the ring remained at home, the light of its tiny sun swallowed by the gloom of her dresser drawer.

Del glanced at Celia's empty office, then sat down at her desk for the first time in days. She stared at an overflowing in-tray and an empty out-tray. A few colleagues called hello, but their greetings were hard to hear over Tiny's ear-splitting cries, audible even through the building's closed door. Why hadn't she thought to bring earplugs?

Del thumbed through the huge pile of memos – records of phone calls fielded by the staff on her behalf while she'd been away. They all had *Shaw* scribbled at the top. She glanced at a few. Liz from Wylies Flat wanted to report her own unfortunate experience with the mayor. Interesting. Del slipped the note into her desk drawer. Hannah Bent of Singleton had rung to say that she supported Del one hundred per cent. So had Paul Balfe and Mrs Ada Lawson of Bobin. John of Upper Lansdowne, on the other hand, hoped that she'd die and burn in hell. His foul threats reminded her of why she'd shut down her social media accounts in the wake of the article.

Sentiments seemed to be evenly divided between support and condemnation. In other circumstances, she might have relished the controversy. She would certainly have kept digging, hoping to uncover more layers of the scandal. For a split second she wished that Nick wasn't a Shaw, and that she could rightly lay claim to the story.

'Excuse me, Del.' An uncommonly tall man dressed in a police uniform stood by her desk. 'Senior Constable Clancy Tucker.'

'I know who you are, Clancy. What's up?'

'I've received an animal welfare complaint about your dog. Would you step outside, please?'

Del groaned and followed Clancy out the door. Tiny spotted her as she exited the building, and he whined an excited welcome

'You can't leave him in the car like that.' Clancy tousled Tiny's head.

'But it's not hot, and look – I left the windows down.'

'Even so, we've had several complaints. If you do it again, I'll inform the RSPCA. They might even impound him.'

'I can only hope,' Del said glumly.

Clancy grinned and opened the car door. Tiny bounded out, forgetting about the cast on his leg, and fell flat on his face with a shriek.

'Oh, Tiny.' Del sighed and helped the dog to his feet. 'When will you ever learn?' He wagged his tail so hard it whipped her bare legs. 'Ow! Stop that.' She shot Clancy a look of pure exasperation. 'What on earth am I supposed to do with him? Vera won't let me leave him at the guesthouse.'

Clancy bent to scratch the dog's ears. 'Why not tie him up here in the shade with some water? I think I have a bowl in my car.'

Tiny was equally unhappy with this new arrangement. His howls echoed right through the office – and all the way down the street. Passers-by began complaining to Debbie in reception, some irate at the noise, others concerned for Tiny's welfare.

Del, whose desk was near the door, couldn't help overhearing every comment.

A young woman said, 'I'll call the RSPCA.'

'Promises, promises,' Del muttered.

Celia emerged from her office and glared at Del. She must have sneaked in the back way. 'Shut that dog up,' she snapped, 'and then come to see me.'

Of all the nerve. Where did Celia get off acting like the aggrieved one here?

Del was still fuming when she went to fetch Tiny.

The two women stood facing each other, bristling like two dogs about to fight.

'Where's Nick?' asked Del.

'I don't know,' said Celia. 'I'd tell you if I did.'

Del snorted. 'And I'm supposed to believe that?'

Celia's face was a mask of self-control. 'Suit yourself. Oh, and get that damned dog out of my office.'

Del ignored the request and continued, 'I should sue you. That's what Carson's doing, right?' She gave herself a mental kick. Her plan was to placate her boss, not antagonise her.

Celia shrugged. 'Mere bluster. He won't sue.'

There was that tingle again, insisting that the story was more than a blatant lie. Celia seemed so sure of herself. So why not run the article under her own by-line?

Tiny was amusing himself by chewing a chair leg. At least he was quiet now.

Celia frowned at the dog, tapping her foot impatiently, then made a grab for his collar. To Del's surprise, Tiny growled and bared his teeth. Celia stepped back. Del had never seen the dog growl before. He climbed up a few notches in her estimation. Clearly Tiny was a fine judge of character.

'I don't want to argue.' Del sat down and tried to collect her thoughts. 'I want to understand.'

Celia's stern face softened. 'All right.' She sat down too. 'I owe you that. But there's only so much I'm prepared to tell.'

Del listened with rapt attention as Celia told her story.

'Stacey Turner came to me six months ago. At first, I thought she was just a peeved employee. But then she showed me the sex tape.' Celia fiddled with her mobile for a few moments. 'Have a look. I made a copy.'

'I thought she didn't want to show it to anyone?'

'You don't count.' Celia handed over the phone. 'Stacey thinks you've seen it anyway, since you wrote the feature.'

Del bit her tongue and viewed the video. It was brief but conclusive, taken mid-act, with Carson's red, sweaty face and naked torso clearly visible. Incontrovertible proof of his guilt. Damn that man! This changed everything. What would she say to Nick now?

Celia took a manila folder from her filing cabinet. 'Have a look.'

Del took her time reading through the documents. Her boss had done her homework – sworn statements from a dozen women accusing Carson of coercing them into having sex.

'How did you get these?' Del held up one of the statements. 'This one alleges a rape that happened twenty years ago.'

'It seems our mayor has been a serial abuser for decades.' Celia took a pack of cigarettes and an ashtray from her desk drawer. 'Do you mind?' She lit up and took a deep breath before adding, 'There's more. Stacey told me that Carson pushed dodgy mining approvals through Council. No environmental impact studies. No threatened species assessments. Stacey turned a blind eye, but I doubt she'll make a formal statement about it. She'd incriminate herself in the process.'

Del's tingle had turned into a loud buzz. 'Is that what the corruption commission is chasing?'

'Who knows? An insider confirmed that Carson's a person of interest. That's all I have. ICAC investigations can drag on for years.'

Celia stubbed her cigarette, closed her eyes and put a hand to her chest. She looked suddenly older than her fifty years – hollowed out and empty. This strange situation was taking its toll on them both.

For a long while nobody spoke, Tiny's gnawing teeth on the chair leg the only sound in the room.

'What do you think Carson will do?' Del asked at last. 'And you're right – he can't sue. That would really open a can of worms.'

'My guess is he'll tough it out – deny everything, make a lot of noise and hope it blows over.'

Del slapped the manila folder. 'And these women?'

'Carson has deep pockets.'

Del felt her anger rising. 'So, he'll pay them off?'

'And the bastard will probably get away with it.' Celia gave Del a searching look. 'So far there's no proof he's done anything illegal.'

Del sat, open-mouthed, as the penny finally dropped. 'You want me to stay on this when I move to Sydney, don't you? You want me to break this story.'

'Why not? It's big and you're the best. I've no doubt that the *Sydney Morning Herald* will back you all the way. They've got the resources, and I don't. But my name must be kept out of it.'

'Why?'

'I can't say.'

Del shook her head in disbelief. 'Where's Nick?'

'I don't know.' Celia's mobile rang. She answered it, glanced across at Del and then handed her the phone. 'Why don't you ask him yourself?'

CHAPTER 12

D el parked off the road behind a screen of wattle trees, her mind awhirl. She and Tiny walked the last few hundred metres to Westbrook. The last thing she wanted was for Carson to notice her car.

They stepped onto a low bank to the left of the gates and made their way along the wall as Nick had advised. He'd been distant, curt even, on the phone, but it had still been wonderful to hear his voice after so long. Del couldn't wait to see him. Although, she had no idea why he'd refused to meet her in town. It seemed reckless to risk running into Carson before she'd had a chance to properly explain herself.

'Come on, Tiny.' He wanted to stop and sniff every stick and bush he passed. She tugged impatiently at the lead. 'We'll never get there at this rate.' After a few minutes they reached an ivy-covered timber gate set in the wall. Del pushed her way through, then headed up the hill towards the cottage.

Nick was waiting for her on the verandah, bare-chested and with his plastered arm in a sling. Del took in his shockingly battered face and bruised torso as she helped Tiny up the steps.

'Good grief. What happened to you?'

Nick beckoned her inside. She glanced around. How strange! The cottage looked exactly the same as it had on their engagement night. The same bowl of nuts on the coffee table. A copy of *House & Garden* lay open at the same page she'd turned to more than ten days ago. It was like going back in time.

Nick pulled away when she tried to hug him. 'Who's this?' He stared at Tiny. 'I thought you didn't like dogs?'

Del recounted the story of Tiny's rescue. 'So, you see, it's his fault I was late getting here last Saturday. I tried ringing a hundred times, but your phone just went to voicemail.'

If Nick was listening, she couldn't tell. He scratched Tiny's ears with his foot. 'This dog looks half-starved.' Tiny rolled over for a tummy rub. 'You did a good thing, Del.'

His approving words brought a surge of relief, and hope flickered alive. They'd find their way back to each other; she had to believe it.

Del continued with her story. 'And when I finally made it back to Westbrook, the gates were locked. It took me ages. Red River was flooded, remember?'

Nick's face remained impassive, except for a grimace when he moved his shoulder.

'Your poor arm. Now I know why you couldn't come into town. Are you going to explain what happened?'

'You're the one who needs to explain,' he said. 'Why did you write those filthy lies about my father?'

Del gulped a draught of air deep into her lungs. At last. Here was her chance to fix things. 'I didn't write them. This will sound crazy, I know, but Celia Bloom set me up. She tampered with my article. Changed it. The allegations came from her.'

Nick's eyes narrowed. 'That makes no sense. Why would she do that? Dad and Celia have been friends for years.'

'I don't know. I was as shocked as you were.'

Nick was staring, his eyes boring into her – searching for any sign of deceit. It broke her heart to see the lack of trust in his gaze. Yet, if he loved her, surely he'd be able to see that she was telling the truth.

At last the hard line of his mouth softened. Nick reached for her hand. Del felt a sudden lightness as the tension of the past week drained away. He drew her into a close embrace, careless of his injuries, and her fingers tenderly traced the broad yellow bruise on his chest. Nick's lips sought hers in a kiss full of passion and need, one that left her dizzy with desire. She closed her eyes and let it take her back to a happier time, wishing the kiss would last forever.

Tiny spoiled the moment. Eager to make it a group hug, he jumped up to join in. Standing on hind legs, his head was just about level with Nick's.

'Stop it!' Del struggled to push the dog away. 'Get down'

Too late. Tiny's plaster cast crashed into Nick's cast, causing them both to howl with pain, overbalance and tumble to the floor.

'Oh dear.' Del looked down at a groaning Nick. 'I'm sorry. Tiny doesn't know his own strength.'

'Obviously.' Tiny was half sitting on his hapless victim and enthusiastically licking his face. Nick managed a smile as she helped him to his feet.

'You still haven't said why you're so beat up.'

Nick grimaced and rubbed his side. 'My car took a swan dive off the Red River bridge.'

'Bloody hell!' Del put two and two together. 'I was stopped by the SES on my way to your house last week. They'd closed the road and said a swift water rescue was underway – a man trapped between his car and the bridge. That was you?'

Nick inclined his head. 'Apparently so. Now, how about you help me put some clothes on? We have to get up to the house and talk to Carson.'

Del's buoyant mood began to sink. It must have showed on her face.

Nick gave her a searching look. 'Del, what's wrong?'

'You go, honey.' She couldn't hide the stammer in her voice. 'I think I'll stay here.'

'No way.' He shook his head firmly. 'My parents need to hear your explanation straight from the horse's mouth . . . However far-fetched it might sound,' he added. 'Here's an idea. We'll hold a family press conference. You'll denounce Celia's lies and declare your full support for my father. You'll call for the paper to issue an apology and a full retraction. Dad will get behind you if he believes you're genuine. He might even fund a fraud suit against the *Gazette* on your behalf.'

Del didn't trust herself to speak. She couldn't even meet Nick's eye. The ticking of the kitchen wall clock only magnified the silence.

'Come on, Del,' said Nick, impatiently. 'What do you say? Do we have a plan?'

Del swallowed hard. What to do? Against all odds, Nick had believed her – believed in her innocence. She had a chance to stay with the man she loved. They could continue their perfect lives together and pick up where they'd left off. Get married. Travel. Maybe start a family one day. All this could be theirs if Del just kept her mouth shut about Carson. How hard could it be? She hadn't even known the extent of his crimes until today.

But on the other hand, didn't she owe something to those women who'd come forward to Celia and made statements? That was a brave thing. They'd put their reputations on the line, disclosed a pain kept hidden, sometimes for years. The statements had one thing in common, other than the perpetrator. In each case the woman's career had been disrupted, and in some cases destroyed altogether. Their lives had been unalterably changed for the worse because of Carson.

Del thought back to the statement of Marie Mason. The name had firmly lodged itself in Del's brain, as had the awful circumstances of the young woman's alleged abuse. Twenty years ago she'd been employed as Carson's personal assistant – her first job after completing a business certificate at Taree TAFE. According to Marie, she'd been a naive, starstruck teenager, thrilled to be employed by Winga's handsome and charismatic young mayor. When the sexual innuendos started, she tried to shrug them off. When the inappropriate touching started, she tried to ignore it. One evening Carson asked her to work late. She'd been unsure, uncomfortable about the idea of being alone with him. But she'd also been determined to keep her dream job. Everyone told her how lucky she was to have scored such a plum position at her age.

When the rest of the staff went home that night, Carson confronted Marie in the rest room, tore off her clothes and raped her. She'd been a virgin. When she fought, he gave her a black eye. That's what she'd said in her statement. She resigned. She didn't receive a reference.

Apparently, Marie never told anyone about the rape. Ashamed, and with her confidence destroyed, she drifted into drug addiction. A string of failed relationships followed. She bore a daughter who was removed by social services and grew up in foster care. 'Carson Shaw stole my youth and innocence. He stole my bright future. I thought I'd never have the courage to admit what he did to me, but I won't let that secret fester inside me a moment longer. I want to tell my story. I want justice.' The statement had more than the ring of truth about it. It positively oozed credibility.

Del's stomach clenched hard, and she couldn't catch her breath. How could she support Carson after reading Marie's heartbreaking statement? How could she swear that Stacey Turner was a liar, when Del knew for a fact that she wasn't?

Nick was staring at her with puzzled green eyes. 'Sweetheart, are you all right?'

Her mouth opened, then shut again. She wanted to scream that no, she wasn't all right. She wanted to confess her misgivings about Carson. She wanted to tell Nick that it would be a cold day in hell before she'd publicly defend his father.

'I feel sick. Perhaps some fresh air.' Del moved out to the verandah, with Tiny limping behind.

Nick followed them, looking uncertain. He lifted his injured arm a fraction. 'Will you help me get dressed?'

She shot him a tight smile. They moved to the bedroom and she chose a roomy black polo shirt. When she leaned close to help his arm through, Nick ventured a kiss. Del dodged it, pretending to be busy with his collar. She was too tense, holding too much back. If she kept quiet about Carson, the pretence would poison every second she spent with Nick.

Nick checked himself in the wardrobe mirror and adjusted his sling. 'Righto. That's as good as I'll get.' He ran a hand through his hair. 'Let's head up to the main house.'

Del didn't move. How much to tell him? Tiny whined and leaned against her leg.

'Sweetheart, are you coming?'

Del sighed and patted the bed. One way or another, she was about to break Nick's heart. 'Sit down, honey. We need to talk.'

Nick frowned and bit his bottom lip. He looked bewildered when Del finished explaining, as if she'd just told him that white was black or up was down.

'So, you're saying that you didn't write the allegations in that article, but that you believe them to be true.'

'Yes.' It felt like signing her own death warrant.

'You believe that my father's been cheating on my mother?'

'Yes.' She wanted to say more, but something sharp lodged in her throat. Nick adored his father and was fiercely loyal to him. Growing up with a mother who had a mental illness had caused an intense bond to form between father and son – a co-dependency. They'd so often only had each other.

Del felt the sting of impending tears. What she'd said already had crushed Nick. How could she now tell him that Carson hadn't merely cheated? That she suspected he'd been a serial sexual predator for years? At the least, using power and coercive control over his victims, and at the very worst, a violent rapist.

'Do you have proof?' he asked.

'Of Stacey Turner's claims? Celia does, yes.'

She studied Nick's face. Hurt and confusion was giving way to anger.

'Don't give me that *Celia* crap.' A pulse started in his cheek. 'What sort of a fool do you think I am?'

'It's true, Nick. Do you really think I'd publish that stuff about your father? I'd have come to you about it, not splashed it all over the paper.'

'Oh, really. Even if it meant losing the exclusive?'

She knew how upset he was. She knew he was shocked and confused. But his caustic tone of voice still hurt. 'If you don't believe me, just say so.'

'I don't know what to believe.' Nick closed his eyes, resting his forehead in the heel of his hand. Del tentatively touched his arm and he shrugged it away. 'Go home, Del. I need to think.' He stood up and marched from the room.

Tiny put his head in her lap and Del let the tears come. She picked up a pillow and buried her face in it. Nick's faint, comforting scent lingered in the weave. She took deep, steadying breaths until her sobs subsided.

'Come on, Tiny,' she said at last. 'Time to go.'

Nick was nowhere to be seen as Del left the cottage and made her way through the garden to the gate. She felt numb, with a tightness in her chest that would not lift. She wondered idly why Nick hadn't asked about her missing ring. Maybe he was glad she wasn't wearing it.

CHAPTER 13

Nick sat on a garden seat halfway up the hill between his cottage and the main house. From his vantage point he watched Del and Tiny reach the gate. She fumbled for a while with the rusty latch. He was irrationally pleased by the delay, as if it might buy him enough time to sprint down the hill after her. He almost did just that. It seemed absurd to let her go after he'd been so desperate to find her.

Then Nick thought of his mother, and of the shame Del's article had caused her. He imagined her descending once more into paranoia and depression. What if this time she didn't have the strength to climb back out? His jaw clenched and his teeth began a slow involuntary grind. As a child, when Mum went away to the clinic, it used to happen all the time. He thought he'd outgrown the habit.

The gate opened at the bottom of the garden and Del disappeared. Nick felt a sharp pang of loss to see her go and had to wait for the pain to subside. His mother was the important one right now. He had to see her – to find out how she was doing before making any decision about Del. Not at lunchtime, with Carson blustering and accusing and threatening to sue everyone he could think of. Not that Nick blamed him for it. A big part of him felt the same way. But he needed to see Mum on her own, in the quiet of the guest wing suite. That's where she always went when she fell into a dark hole.

Nick took a final glance at the closed gate and then started walking up the hill to the house.

He found his mother asleep, with Winston curled at her feet. She looked so peaceful, lying atop the quilted blue bedspread, her hair fanned out on the satin pillow. Relaxed, like she didn't have a care in the world. Maybe he was wrong. Maybe she did have the strength to resist another slide into the abyss.

That's when he saw the pill bottles. Four of them, lined up neatly beside their lids in an open dresser drawer. A half-filled glass of water stood on the nightstand, alongside a toppled crystal jug. A sudden fear lifted the hair on the nape of his neck and his hands grew clammy.

'Mum?' Nick shook her cold shoulder. 'Mum, wake up!'

Nick stumbled backwards, almost falling and his mouth opened in a primal scream. He called triple zero and began a desperate attempt at CPR, but deep down inside he knew it was too late.

Del was sitting in the kitchen at the Vines Guesthouse, sharing a sandwich with Tiny, when Celia rang with the terrible news.

'I thought you should hear this from me before it hits the headlines. An ambulance attended Westbrook at around 1 pm today. They found the body of a fifty-year-old woman. She was declared dead at the scene. The driver told me off the record that it was Natalie Shaw, and Sergeant Bilson has confirmed it.'

Del almost dropped the phone. 'Nick's mother is dead?'

'It seems there were no suspicious circumstances. A probable suicide.'

Suicide. Bile rose in Del's throat at the very sound of the word. She knew what it was like to lose a parent like that, albeit through physician-assisted suicide in her father's case. She knew about the shock and complicated grief, the guilt and self-reproach and bitter recriminations.

Del's first instinct was to go to Nick. He'd be completely devastated. But how could she? Nick would never want to see her again. Del could barely speak through her anger and despair. 'This is your fault, Celia. Although, of course, everyone will blame me. You knew how fragile Natalie was. What you did was criminal, in more ways than one.'

'Was it criminal to tell the truth about Carson?' For the first time, Celia sounded unsure of herself.

'Using my by-line? Yes! And it was also criminal not to warn the man first. With some prior notice he might have been able to prepare his wife for the coming scandal.'

For a long while Celia stayed silent on the end of the phone. Del began to think she was no longer there.

'I'm truly sorry about Natalie,' said Celia, her voice breaking. 'She was a good woman, and far better than Carson deserved.'

'You should have thought of that before you betrayed your profession and decided to take me down with you.'

A muffled sob came through the line. Was Celia crying? Perhaps, in this moment of weakness, Celia would finally come clean.

'Why use me to attack Carson?' asked Del. 'Why not simply do it yourself?'

'I'm sorry,' Celia said again. 'I'm sorry for you and for Natalie and for Nick. But I won't tell you why I did it. I'll never tell.'

Del ended the call and slid to the floor. Damn Celia. Damn Carson. They'd ruined everything. The dam broke and she wept aloud, rocking back and forth, clutching Tiny to her, burying her face in his shaggy fur. She wept for Natalie and Nick and the women that Carson had victimised for years. She wept for herself – for her shining future, now turned to dead dreams.

And as the paralysing horror built so that she could barely draw breath, a sudden, sickening realisation hit her. Words written on a page could kill. It made no difference if they were true or not. They could divide lovers and tear families apart and destroy lives. Of course, she'd known it intellectually. How many times had people told her? How many times had people tried to make her understand?

Even her own mother. 'I'm proud of you, darling,' she'd said when Del had her first article published. 'You're going to change this world for the better. But never forget that there are real people behind your stories.'

'You don't need to tell me that, Mum,' she'd said with a dismissive roll of her eyes

But having an intellectual understanding of something and living through it yourself were two very different things. Del knew that now. And there was something else she knew with indisputable certainty. She didn't want to be an investigative reporter. She didn't want to be responsible for ruining people's lives, even unintentionally. She never wanted to write another word.

An unfamiliar wave of homesickness hit her as a knock came at the back door.

'It's just me, lass. Good news,' called Vera, opening the door without an invitation in that annoying way she had. 'Brooke has a place for young Tiny. She can pick him up tomorrow.'

Tiny whined and pawed at Del's arm.

'Are you there, lass? Did you hear me?'

'Yes, I heard you, Vera. Thank you.'

Del waited until she heard the door close again, and then she tried to get off the floor. Her leg had gone to sleep. It felt like a dead lump of wood. She held on to Tiny's collar and he helped pull her to her feet.

'I'm going to ring Frank Walker and turn down the Sydney job,' she told him.

An unimaginable thing to say, even as recently as yesterday. But Tiny simply wagged his tail as if he agreed with her. Del stared out the window. The garden view that had previously looked so pretty, now seemed unfriendly and alien. She couldn't stay here in Winga. Without a job. Without Nick. What was the point?

'And then I might ring my mother.' Tiny gave two short sharp barks. Del had never heard him do that before. Howling and whining, yes, but not barking. It seemed like a sign. 'Tiny, let's go home to kingfisher country.'

CHAPTER 14

Afternoon shadows had grown long by the time Del parked at the rusty farm gate leading to Kingfisher Farm – five hundred hectares of prime grazing country in the foothills of the Yenga Ranges. The property stretched from the lower river flats right up to the edge of the national park.

She'd passed through her historic home town of Berrimilla twenty minutes earlier. The place hadn't changed much: a post office, a church, a primary school, a sports ground, a general and produce store, a bakery and a community hall. The only difference was a sign outside the old hardware shop that read 'Berrimilla Vet Clinic'. That would be useful; Tiny would need his cast off soon.

The township was nestled in the heart of Kingfisher Valley, between Yenga National Park to the west and the looming peaks of Mount Morton to the east. It had been built on the back of a gold rush, but not the conventional kind. Her forefathers had been timber-cutters – harvesters of red gold. They hauled valuable red cedar logs from the mountain forests with bullock teams and floated them down the river. As the prized timber grew rarer, the Fisher family applied for a land grant and had been farming there ever since, running cattle and fat lambs. Del had helped Dad plant a small vineyard before he became too ill to work. She wondered how it was going.

Del and Tiny got out of the car and looked around. There was an old adage that said you could never go home again. It came from the title of a 1940 Thomas Wolfe novel that she'd studied at university. It referred to the fact that so much will have altered since you left, it's not the same place anymore. That where you grew up existed only in your memory.

But that wasn't true. Standing at the gateway to her childhood home, Del could have been fifteen again. So little had changed. True, the gate was a bit rustier and the dirt track a little more rutted. And the avenue of rainforest saplings her father had planted that last year before Del left was now growing leafy and strong. But the feel of the place was the same. The familiar fragrance of rose myrtle leaves and the whipbirds calling in stereo. Even the great gleaming web of a St Andrew's cross spider made her feel at home. She hadn't expected that. She hadn't expected her gut to say that she'd made the right decision.

Del unlatched the gate, deftly flipping the extra link on the chain that had been put there years ago to stop her clever old pony from opening it. She called for Tiny to get back in the car. Her fingers traced the steering wheel before grasping it, firmly.

'Right,' she said. 'Let's do it.' So far this had been easier than she thought. If only her father was waiting at the top of the hill, it would have been a perfect homecoming.

A voice sang out. 'Yoo-hoo, darling! Hello!'

Del looked up to see her mother, Darby, hurrying down the track and waving her arms. Mum must have been watching for the car. Del imagined her sitting in the one corner of the verandah with a view of the gate, the way she used to do when waiting for Dad to return from dialysis treatments. He wouldn't let anyone go with him towards the end. *No need for us all to be bored witless,* he'd say.

At the sight of her mother, Del's positive feelings fled. Coming home to Berrimilla wasn't a good idea after all. She would have reversed the car around and fled if she hadn't been paralysed by a range of conflicting emotions: anticipation and dread, happiness and sadness, hatred and love. Because there were times when she *had* hated her mother. Darby was the one who'd helped Dad get the pills. She'd supported and enabled him to take his own life. She'd called it euthanasia. For a long time, Del had thought of it as murder.

Darby appeared at the car window, accompanied by two border collies. Del hadn't seen her mother for eight years, and she'd expected her to look a little older. But the face that beamed through the window had more than a few extra frown lines. Darby's sun-reddened skin bore a network of new wrinkles, with deeper creases on the forehead. Her wavy fair hair was peppered with grey and was pure silver at the temples. She'd put on weight and looked weary and weather-worn, older than her fifty years. Fifty years – the same age as Natalie Shaw. Del swallowed hard, thinking of Nick and the pain he was going through. She felt a sudden rush of gratitude that she still had her mother.

Darby tapped at the glass. Del hesitated to wind down the window. What would she say? Panic rose as Del's throat grew dry as sandpaper and she became utterly tongue-tied. It had been years since she'd spoken to her mother face to face. The bitterness and rancour of those parting words still haunted her. Despite the role Mum had played in her father's death, she hadn't deserved such venom. Back then Del had believed that she possessed a monopoly on grief.

'Who's this gorgeous fellow?' Darby pointed to Tiny, who was wiggling with a surfeit of goofy friendliness on the back seat. 'Poor thing. What happened to his leg?'

How grateful Del was for the dog at that moment. She could have hugged him. Tiny was just the circuit breaker Del needed when it came to her mother. She could safely talk about him without touching on more sensitive topics. It would be like talking about the weather, but less banal.

'That's my dog.' Darby looked both surprised and pleased at Del's answer. 'I'll tell you about him up at the house.'

Del exhaled. There – that hadn't been so hard. *I can do this*, Del told herself. She'd take it bit by bit and hope it got easier. *And whatever happens, don't talk about Dad.*

'Hop in,' Del said to her mother. 'I'll give you a lift up to the house.'

Del wandered through the old weatherboard farmhouse where she'd grown up. Picking up a knick-knack here, pulling a book from a shelf there, running her hand across the longcase clock in the hall. Her great-great-grandfather, Thomas Fisher, had crafted the case from local red cedar more than a century ago. The smooth, familiar carvings felt comforting beneath her fingertips.

Del returned to the kitchen where Tiny had made friends with the collies. The three of them were happily gnawing on lamb shanks. Tiny hadn't even noticed her leave the room. No howling, no crying, no separation anxiety at all. It felt strange to no longer have the dog as her shadow.

'Where's Rocky?' asked Del, momentarily forgetting how much time had passed. Rocky was Dad's faithful kelpie, who'd stayed by his side right until the end.

Darby looked up from where she was chopping vegetables. 'He passed not long after your father. A snake bite. I have Jimmy and Zara now.'

The collies patted their tails on the floor when they heard their names. Del took a closer look at her mother's face, at the moistness around her eyes. Was she crying, or was it merely the effect of slicing onions? 'Want some help?'

Darby shook her head. 'Almost finished.' She slid chunky vegetables into the slow cooker, along with a bottle of preserved tomatoes, several cloves of garlic and a plate of diced meat. 'Lamb stew.' She met Del's eyes uncertainly. 'It used to be your favourite. Of course, that was some time ago ... '

'Stew's fine, Mum.'

Del's eyes travelled round the kitchen. They landed on a collection of bills poking from the back of the dresser. Mum was so old-fashioned.

Who received paper bills anymore? Del picked one up – a reminder about the produce store account. In fact, most of them bore red overdue warnings. It hadn't occurred to her that Mum might be struggling financially following Dad's death. If she was honest with herself, she'd been so angry to begin with that she wouldn't have cared. And in the intervening years, when Del was off chasing her dreams, she'd thought about her mother less and less. It was easier that way. Thinking of Mum inevitably led to thinking of Dad, and the crippling grief would bubble up again.

Del took a quick tour outside while Darby cooked dinner. Maybe Thomas Wolfe was right after all. The farm *had* changed. There was a depressing, rundown quality about it. Weeds abounded, with clumps of blackberries, thistles and gorse dotting the paddocks beyond the house. Fences sagged and were patched in places with scrap bits of wire netting. A few stray sheep jumped back through a weak point in a fence when they saw her.

What really upset her was the state of the vineyard. Nine years ago, she'd helped her father plant out the hectare of hillside with shiraz varieties. The two of them had carried the dormant vines, thirty or forty at a time, to the prepared ground, in water-filled buckets so they didn't dry out. Then they'd lovingly buried the roots in the rich mountain loam.

Her father had harboured high hopes for his little vineyard, planning to expand it each year and, in the meantime, learn everything he could about winemaking. He'd even designed a mock-up label, Bluebird Shiraz, displaying a pair of his beloved kingfishers. Del smiled, thinking of how Dad always threw himself into projects with a passion. But he didn't live long enough to see his cherished vines bear fruit. And now they sprawled across the weedy slope, unloved and untended, running wild. Many had collapsed from their wire frames altogether.

It was mid-August, and bud break wouldn't happen for a few more weeks. Del knew that, but she couldn't help thinking that the bare vines were all dead. Yet when she nicked the bark of a nearby plant with her fingernail, the living green tissue showed underneath.

Del lifted a fallen vine and draped it over a trellis. Then she moved on to the next one. Each rescue soothed her. Mum had no right to abandon the planting this way. And here came that familiar surge of resentment. Del braced herself against it. If this arrangement was going to work, she needed to forgive her mother, or at least let go of her bitterness. Blaming Mum wouldn't bring Dad back.

Del turned to go, unable to face the neglected hillside any longer. But she'd bite her tongue when she went back inside. She wouldn't let Mum know how disappointed she was to see the vines that way.

The tragedy of Natalie's death had brought home how lucky she was to still have her mother. Del tried not to think of Nick, and of how broken he must be. She failed. A flood of self-pity claimed her. *What about me?* she thought. She'd lost a lot too. Her dream job and her career. She'd lost her father, and although the bereavement wasn't as recent as Nick's, here at Kingfisher Farm it felt brand new. And through no fault of her own she'd lost Nick as well – the love of her life. It was impossible to imagine a future without him. When she tried, there was nothing but blankness. And there among the vines Del knelt and wept.

CHAPTER 15

For the first few weeks at Kingfisher Farm, Del mainly rested and tried to recover her equilibrium. She felt vaguely disconnected from the world and refused to watch the news. She spent her spare time reading old novels plucked from the jumbled bookshelf in the hall. It held a small but eclectic collection and Del rather liked the limited range. Fewer decisions to make, and it forced her to read out of her comfort zone: *The Harp in the South*, *Remembering Babylon*, *Gould's Book of Fish* – books she would never have normally chosen.

Some particularly spoke to her, such as *My Brilliant Career* by Miles Franklin and *The Getting of Wisdom* by Henry Handel Richardson. These books were published more than a century ago, yet at times they seemed to talk about Del's own life. It annoyed her no end that female authors had been forced to use male names in order to get published. Thank goodness times had changed. Then Del thought about the women that Carson had preyed upon and their ruined careers. It was still a man's world.

One morning, Darby noticed Del sitting on the porch reading *Jillaroo* by Rachael Treasure. 'I gave you that book for your birthday,' she said. 'Do you remember?'

Del remembered, all right. She'd scanned the blurb – something about a young woman choosing between plains cropping or farming in the mountains, with a hot romance thrown in. Then she'd put it on her shelf, unread. Seventeen-year-old Del had dreams of forging a career in journalism. Reading about a girl whose heart belonged to the land held no appeal back then.

But now Del thought the story was fascinating, and she found that she enjoyed discussing it with Darby, who was a voracious reader. This led to more discussions about books, and even several trips together to the mobile library. After browsing the library's selection, they sat down for coffee and cake at the Berrimilla Bakery and showed each other what they'd borrowed. But their conversations never became personal.

A subtle tension existed between Del and her mother. Dad's death, and the manner of his passing, remained the great unmentioned. Del was wary of the almost unconscious resentment still simmering inside of her. Frightened to confront it. Frightened that it might burst free and ruin the tentative relationship she was building with Darby.

Sometimes she noticed Darby quietly watching her and sensed that she wanted to talk about Dad. But she never did. Del was grateful for that. She was also grateful that Darby didn't pry into her personal life. She must have read the article about Carson; she was a rusted-on reader of the *Winga Gazette*. And she must have known about the scandal it had caused. But she'd never mentioned it – not once. And since Darby had no idea about Del's romance with Nick, that subject never came up either. Strange, to live only in the here and now, as if her recent past had never existed.

When Del felt settled enough, she went to visit her father's grave. Well, not his grave exactly. Apparently, Darby had spread his ashes about the trunk of a giant red cedar – the tallest in an avenue of trees flanking the road into Berrimilla. They'd been planted more than a century ago by Thomas Fisher, known as the town's founding father.

Del hadn't been there to see Dad's ashes scattered. She had left town straight after the funeral, refusing to take her mother's calls.

She'd briefly returned for the laying of a memorial plaque for Dad. The Council donated it and Mayor Carson Shaw himself had come up from Winga and laid it at the foot of the tree. The *Gazette* had covered it.

'This plaque is more than a tribute to your departed loved one,' Carson had said to the crowd. It seemed like the whole town had turned up. Dad had been a popular member of the Berrimilla community, always ready to lend a helping hand when needed and generous to a fault. Many people were saddened by his passing. 'Allan Fisher's life stands for the long line of pioneers who helped settle our beautiful region,' said Carson. 'On behalf of the Central Ranges Council, I'm honoured to provide this memorial to a fine man.'

Darby had been so pleased, so proud for Dad to be publicly honoured in that way. 'Our mayor is a wonderful person,' she'd said. And even Del, through her anger and grief, had considered it a kind gesture. How wrong they'd been about the man. For Carson, it was always about the photo op. And when Del had met him two years later, when she was with Nick, he didn't remember the memorial in Berrimilla at all.

After a while, Del began to take on a few simple chores at the farm, looking after the chooks and vegetable garden. Helping around the house and making lunches. Darby wouldn't let her prepare the evening meal, though, and Del was just as pleased. Her mother's comforting home cooking was going a long way to helping her heal.

Del soon learned her mother's routine. With the sometime assistance of a local man, Ken Tucker, Darby managed sixty or so Angus breeders and a flock of crossbred Merino sheep – fewer than half the animals they'd had when Dad was alive. When Del asked about that, she was shocked to learn that her mother had sold off two hundred hectares of prime river flats in order to repay a line of credit they'd taken out when Dad became ill. Kingfisher Farm was a little over half its original size, but it was still a lot for Mum to manage on her own.

Darby checked the stock each morning, rising early and heading out on the quad bike, with Jimmy and Zara perched on the back. Tiny had taken a shine to Darby, and on the first day he'd clumsily tried to climb aboard too.

'No, Tiny,' Darby had chided gently. 'Not with that leg. You'd better stay here.'

Del had smiled. Even once Tiny's leg was healed, she doubted the ungainly pup could ever balance on the bike the way Mum's collies did. Darby returned midmorning, sometimes with an orphan lamb on board, or a sickly triplet. If so, she'd spend a lot of time feeding them and settling them comfortably in the shearing shed pens. Darby had a tender heart. If no young animals needed care, she did odd jobs until twelve o'clock, like tending to her three rambunctious rams and two stud bulls, who were currently separated from their ladies and constantly testing the hot wires keeping them apart. She never tended the vineyard, saying she didn't have time. Del could see now it was a fair claim.

At twelve o'clock Darby came inside to eat cold lamb sandwiches and watch *Dr Phil* on television. After lunch she'd go out again to mend fences or spray weeds or check on the water troughs. After dinner she usually spent time on paperwork, deciding when to sell a pen of sheep or send some cattle to market. Juggling bills and accounts. Darby worked hard, but without Dad to help, it wasn't enough. Slowly but surely the farm was getting on top of her. Yet she never complained. Even when Darby seemed bone weary, she tackled jobs with a smile and never shirked a difficult task. Del felt a growing admiration and sympathy for her mother.

Twice a week Darby went into Berrimilla to have dinner with friends at the quaint little pub. Sometimes Ken picked her up and dropped her off again. Del wondered if they were romantically involved. If they were, Mum did a good job of hiding it. Probably just as well. However irrational it might be, Del wasn't ready to see her mother with anybody else. Darby always asked her daughter along, but Del wasn't ready for a parma and small talk with strangers. Maybe she never would be.

'I'm going into town,' said Del one morning. 'Tiny needs to have his cast checked at the vet. Is there anything you need, Mum?'

'Some plain yoghurt. I was thinking of lamb kofta for dinner. Here, let me give you some money.'

Del waved the offer away and escaped out the door with Tiny. After a month at Kingfisher Farm she was growing heartily sick of lamb: lamb roast, lamb chops, lamb stews, lamb curries, lamb kebabs, lamb salads. The meat formed the basis of almost every meal. But she didn't say anything to Darby. Killing a valuable steer for the table would be an extravagance. It would yield far too much meat for two people and three dogs, even using the big freezer on the back porch. Butchering a fat lamb was far more practical.

Del had been looking forward to tasting her childhood-favourite dinner – creamy chicken casserole – but it didn't appear on the menu. Darby was unusually sentimental for a farmer. As often as not the poddy lambs she hand-raised stayed on as bossy pets. Del had found a couple of the little bandits breaking in to the vegetable garden just that morning.

And Darby was also inordinately fond of her hens and refused to kill them. When Dad was alive, he owned a vicious red rooster called Devil who wouldn't let Darby anywhere near the chicken run. Devil did his duty by the chooks, who regularly went broody and hatched troops of fluffy yellow chicks. Dad raised the cockerels for midweek roasts and kept the pullets as replacement laying hens. Old layers went into the pressure cooker to make soups, stews and tasty stock, and the farm always had more eggs than it could use.

But Devil had died long ago, which meant no new chicks had been born for years. Darby bought a few young pullets from her neighbours, but her ageing hens lived out a happy retirement. She fed them kitchen scraps and let them out for a daily scratch around the garden. She'd given them names – something Dad had warned against.

'They're not pets, love,' he'd chide gently. 'You have to be practical. You're a farmer now.'

Well, yes, she was, but she hadn't been born to it. Darby was a young nurse when she first met Dad at a wedding in Sydney.

According to them both it was love at first sight. Six months later they married, and Darby moved to Kingfisher Farm. She'd never looked back, and she had taken to life in the bush with a passion that matched her husband's. They'd had the happiest of marriages, and Del had enjoyed a magical childhood. Out from dawn to dusk with her friends – building forts, riding horses, catching yabbies in the dam. Swimming in Kingfisher Creek. As a girl she couldn't ever remember feeling unsafe or unloved.

Del frowned and bundled Tiny into the car. She had to stop her recollections there, before her father was diagnosed with kidney disease. Before the months of dialysis, the failed transplant and his outrageous decision to refuse further treatment. Before the arguments and the anguish and the final rift with her mother. No, Del wouldn't go there. If she did, she'd have to turn around and leave Kingfisher Farm that very day.

CHAPTER 16

D el bumped down the rutted drive, determined to keep her thoughts firmly on the here and now. She took it too fast, and the car pitched in and out of the deepest potholes, flinging its occupants about. Tiny whined in protest.

'Sorry, boy. Who'd have thought you could get seasick this far from the ocean?'

Del returned to the problem of the farm's lamb-heavy menu. Maybe she'd offer to cook a few vegetarian meals each week, using the abundant fresh produce from the garden. She'd need to Google some recipes. Until now, Del had avoided using the internet, such as it was. The farm had terrible reception. She hadn't even looked at Mum's copies of the *Winga Gazette*. She couldn't face it. But she also couldn't shut out the world forever. It was time to take baby steps out of her seclusion – time to stop mooching about feeling sorry for herself.

For Del had a more important reason to go online than searching for recipes. Spring had come. The world was renewing itself. And she wanted to restore the vineyard. The plan had come to her during a string of sleepless nights. She couldn't bear how aimless her life had become. In the space of one week she'd gone from an ambitious and driven career journalist to being unemployed and living in her old bedroom at her mother's house. She craved direction in her life, yet, after experiencing so much loss, she hadn't imagined anything would inspire her again.

But Dad's neglected vines had. They presented Del with the perfect opportunity to throw herself into a new project and honour her father at the same time. Her own dreams might have died, but she could still make his come true. Del would produce a vintage – bottles of fine wine with Dad's own Bluebird label attached. The idea energised her so that she almost felt happy – such an unfamiliar emotion that she barely recognised it. And when Del got out of the car at the Berrimilla Vet Clinic, she walked with a fresh spring in her step.

Dr Pam Bryant gave Tiny a final once-over and smiled. 'He's doing well. Two more weeks and that cast can come off.'

An image of Nick and his broken arm came to her. 'Do human bones and dog bones heal at the same time?'

'Why, yes,' said Pam. 'Generally they do. It depends on the break, of course.' She gave Tiny an affectionate pat. 'You told the nurse that he's a bitzer – breed unknown. Don't you know what kind of dog he is?'

'Um ... ' Del took a long look at her dog and shrugged. 'A cross between a greyhound and a bear?'

Pam laughed. 'Wrong. He's a wolfhound – a fine example of the tallest breed in the world. They were once used to drag men off horseback in battle and to hunt stags and wolves. They also have a strong chase instinct, so you'd better watch him around your mum's sheep.'

'What would a wolfhound be doing roaming the paddocks as a half-starved stray? You could count each bone in his spine when I first found him.'

'My guess is that pig shooters bought him as a breeding dog – to add size and endurance to their pack,' said Pam. 'There are plenty of feral pigs in the nearby hills. He probably got lost on a hunt, or maybe ran away. It would have hurt them to lose such a valuable dog.'

'Pig hunting?' Del had researched the subject for an article a few months ago, and she knew just how barbaric it was. Hunting pigs with dogs involved the pack flushing out a pig and chasing it until it was exhausted or cornered. They then attacked and held the terrified animal until the men arrived. It meant a cruel death for the pig, and the risk of serious injury for the dogs. Training methods included setting packs onto confined pigs that had been captured specifically for the purpose. The thought of her gentle Tiny being brutalised like that, or being gored by a wild boar, made Del feel sick.

'Is that what happened to you?' She hugged the dog's shaggy grey neck. 'Poor baby.' He whined, closed his eyes and pushed his head against her.

'Tiny certainly was lucky to wind up with you,' said a beaming Pam. 'And since he's not desexed, shall I make an appointment to do that after his cast comes off?'

'Right then, book him in.'

Del hoped that Nick was recovering as well as Tiny was. 'Come on, boy,' she said after she'd paid for the consultation. 'Next stop, the post office.'

Such a shame to slip the dazzling ring into the dull brown envelope. She seemed to be always hiding its light. But it couldn't be helped. She needed to close that chapter of her life. The ring belonged to Nick.

Del took one last peek. Her mind travelled back to the evening when she'd first seen the beautiful ring. The night when Nick proposed. The best night of her life. But her happiness had been like the crimson daylilies that graced Mum's garden in summer. They lasted for a single day.

Bloody Celia. She'd never get what she deserved now, but Del hoped that Carson would. The only good thing to come out of this whole mess would be if that bastard could finally be held accountable for the pain he'd caused. Carson had already stepped down as mayor, citing grief over his wife's death. Darby had told her so, even though Del had asked her not to mention the news. Carson's resignation was a good start, but she didn't want it to end there. As it stood, the man remained a sympathetic figure, a loving husband retiring to grieve in private. Del wanted Carson exposed. She wanted the world to know what an appalling person he was. She wanted Nick to know too. Loyal, trusting Nick. He deserved to know the truth. And however much Del resented Celia, she hoped her former boss would keep digging into Carson's past.

'Dogs shouldn't be in the post office,' grumbled the man in the queue ahead of her.

'Oh, stop it, Fred,' said the middle-aged postmistress standing behind the counter. Del recognised her but couldn't remember her name. 'Can't you see the poor thing's hurt?' She gestured for Del to come forward. 'I'll deal with you first, love,' she said. 'Let you get your doggy home, eh?'

Fred muttered something under his breath, but moved aside.

'My name's April,' said the woman. 'And you must be Del, Darby's girl. Heard you were back. I remember when you were just a little tacker up at the school here. Bright as a button you were. Anyway, how can I help?'

Del stepped forward, embarrassed to be recognised, and wishing Darby had kept her mouth shut. All the locals would know that she'd written that article, and she was bound to face some hostility from Carson Shaw fans. She addressed the envelope and sealed the ring box inside, together with a brief handwritten letter. She'd held herself on a tight rein while writing it, keeping it formal. Scared that if she unleashed her feelings they'd overwhelm her and she wouldn't be able to write it at all.

Dearest Nick,

Please accept the return of the engagement ring you gave me. I simply adore it, but since we won't be married now, I can't keep it.

Please also accept my deepest sympathies upon the death of your mother, Natalie. She was always very kind to me. I know how much you loved her, and how heartbroken you must be.

I didn't make those allegations against your father, but I don't think that matters any more. Too much damage has been done, and the last thing I want is to add to your pain by defending myself. I've turned my back on journalism. I won't take that job in Sydney. I'll never write again. But I will always love you. Have a wonderful life.

Eternally yours,

Del

She spent a long time staring at the envelope, unwilling to hand it over and thus conclude the final chapter of her love affair with Nick Shaw.

The man behind her shuffled his feet and *harrumphed* loudly.

April smiled in an encouraging way and held out her hand. 'Have you finished with it, love?' Del reluctantly let her take it. 'Do you want express postage?'

'Yes,' said Del. 'And insurance, and signature on delivery. I want the works.'

'Card or cash?'

Del presented her card. She watched as April postmarked the envelope and tossed it carelessly into a postal bag. Del flinched to see it. 'Come on, Tiny,' she said, and turned to leave.

'Before you go, can I ask you to sign our petition?' April pointed to a sheaf of papers stapled in one corner. 'It's to stop the coal mine. Here's a pen.'

Del moved the papers further down the countertop to make way for the grumpy man. She considered petitions the most useless form of activism. Signing one of them was almost always a pointless exercise, serving no purpose except to make petitioners feel good about themselves. Still, if it would please April, what was the harm?

It was addressed to Premier Gordon and read:

A study prepared by the NSW Nature Conservation Council warns that any expansion of the Mount Morton mine will have the following impacts:

1. The decline of nearby Berrimilla village due to increased noise, dust and a decrease in property values.

2. The encroachment of mining operations on prime agricultural land.

3. The contamination of groundwater.

4. The destruction of five hundred hectares of koala and regent honeyeater habitat.

The Mount Morton mine expansion should not go ahead. Local residents, farmers and wildlife must be protected! Please sign the petition.

The Mount Morton mine. Carson had mentioned plans to expand its operations when she interviewed him for the feature article. He'd boasted about the jobs he'd create and the investment he intended to make in local communities. At the time Del hadn't put two and two together. She hadn't realised that Carson was talking about Kingfisher Valley.

Del slowly flipped through the long list of names. She recognised a lot of them from her childhood. The Carter family, the Bairds and the Alders. She'd gone to school with Ashleigh Jamieson and Bruce Burrows. And look, there was Ken Tucker's name and her own mother's as well. Darby had written three big exclamation marks after her signature. There was clearly a good deal of community opposition to the mine expansion. Not that it would do any good. Big corporations always won in the end.

Del put the petition down. She wouldn't be signing it after all. The last thing she wanted was to cause Nick more trouble.

CHAPTER 17

Nick clumsily sorted through Westbrook's morning mail with his one good hand. Carson usually insisted on doing it himself, but he seemed to have lost interest. He'd lost interest in a lot of things lately.

Nick's skin was crawling under the cast. He'd give an arm and a leg just to scratch it for ten seconds. But he had to wait two more weeks for the bloody thing to come off. That wasn't the only thing he was looking forward to. Today was the last day of being stuck at home. He'd return to work tomorrow and discover what sort of a mess he'd have to deal with. Nick didn't have as much confidence in the brilliance of young Geoff Tyler as his father did. And it would be good to have some sort of purpose back in his life. Something to take his mind off all the loss. It would also be good to be working side by side with his father again. Nobody understood what Carson was going through like Nick did. The two of them were united by sorrow.

Nick's grief came in waves. Sometimes the tide overwhelmed him with sadness. Sometimes the waves weakened, letting good memories flood in: Mum's smile, her warmth, the funny or sweet things that she'd said. And he found the surest way to ease his misery was to support Carson in his. It was what Mum would have wanted – one last thing he could do for her.

Carson had not been coping in the month since Mum died. Nick had encouraged him to take bereavement leave, but he'd insisted on soldiering on. Even so, he'd barely gone in to the office. And according to Max, his personal assistant, when he did he was all over the place. Losing his temper. Forgetting things. Missing meetings and making mistakes. Nick thought back to all the times his father had been there for him when Mum was ill. It had been just the two of them for much of his childhood, and Carson had been a good single dad. A bit overbearing, perhaps. That was Carson's way. But he'd also been strong and supportive – offering unconditional love. It was time to return the favour.

Last week Carson had stepped down as mayor, citing personal reasons. He hadn't warned Nick, who'd found out about it by listening to the local radio news. The resignation had been met with an outpouring of public sympathy. But there were some who viewed it as a capitulation – an admission of guilt.

'This isn't like you, Dad,' Nick had said. 'You're a fighter. You should be suing the pants off that gutter press. By resigning, you're simply adding fuel to the scandalmongers' fires.'

Carson had looked grim. 'I can't do it, son. Maybe before, but not now – not without your mother.'

Nick had moved in to the main house and employed a live-in chef so Mrs Marlow wouldn't have to cook now that Mum was gone. Natalie had been an enthusiastic and accomplished chef, who was always happiest in the kitchen when she was well. But Nick needn't have bothered. Carson, who formerly had the heartiest appetite of any man he knew, was barely eating. He wasn't shaving, and his short grey beard grew in odd contrast to the deep brown of his dyed hair. That morning Carson had actually emerged from his room wearing track-pants. Nick didn't know he owned any. He couldn't shake the fear that he might lose his father to depression, as well as his mother.

As Nick finished going through the mail, a handwritten envelope caught his eye. Something jagged stuck in his throat as he recognised

Del's sprawling script. He opened the envelope with fumbling fingers and extracted the little velvet box enclosed within.

Nick turned it over in his fingers a few times before lifting the lid. He stared at the jewelled band in astonishment. It looked exactly like the antique engagement ring he'd bought for Del. But it couldn't be. That ring lay in the safe at the top of his wardrobe. He'd never had a chance to give it to her. He went to the bedroom and checked the safe; the ring was gone. It didn't make any sense.

Nick checked the envelope again and found something else – a letter from Del. He hadn't seen the slip of paper at first. And when he read her note, he understood. A wave of longing and regret turned his legs to jelly. He *had* asked Del to marry him, and he'd given her the ring, though he couldn't remember doing it. He felt an absurd thrill to know that she'd said yes. It must have happened during the shadowy, forgotten weeks before his accident.

It was hard to believe that Del was turning down her dream Sydney job. And what had she said about giving up writing? Nick reread the letter for the third time. *I'll never write again. But I will always love you. Have a wonderful life.*

He stifled the urge to cry out to the empty room – to scream that he loved her too and always would. A sharp pain in his chest made him gasp. He hadn't thought his heart could hurt any more. Was Del quitting journalism because of guilt? She still denied writing the allegations made in the article, but she was right when she said it didn't matter any more. Even if her improbable story about Celia changing her copy was true, he and Del were finished.

Nick couldn't be with someone who believed those dreadful things about his father. He'd seen firsthand Carson's anguish at the death of his wife. Carson had collapsed at the funeral in tears, in front of everyone. Nobody could fake that kind of devotion. True, Nick was still perplexed about why his father hadn't followed through with his libel suit against the *Winga Gazette*. He'd even briefly wondered if Dad doubted his prospects of success – but only for a nanosecond. It was more likely that his plans to sue had been derailed by grief.

Nick clutched the ring, sat down at the kitchen table and closed his eyes. Thinking of Del. Desperate to remember proposing to her. Snippets of lost time were returning to him since he'd come home. An argument with his father about the environmental recovery plan for the Mount Morton mine. Presenting his auditor's report to the board of directors. He even remembered taking Winston to the vet for his annual shots. A quick check of the vaccination certificate showed that trip took place two days before his dash across the flooded Red River bridge. He might never forgive himself for that folly. He still couldn't believe he'd been so foolish.

So, if he could remember something as mundane as a vet visit, why the hell couldn't he remember getting engaged? Nick wondered how it had gone down. He'd had a range of ideas in mind. Taking Del to Sydney and booking out an entire restaurant just for the two of them. Maybe popping the question during a walk along their favourite beach, or at at quiet dinner at home. He'd even thought about a trip to Paris. But that hadn't happened – he'd checked his passport. He could barely restrain himself from phoning Del then and there to find out.

Not knowing was maddening. How he wished he could go back in time and experience the joy of that occasion. Because it would have been joyful, a moment filled with the excitement of sharing their future together. But something else puzzled him. Why hadn't anyone else mentioned it? He wouldn't have got engaged without telling his friends and family. Mum, in particular, would have been thrilled. She liked Del and would have welcomed her with open arms.

It took a moment for him to realise that his mother was, in fact, dead, and that it was Del's fault. It still felt like a bad dream. Nick often pictured Mum in the room, alone, humiliated and afraid. He tried to imagine what she'd been thinking and feeling in the days and hours before taking the pills. The worst thing was that he'd never know. These imaginings haunted him, leading to nights without sleep and days lived in a kind of blur.

Nick put the ring back in its box and shoved it across to the other side of the table. Damn it – he'd give anything to make his thoughts stay still for a while. Maybe he should go to the doctor and get some sleeping pills. Maybe he should see a psychologist. Nick surprised himself then by wondering what advice Del might give him. She was such a practical person, not given to flights of fancy. She believed that the answers to problems lay in thorough research. Gathering as much information as possible, no matter how difficult or painful that process might be.

'What should I do?' he said aloud, and Del answered him in his head.

There is a way to understand what your mother was going through before she died. You know there is. Do the research. Read her diaries.

Trust Del to come up with something like that. The investigative reporter in her wasn't dead after all. Nick pictured his mother on the day she died, the way he'd done dozens of time before. But this time his mind's eye travelled around her room. He took in the Arthur Streeton painting on the wall and the antique colonial armoire in the corner. Was that where Mum had kept her notebooks? Or maybe they were in the drawers of the French provincial nightstand. She'd always been a dedicated and prolific diarist.

Nick went to the kitchen window. It looked out onto a bed of fragrant yellow roses, Mum's favourite flowers. He took a deep breath. Could he do it? Could he brave going into his mother's room to search for her diaries? He wished he was as fearless as Del; she would do anything to uncover the truth

Winston scratched at the back door and Nick let him in. The dog had been there with Mum during her final moments. Nick rubbed his ears, the way he liked.

'If only you could talk, eh?'

Winston whined and wagged his tail.

'Come on, boy. I have something important I need to do, and I could use your moral support."

CHAPTER 18

A weight lifted from Del's shoulders after she sent the letter to Nick. In the days that followed, it became possible to think about him without a crippling pang of heartbreak. Instead she felt just a dull ache of loss. Painful as that was, it wasn't enough to stop her living her life.

Del was taking an active interest in the running of Kingfisher Farm now, and she needed to make a business plan. So, one morning she sat down at the kitchen table with a pot of tea, some toast and her laptop. Time to make a list of pros and cons. Right. On the pro side, beef values were up and cattle were fetching high prices at market. Since the farm was understocked, there was the potential to run many more head in the future. Del had also been researching viticulture enterprises as fast as Mum's dodgy internet connection would allow. If maintained properly, the vineyards could provide a handy new income stream.

Then there was the con side. That was a longer list. There were the sheep, for starters: an ageing flock of crossbred Merinos. They were a liability. Lamb and wool prices had plummeted, and even with the collies' help, Darby said that she never managed to muster them all.

Up at the higher reaches of Kingfisher Farm, where the boundary fences were in disrepair, stock frequently escaped into the national park. Ram lambs that missed the musters bred with their mothers and sisters, leading to a sickly, inbred flock. And foxes were taking lambs, too. Del's father had always brought the lambing ewes down to the protected paddocks near the house. Ewes giving birth up in the mountains were vulnerable.

Another con, linked to the sheep problem, was maintenance. The fences needed repairs, as did the shearing shed roof. The driveway and tracks needed gravel. The ancient stock-tank pumps that operated the water troughs kept cutting out. They needed replacing with something under thirty years old; an up-to-date pumping system with a digital pressure and flow readout. One that could operate the new drip irrigation system Del wanted for the vineyards. And something needed to be done about the internet. A business couldn't run efficiently with such slow speeds.

Del methodically made a list of the positives, the negatives and what needed to be done. Of course, modernising the farm would require money – something that Darby didn't seem to have much of. After making a rough estimate of the costs, Del had decided to invest her own funds. She had a moderate amount of savings and no expenses to speak of while living with Darby. Del would make her father proud by putting Kingfisher Farm back on its feet. The prospect helped blunt the aching sense of loss she still felt.

First, she'd order a StarNet satellite dish. It would replace the farm's dodgy NBN connection that lagged and constantly dropped out. Del had previously researched SpaceX's low-orbit satellite service for an article about rural telecommunication problems. She'd interviewed more than a dozen remote users. And the consensus? StarNet was a winner, providing fast and reliable uncapped internet for far-flung farms all over the Central Ranges. Del couldn't wait to tell Darby that she'd finally be able to stream Netflix.

Next, she'd spend a day visiting her friend, Kim Khan, who lived up at Tingo an hour away. Kim may well be Del's closest confidant, but she hadn't spoken to her since those awful weeks after Nick proposed.

A qualified botanist, Kim worked part-time with the environment department, advising landholders on bush regeneration. She and her husband, Taj, ran a rainforest nursery, propagating and growing a rich variety of plants native to the Central Ranges. They aimed to conserve those species and make them available to home gardeners, farmers, and restoration schemes.

They also bred Maremma livestock guardian dogs. Kim and Taj had reintroduced dingoes to their wild two hundred hectares of land on the edge of Tarringtops National Park. At first locals had been up in arms. That's how Del had originally met Kim – by interviewing her about the controversial program. But the pair had supplied their Maremmas to nearby farmers, who hadn't lost a single sheep to the dingoes since. Yes, livestock guardian dogs were just what Kingfisher Farm needed.

Tiny pricked up his ears and pawed at Del's arm. 'Would you like that?' she asked, stroking his ears, and giving him a piece of buttered toast. 'Would you and the collies enjoy more canine company?'

Darby came in and tossed her hat at the peg on the wall. 'Got it in one,' she called triumphantly.

Tiny barked his approval, then raced joyfully around the kitchen, tail lashing in excitement. Since his cast had come off, he wanted to travel everywhere at top speed. Oddly enough, he seemed to be just as clumsy as before, and missed the turn. He tried to stop himself as he cannoned towards the dresser, skidding on the wooden floor.

'No!' called Darby.

Too late – Tiny made a direct hit. The overflowing pile of bills and papers on top of the dresser went flying, and Del neatly fielded a plate dislodged from the rack.

'Well caught,' said Darby, with a little clap. 'Now put him outside. He's like a bull in a china shop since that cast came off.'

Del obliged. When she came back inside and sat down, Darby peered over her shoulder. 'What's all this then?'

Del hesitated. She hadn't consulted Darby about her scheme. So far, their conversations had been confined to superficialities. The weather. Market prices. Whether or not 'jokey' was a legitimate Scrabble word. But she could hardly go ahead with these changes without Darby's approval.

'I'm making a business plan for the farm,' Del said at last.

Darby stared at her and took a step back. She spread her fingers like a fan against her heart. 'So, this means ... '

'It means I'm staying.' Del bit her lip. For some reason she'd almost snapped the words. 'If you'll have me, of course.'

Darby sat down too, close enough for Del to feel her faintly trembling. She indicated the laptop. 'Show me.'

Del pushed it across the table. 'It's nothing much. Just a rough list of pros and cons.'

Darby read through it and chuckled. '*Stop Mum making pets of chooks and lambs.* You sound just like your father.'

For once, the mention of Dad didn't cause a pang of pain. Del smiled. 'I do, don't I?'

'This all sounds great,' said Darby, 'but truth is, the place has a cashflow problem at the moment.'

'Mum, I have savings. I want to invest in the farm.'

Darby looked nonplussed. She read through the list again. 'You want to restore the vineyard?'

Del's usual guard with her mother slipped, overcome by a surging enthusiasm. 'That vineyard was Dad's dream. Kingfisher Farm's own vintage. Remember?'

Del pushed back her chair and ran to her room to fetch the prized album of Dad's photos.

'See?' She turned to the back. 'He had this mocked up. Bluebird Shiraz.'

'Ah.' Darby ran her finger down the label. The pair of bright blue kingfishers looked real enough to fly off the page. 'Of course I remember. It was my dream too.'

'Then why, Mum? Those vines have been neglected for years. Why didn't you look after them?'

Darby shook her head. 'It was too painful. I see those vines and I see your father. I see him full of hope for the future, like he was that weekend you planted them.' Darby's face slowly crumpled, and her body sagged. 'There's never even been a harvest. I just leave the grapes for the birds.'

To Del's horror, Darby burst into tears. Not just ordinary tears. They blinded her eyes and flooded down her cheeks. More anguished than the tears Del herself had cried when she'd lost Nick. Darby buried her face in the palm of her hands and sobbed through her fingers.

Del didn't know where to look. She'd spent the last eight years avoiding any sort of emotional connection with Darby. And yet here she was, standing in the home where she'd grown up, immersed in her mother's misery.

Del put a tentative hand on Darby's shoulder, furiously thinking of what to say. She'd learned to harden her heart to her mother. Consoling words didn't come easily.

'Don't cry, Mum,' Del said at last. And then, paradoxically, she began to cry too. Her dammed-up emotions burst through the flood-gates and suddenly they were weeping together, sharing their heart-break at the loss of a father, a husband and a friend. Sharing their pain and grief in a way that hadn't happened eight years ago.

Darby had helped Dad die. She could have encouraged him to go back on dialysis and wait for a second kidney to become available. He might have lived for years. But instead she'd assisted him in procuring the pills that took his life. Del had thought that she'd never be able to forgive her mother. But spending these weeks home at Kingfisher Farm had given her a new perspective.

Up until now, she'd only seen her father's death through the lens of her own grief. Now she was starting to see it through her mother's as well. And a realisation hit her. Yes, Dad had loved his vines. Restoring them would indeed honour him. But he'd loved Darby far, far more. How he'd hate to see his wife and daughter at odds. Restoring her relationship with Darby would honour Dad more than anything else Del could do. It wouldn't be easy, though. Even now, she could feel the old bitterness lurking close.

Del took a box of tissues from the shelf, blew her nose, and then offered one to Darby. And for the first time in eight years, she hugged her mother.

CHAPTER 19

It was a glorious spring morning and the perfect day for a drive. Del passed through the tiny town of Tingo and took the turn-off onto Bangalow Road. The road wound through steep green paddocks until half an hour later it was swallowed by tall timber. Thick stands of subtropical rainforest trees towered into the blue sky above. In places, the tangle of broad leaves and matted branches blocked out the sun.

Finally, she crossed the narrow bridge over Cedar Creek, and after a few minutes she saw the familiar line of lilly pillies she was looking for. 'We're here, Tiny.'

She pulled up at the white timber gate. A spanking new sign to the left read 'Journey's End Rainforest Nursery'. The letters were surrounded by hand-painted flowers, foliage and a prick-eared dingo head, all drawn with great delicacy. That would be Taj's work. Kim's husband was a talented artist.

She waited for the solar mechanism to automatically open the gate, then zoomed through, always worried it would slam shut too soon. A group of little wallabies bounded away from the car. A line of silver quandongs flanked the drive, their smooth buttressed trunks topped with fragrant white flowers and the pink flush of new leaves.

Later in the year they'd be smothered in iridescent blue berries – a feast for the birds and flying foxes. Such graceful trees. Del imagined a stand of them at Kingfisher Farm. Maybe Kim would have some seedlings for sale.

Tiny tumbled from the car, barking with delight. A flurry of answering yelps came from behind the modest farmhouse. It would have looked like any of a dozen houses that she'd passed on the way here, if it wasn't for the art. Colourful murals covered the weatherboard walls. Paintings of rainforest glades sheltering wallabies, possums and quolls. A dingo peered from behind a lichen-covered boulder. Leadlight flowers burst from windowpanes. Climbing vines wound their way up verandah posts, and a bronze eagle, broad wings unfurled, was landing on the chimney. The building blended seamlessly with its forest surrounds.

'Del!' a voice sang out. 'Up here.'

Tiny tore up the mossy path towards a pair of large greenhouses. Kim stood in front of them, wearing denim overalls and holding a watering can. She was a tall, slim woman, a few years older than Del, with kind eyes and a messy blonde bob. Two large white Maremmas stood on her left, and a small brown terrier stood on her right. When they saw Tiny, they started barking loudly. This only made him gallop faster, tail lashing from side to side with excitement.

He bounded around the other three dogs in great, joyful circles. Deciding Tiny was harmless, the terrier stopped yapping and started chasing him instead. The Maremmas play-bowed and joined in on the game.

Del reached Kim and gave a her a heartfelt hug. 'What's that for?' she asked, when Del finally let her go. 'You're not normally much of a hugger.'

'It must be something in the water,' said Del, with a grin. 'I even hugged my mother yesterday.'

Kim raised her brows, 'So, how's it going between you two, then?'

Del held out her hand and rocked it slightly. 'Comme ci, comme ça.'

'Well, I'd call that okay,' said Kim. 'And this must be your stray.

He's huge!' She pointed to Tiny, who was on his back, long legs akimbo, being jumped on by the other dogs in a mock fight. 'He won't chase my sheep, will he?'

'No way,' said Del, as Tiny extricated himself and took off down the hill with the dogs at his heels. 'Back at the farm he sits with the poddy lambs while Mum bottle feeds them, then gently licks the spilt milk from their faces.' She lowered her voice and leaned close to Kim, 'I don't think he knows he's a wolfhound.'

'Oi! Lily, Snowball, Scout – leave off!' Kim laughed as the dogs ran to them. 'Maybe we'll make him an honorary Maremma.'

The two friends walked down to the house.

'Where's Taj?' asked Del.

'Away. He's working on the Lord Howe Island World Heritage Project. Supervising the delivery of thousands of our own seedlings,' said Kim, proudly. 'We're the go-to people now for all sorts of bush regeneration groups.'

Del was duly impressed. She was also glad that Taj was away. Much as she loved the man, it would be good to have Kim to herself.

Kim gave Del a tour of the nursery, which had grown since Del's last visit just a few months ago. There was an additional shadehouse for propagating the native orchids that Kim loved so much, and two wide terraces making room for a broader range of advanced plants, not to mention the extra platforms for tubestock, and a fernery.

'Are they new polytunnels over there?' asked Del. 'You and Taj must have been working day and night.'

Kim indicated the scene with a broad sweep of her arm. The breathtaking views across the range. The rows of thriving native plants, many in full bloom. The tree ferns and stag ferns germinating naturally in pots and under walkways. The place was bursting with life.

Kim's face broke into a broad grin. 'You call this working? Come on. I'll show you Frosty's new litter. Nine puppies!'

After lunch, Kim drove them up a rutted track to the highest point of the property – a ridge line bordering the national park. Across the valley, a waterfall plunged two hundred metres down a steep gorge, its silver ribbon breaking into tiny rainbows on the boulders below. A trick of the light made the cascading water seem close enough to touch.

'It's so beautiful, it doesn't seem real,' whispered Del.

'That's just how I felt when I first saw it.' Kim plucked an aromatic leaf from a native mint bush, crushed it between her fingers and put it to her nose. 'I never get tired of that smell, do you?'

Del did the same thing. She shut her eyes and inhaled, taking the sweet, minty fragrance deep into her lungs. The scent brought with it a precious rush of childhood memories. Family picnics by the river. Catching tadpoles. Fishing with her father. She wanted to hold on to them and was loath to open her eyes. When she did, Kim was watching her with eyes as keen as a kingfisher's.

'Your place is a bit like mine,' said Kim. 'It borders a national park, right? What's the view like from the top of the farm?'

Del didn't know, despite having made the trip to the northern boundary just last week. She'd gone to check the state of the fences, and that's what she'd done – all she'd done. She hadn't stopped to smell the mint. She hadn't paused to gaze across the ranges.

Kim put a hand on her shoulder. 'Taj is away. Jake's got himself an apprenticeship in Taree, and Abbey's off on a school camp. So, since I'm home alone, why not stay the night? We can have a few wines, and talk. What do you say?'

'I'll have to ring Mum,' said Del, feeling like she was fifteen again.

The two friends skewered some marinated chicken pieces and tossed a green salad. While the kebabs cooked on the verandah grill, Kim opened a bottle of red and poured them both a glass.

'Can I help with anything?' asked Del.

'Yes – stop the dogs from stealing our dinner.' Del laughed, and shooed them away from the barbeque. 'Otherwise, just relax and enjoy the view.'

Yes, that's exactly what she would do. Stop worrying about every-thing and simply breathe. Del sat down and picked up a folder lying on the table – the nursery's stock book. It read like a 'Who's Who' of iconic subtropical rainforest trees: black booyong, flame tree, sassafras, tamarind, rosewood, yellow carabeen, Moreton Bay fig, plum pine, cork-wood. The list went on and on, a catalogue of Kim's success as a botanist.

'How do you do it?' Del asked as Kim placed the meal on the table.

'Do what?'

'You're not that much older than me, but you have life all sorted: a gorgeous husband, kids, a passion for what you do. By comparison, my life is a mess.'

Kim topped up Del's wine and seemed to take a moment to compose herself. 'I came to Journey's End after my husband was killed in Afghanistan. So mired in grief that I couldn't work – couldn't do much of anything, actually. Jake was acting out badly enough to be expelled from school. Oh, and my dog had just died. How's that for a messy life?'

Del's cheeks burned with shame. She'd been so focused on herself that she'd forgotten about the trials Kim had been through. A grief-stricken young widow, left all alone in the world. Moving to the bush to start a new life for herself and her children. It had been hard. It had taken courage. But Kim had put her broken life back together, finding love again and making her conservation dream a reality.

For a while, the two friends ate in silence, and twilight's curtain descended over the mountains. They'd almost finished their bottle of wine before Del finally opened up about her plans for the farm.

Kim listened with rising enthusiasm. 'I love it! Establishing your own vineyard? Putting the farm back on track? That's exciting. But I never saw you as the agricultural type.'

'Neither did I.' Del offered a wry smile. 'I swore when I left that I'd never run the farm.'

A soft breeze lifted her hair and an owl hooted from somewhere out in the darkness. Del shut her eyes, imagining for a moment that she was sitting on Nick's verandah, basking in the warm glow of his marriage proposal.

Kim nodded sagely. 'How life can change, eh? Tell me, are you getting over Nick?'

Could Kim read her mind? Del gulped down the rest of her wine. 'I'm trying. Throwing myself into work helps.'

'You know Nick's behind the push to expand the mine out your way, don't you?'

Del's breath caught in her throat.

Kim disappeared inside briefly and emerged with another bottle of wine in one hand and a glossy pamphlet in the other. She handed the pamphlet over and Del's heart missed a beat. Nick's smiling picture dominated a front page headed 'Westcorp Mining – Growing with Your Community'.

It wasn't one of those formal corporate photographs, with him wearing a suit and tie. Instead, he leaned casually against a tree trunk. Yellow roses bloomed in the background. Del recognised the roses, and the rough-grooved bark of the elm tree shading his cottage at Westbrook.

Del held out her glass. 'I need another drink.'

Kim obliged by opening the second bottle of wine.

Del examined the image more closely. Nick wore an open-necked drill shirt with rolled-up sleeves, and he had a boyish grin on his handsome face – the epitome of casual, country charm. The photo was a public relations triumph, designed to appeal to the rural community that Nick wanted to win over. It occurred to Del that he wouldn't know she was part of that community. In the four years that she'd known Nick, Del had never spoken about Darby or Kingfisher Farm. She'd merely talked in vague terms about growing up in the Central Ranges

'My father died years ago, and I'm estranged from my mother,' she'd said.

'Can't you tell me more than that?' Nick had pleaded.

She'd shaken her head. 'Please, I don't want to talk about it. Maybe one day . . .'

He hadn't pressed the issue. Instead, he'd kissed her and said, 'When you're ready, I'll listen.'

Del felt herself choking up. Nick was the most loving, most under-standing man in the world. She took another look at his smiling face on the pamphlet. A flash of anger made her toss the brochure across the table. 'How dare Nick look so damn cheerful.' Del slapped a mosquito on her arm, leaving a smear of blood. 'Like he hasn't a care in the world.'

'That's a bit unfair.' Kim looked at the photo. 'I've only met Nick a few times, but even I can tell that he's posing for the camera. It's a fake smile. It doesn't mean he's happy.'

'Well, you could have fooled me.' Del snatched back the pamphlet and glared at it.

Kim seemed bemused. 'You're talking about a man you fell in love with. A man who wanted to marry you a few months ago. A man who's just lost his mother and found her dead body. Do you think he's so shallow that he's simply put all of that behind him?'

Kim was right. Nick had been through a lot. She had no right to judge him in any way, especially since she herself was indirectly behind his misery. And anyway, she still loved him. That would never change. Didn't she want him to be happy? She recalled the words of the note she'd written him. *Have a wonderful life*, she'd said, and she'd meant it. Never again would she begrudge Nick his happiness.

Kim pointed to the pamphlet. 'Where do you stand on the mine?'

'I haven't thought much about it,' said Del. 'My mum's dead against it, though.'

'So am I,' said Kim.

'A conservationist like you opposed to a coal mine? Who'd have thought?'

Kim laughed. 'I suppose it does go with the territory.'

'The thing is, I can see both sides,' said Del. 'Mining companies invest heavily in communities. They create lots of jobs. As long as the environmental protections are there, I don't see anything wrong with it. Now, can we talk about something else, please?'

Del reached down to stroke Tiny, who was snoozing under her chair. Now that she knew Nick was spearheading the mine expansion, she was more determined than ever not to join any opposition to it. Let Nick succeed and make his father proud. Let him have the wonderful life that she wished for him.

'I'm making a solemn vow,' said Del, somewhat drunkenly. 'And, Kim, I need you to be my witness.'

'Deal.'

Del raised her glass. 'I hereby swear that I'm giving up men.'

CHAPTER 20

When Del got up the next morning, Kim was making pancakes and both of them were nursing hangovers. They didn't chat much. They'd done all their talking the night before, staying up into the wee small hours, discussing everything under the sun. Life, love, philosophy – the state of the world.

Del left after breakfast with a promise to catch up again soon. On the drive home, her mind was awhirl with all they'd discussed, especially her plans for the farm. Kim had been full of help and good advice.

Del told her that Darby was losing lambs to foxes. Kim had promised to give Del two puppies from Frosty's litter. Del told her that the vineyards were being smothered with grass and weeds, but that she didn't want to use herbicides so close to the budding bunches of grapes. Kim had advised her to repair the fences and run sheep in between the rows.

'I've tried that, but the sheep stand on their back legs and strip the leaves.'

'I don't mean your current sheep,' said Kim. 'You should sell those. I mean miniature sheep – Babydolls. They're a rare heritage breed, the original Southdown type, and the Stud Sheep Breeders Association has just opened an Australian studbook. Those little cuties are in huge demand.'

'Why?' asked Del. 'Not much meat or wool on a mini-sheep.'

'They're not raised for meat or wool.'

'Then what's the point of them?'

'They're in demand'—Kim paused dramatically—'for vineyards. At only sixty centimetres tall, they can't reach the grapes, but they remove unwanted shoots from the vine trunks, plus they do all the mowing. And their light weight doesn't compact the soil like heavy machinery does. They also provide natural fertiliser – it's a self-sustaining system.'

'How do you know so much about these Babydolls?'

'Taj runs a small flock to train the Maremmas. He reckons if we're going to have sheep, we may as well have ones whose weanling lambs are worth a thousand dollars a pop. And that's at just twelve weeks.'

'Good grief! Mum's lucky to get three hundred bucks for hers, and that's when they're between six and eight months old.'

Kim had looked annoyingly smug, 'To top it off, Babydolls often have twins and triplets. It's not just vineyards that want them. Orchards do too, and they're all the rage for hobby farmers and popular as children's pets. It's their sweet little woolly faces, I think. They wear a perpetual smile, like dolphins.'

Del was convinced. She couldn't wait to tell Darby about her plans for using miniature sheep to help maintain the vines. Her plans to use livestock guardian dogs to protect the flock. Her plans for breeding Babydolls as an added income stream for the farm. They had a lot to talk about – after she took some paracetamol for her head, that was. But she wouldn't mention her connection to the man in charge of the mine expansion. Darby didn't know about Nick, and Del planned to keep it that way.

Del arrived home at lunchtime to find an old white Toyota Hilux ute parked up at the house. Darby was standing on the porch, deep in conversation with a man wearing a small backpack. He was tall and looked about thirty, with an unruly head of jet-black hair held back with a red bandanna.

Tiny tumbled from the car, howled a greeting and galloped towards them. The man turned and caught sight of Del. He waved, and as she approached the house she was struck by his classic good looks – an arresting face with smiling amber eyes, pronounced cheek-bones and a sharply defined chin. Something bright dangled from his single silver earring. What was it? She couldn't quite see.

The man must have noticed her staring. 'This?' He touched the charm. 'A golden bee. My lucky talisman. Without bees to pollinate the earth, we humans face disaster.'

His voice was deep and musical. To Del's utter surprise, she felt an instant attraction. Unbelievable. Struggling to recover from a broken engagement, and having just sworn off men – and yet here she was, being swayed by the first handsome face she'd seen since coming home to the farm.

Darby beamed when she saw Del. 'Come and meet Vince. I've asked him to stay for lunch. Vince, this is my daughter, Del.'

He reached out his arm. 'Vince Gambino.' As she shook his hand, he turned the full force of his tawny brown eyes upon her. They seemed to burn with an inner fire. Del felt a little mesmerised. 'I'm pleased to meet you ... Del.'

He said her name slowly, with a certain gravity, as if it mattered. A flush of warmth rose from her throat to her cheeks.

'Del is short for Adelaide,' said Darby. 'Such a lovely, old-fashioned name, don't you think? But for some reason she doesn't like it.'

Del groaned. Vince shot her a knowing smile, as if to say, *parents can be so embarrassing.* It made Del feel as if they shared an under-standing. Who was this man?

'Vince is here about the mine,' said Darby. 'Come inside, you two, and I'll make us some lunch.' She smiled at Vince, seeming almost as taken with him as Del was. 'I hope you like lamb and barley soup.'

While Darby fussed over a pot on the stove, Del invited Vince to sit in the kitchen. He put his backpack down at his feet and ran a finger along the old timber tabletop.

'Nice. A single slab of solid cedar. You don't see many of these any more. Homemade, right?'

'Yes,' said Del, delighted that he recognised the importance of the well-loved old table. 'By my great, great grandfather, Thomas Fisher.'

'So, your family has been farming here for generations.'

'Well, yes, although I've only recently returned to Kingfisher Farm – to help my mother out. She's been managing here on her own since my father died and it's become a bit much for her.'

Del didn't usually open up so easily. Vince was easy to talk to. She suddenly wished that she was wearing something other than a baggy T-shirt and old cut-off jeans.

'That's good of you,' he said. 'Although I'm sure living in Berrimilla is no hardship. It's a beautiful part of the world.'

She wasn't really listening. Darby had brought them mugs of hot, sweet tea earlier, and Del was watching Vince's prominent Adam's apple bob up and down as he swallowed.

'Lunch is ready,' called Darby, snapping Del back to reality. 'Del, can you help carry these?'

'Let me.' Vince sprang to his feet and helped ferry the bowls of steaming soup and plates of buttered bread over to the table.

Darby removed her apron and washed her hands at the sink. They all sat down and tucked in.

Vince smacked his lips together approvingly. 'This sure tastes good, Mrs Fisher.'

'Please, call me Darby.'

Vince was right – the soup was delicious. Despite her recent aversion to lamb, Del could feel the rich, nourishing broth chasing away her hangover.

Her curiosity got the better of her. 'Mum says you're here about the mine. Do you work for Westcorp?'

Vince looked suddenly serious. 'Quite the opposite. I'm an environmentalist. I'm visiting people to tell them about the threat the mine poses to Berrimilla and surrounding farms.'

He pulled a pamphlet from his backpack. It wasn't like the slick, glossy brochure that Kim had shown her – the one with Nick's photo on the front. This one looked like it had been made using a home printer.

'Who funds you?' asked Del, the reporter in her making a comeback.

'A hotchpotch of sources.' He wiped his face with a paper napkin. The dark shadow of stubble on his chin suited him. 'A small grant from Greenpeace. Another from Lock the Gate. Mainly I'm funded by donations from concerned members of the public.' Vince anticipated her next question. 'I gave up my job as a graphic designer to become a volunteer. This cause is important to me.'

That explained Vince's clothes. His worn-out jumper and faded jeans probably came from a thrift shop. What an interesting man. So different from Nick, with his Ralph Lauren polo shirts and R. M. Williams moleskin trousers. If she was still at the paper, she'd love to write an article about Vince.

Del began reading the pamphlet. The headline read, 'Stand with us! Protect your community from the Mount Morton Coal Mine'. Its claims echoed the Post Office petition. The expanded mine would cause a decline in living standards due to noise, dust and decreased property values. It would encroach on farmland and contaminate groundwater. It would destroy hectares of koala habitat that was also a home to endangered honeyeaters and gliders.

'People are tired of being bullied,' Vince's voice rang with conviction. 'Mining companies routinely lie to landholders, intimidate communities and threaten legal action against anyone who opposes them.'

'You'll get no argument from me,' said Darby. 'Our progress association is behind the petition. You have my full support.'

Vince turned to Del. 'And what about you? Where do you stand?'

She shook her head and held up her hand. 'Leave me out of it.'

'That's a pity.' Darby sounded disappointed. 'I hoped you might write a letter to the paper for us. Maybe get an article published. You're the best person for the job, considering your background.'

'Background?' asked Vince.

'My daughter is a reporter.'

'*Was* a reporter,' Del corrected.

'Well, yes,' Darby smiled proudly. 'Del's turned her back on all that and has come home to help run the farm.'

'A reporter, eh?' Vince looked thoughtful. 'We could use someone like you. The campaign runs on a shoestring. We can't afford to pay for publicity.'

Vince's enthusiasm was infectious. Despite her vow to never write again, she rather liked the idea of working with this man.

'Please, Del,' said Darby, as she began gathering up the empty plates. 'I'm sure your father would have wanted you to help.'

Del bristled, the old anger flaring again. How dare Darby pretend to know what Dad would have wanted. If it wasn't for her, Dad may well have been there to speak for himself. The remark made her realise how foolish she'd been to consider Vince's proposal, however briefly.

And what about the promise she'd made – the promise not to cause Nick one more moment of heartbreak or trouble? How would he feel if she were to campaign against him? It would confirm his worst fears about her.

Del looked at Vince's hopeful face. He was charming, for sure. Charismatic even – but she'd sworn off men. So many promises she'd made to herself, yet her resolve had almost crumbled at the sight of Vince's dark good looks. What sort of a person was she?

Del glared at her mother. 'I said I don't want to get involved.' She shoved her chair back and stood up. 'And I meant it. So, Vince, if you'll excuse me, I have work to do.'

Del escaped the house, feeling ashamed of herself. She whistled for the dogs, collected her fencing tools and headed for the vineyard – the place where she could still feel her father.

CHAPTER 21

Nick opened the diary for what might have been the hundredth time. With his cast removed, he could use both hands to turn the pages. But that only made it easier for him to find the one near the middle where his mother had written her final, devastating entry. Where her old-fashioned fountain pen had traced her final few letters – an *f*, an *r* and two *es*, *free* – then added a full stop to her life. The blank pages beyond that last word were confronting, making her absence seem terribly real.

He'd wanted to know what his mother had been thinking and feeling in the days and hours before taking the pills. Now he knew. In a sense she'd come back to life through her written words. With a little imagination he could hear her speaking them aloud, could see her standing with the open diary in her hand. That was unsettling enough, but more unsettling was what she'd written on the last page.

I can't exist in a world that knows me as a sad, abandoned creature – an object of nothing but pity. I don't blame Carson. I'm not enough for him, and I never have been. That's not his fault. He loved me anyway. But now my private hell has been exposed, and it's too much. My darling Nick will be better off without his worthless excuse for a mother. Carson won't be chained to a mad woman. Today I will set them both free.

Nick had seen his mother on the morning before she died. He'd witnessed her break with reality. And when he read that final entry, her anguish rang loud and clear. Pain and self-loathing had driven her to her death. Yet he'd been unsure of the meaning of one line.

I'm not enough for him, and never have been.

That could simply mean Natalie felt that she'd never measured up. But could it also mean she thought Carson had strayed outside their marriage? Nick had kept reading, flicking back in time through his mother's life.

He'd stayed up all night, unable to put the diaries aside. He found moments of joy that made him smile. When Natalie described her fiftieth birthday and all the fun she'd had. Or when Nick took her to Sydney to see *The Phantom of the Opera*. But these bright spots were few and far between.

Of course, Natalie had struggled with her mental health for a long time, prone to paranoia and depression. But even knowing this, Nick found it hard to discount all of the disturbing things he read. These were private diaries, meant for her eyes alone. His mother had no reason to lie. What she wrote was what she'd earnestly believed, whether it coincided with reality or not. And what she'd earnestly believed was that Carson had been unfaithful to her – not once, but on many occasions.

Carson has someone else again. I can always tell. He's more affectionate, more attentive. It's out of guilt, I suppose.

Another entry read, *He came home this afternoon with that look in his eye. He's had some girl. I fear that it's one of those apprentices he sponsors. I know it happens. I read the email from a poor girl's mother. I think he must pay them off.*

And another, from only a year or so ago, *My darling is playing away. I can cope with his one-offs, but not with these extended affairs. I've moved into the guest suite. It's the only way I know how to cope. I can't bear to share his bed. He knows I know, yet we never speak of it.*

Nick wanted to dismiss her shocking words as delusions. But although the entries about Carson's infidelity went back years, the tone of them never changed. If they were mere figments of a paranoid imagination, he'd have expected wild accusations followed by periods of insight – periods where Natalie had some understanding of the falseness of her perceptions. That wasn't the case. Through thick and thin, illness and health, happiness and sadness, his mother steadfastly held on to the belief that Carson was a serial philanderer.

Nick desperately didn't want to believe it. Carson had been his rock throughout childhood and right up until the present day. Overbearing and autocratic at times, but his heart was always in the right place. Nick had never once doubted Carson's love, either for himself or for Natalie. And Nick was devoted in return. No son could love and admire their father more than he did.

Still, Nick couldn't ignore the fact that Natalie's diaries supported the allegations made against Carson in the *Winga Gazette*. A faint, niggling doubt gnawed at him. Had he lost the woman he loved in defence of a guilty man? No, he wouldn't allow himself to think that way. His mother had suffered through years of debilitating mental illness, which eventually led to her taking her own life. It was futile to look for a reason beyond that.

He wished Carson would follow through with his threat to sue the *Gazette*. Not doing so was a bad look. Nick resolved to confront his father on the issue. But he'd wait until Carson had had more time to recover from Natalie's death.

Relinquishing the mayoralty had also taken its toll. Carson had thrived in the limelight, proud of his personal connection to thousands of constituents. He'd loved listening to their concerns, which was one of the reasons why he'd been so popular. No community event was too small for him to attend, and it was often joked that he'd turn up to the opening of an envelope.

But since Natalie's death, the once-gregarious Carson had become reluctant to attend public events. At times he seemed almost as depressed as his wife had once been. But with Nick's help, Carson would get through it. Nick wouldn't fail his father the way he'd failed his mother. The 'if onlys' piled up when he lay awake at night thinking of Mum. Thoughts fit to drive a man mad. If only he'd come home from hospital sooner. If only he'd convinced Mum to confide her fears to him. If only he'd gone up to the main house with her on that final, fateful morning. Well, there'd be no regrets or missteps when it came to Dad. Nick didn't plan to put a foot wrong there.

He put the diary back into the large blanket chest in the corner of his walk-in wardrobe. Nick had cleared it out to discretely accommodate the dozens of volumes, all neatly labelled in Mum's flowery script. It was comforting having them close. He'd only gone through a few of them so far. Partly because of the sheer volume of words, and partly because the task was so emotionally taxing. But he'd made himself a promise to read every word.

Nick decided to tackle them anew using a different strategy. Instead of skipping around and browsing random entries, he'd begin at the beginning. He selected six of the earliest volumes he could find, dated more than twenty years ago, and packed them in his suitcase. Thank goodness he'd retrieved the diaries before his father had blocked off the guest wing. Carson hadn't even allowed Mrs Marlow in to clear out Natalie's things.

'Leave it as it is,' he'd said, then brought in a carpenter to board up both entrances. An attempt to seal off the pain of her death perhaps. But it wouldn't work. Natalie inhabited the walls, the furniture, the garden – every inch of Westbrook. Was this what people meant by being haunted? This sense that your deceased loved one remained?

Carson felt it too, Nick could tell. For Nick, his mother was a loving presence. It pleased him to think that she was still around, if only in memory. With her final words she'd promised to set Nick and Carson free. He wanted to think that she'd set herself free instead. Free of her mental torments, free of her human frailties. He hoped that she was finally happy. It comforted him to believe it, even though most of him wished she was still here. But for his father, reminders of Natalie filled him with renewed misery. The mere thought of his grief made Nick ashamed for ever doubting his fidelity to his wife.

Carson didn't know that Nick had the diaries, and, considering their contents, it was best to keep it that way. It would break his father's heart to read them.

Nick had just finished packing when a knock came at the door. That would be Carson, come to say goodbye. He'd given Nick the job of overseeing the northern mine expansion and garnering public support, part of which involved visiting local communities and allaying their concerns.

'There's some trouble brewing up in Kingfisher Valley,' he'd told Nick. 'A residents' association is rallying people against the project. Led by a man called Ken Tucker, an ex-coalminer with a bee in his bonnet apparently. It's just a small movement at the moment, but I want it stopped in its tracks. The last thing we need is some community group launching a challenge in the Land and Environment Court. That could set us back months.'

Nick effectively had carte blanche when it came to investing in the community. He was looking forward to sharing some exciting plans with the people of Kingfisher Valley. A sports ground and community centre for Dungong. Sponsorship programs for local schools, and a brand new mobile library bus. Road upgrades to Berrimilla and Hermit Hill. With so much to offer, Nick was confident that he could win over public opinion.

'Hurry up,' called Carson at the cottage door. 'I haven't got all day

and it's time you were off. It's a four-hour drive to Mount Morton.'
Winston barked in agreement.

Nick grinned. That sounded more like the old Carson. He took a
last look around the cottage and whispered, 'Bye, Mum.'

It would be good to throw himself into something new. Something
to take his mind off losing his mother. Something to take his mind off
losing Del. And, for the umpteenth time, he wondered where in the
world she was.

CHAPTER 22

It was a glorious October day in the mountains. The sun shone from a sky of flawless blue. A fragrant breeze rippled through the grass. Magpies carolled in chorus from atop a tall grey gum, and at that moment there was nowhere else on earth that Del would rather be. She glanced at her watch and realised that she'd forgotten to stop for lunch.

It might have been Sunday, but this was no day of rest. Del had been working since breakfast, trying to get the vineyard ready in time. For tomorrow, her brand-new flock of Babydoll sheep would arrive.

Kim had helped her to find them – two rams and eighteen ewes from a dispersal sale. Their purchase price had eaten into Del's savings, but by buying an entire flock, the average cost per animal was way down.

Del wiped the sweat from her forehead and finished straining the final length of sheep netting on the vineyard's western boundary. With each pull of the ratchet, the ringlock fence grew tighter and tighter until, with a final tweak of the top wire to judge its tension, Del was done.

'Not bad, if I do say so myself. What do you think, Tiny?' The dog whined and thumped his tail on the ground.

Ken Tucker came over from where he was piling up old fence posts. He was a tall man in his mid-fifties, with a leathery face and deep smile lines around his eyes. Del didn't know much about him, other than the fact that he'd helped her mother with the farm over the past few years, but she noticed that he wore no wedding ring.

He also tweaked the top wire. It gave a satisfying twang, and he grunted his approval. 'She's tight as a drum.'

Del smiled, pleased by his gruff praise, and surveyed her handiwork. What a difference the new fence made. Some of Darby's sheep grazed up to it and tested the ringlock in a few places. They gave it a determined try, clearly used to having unimpeded access to the vines, but they couldn't get through. They took a last, longing look at the juicy leaves and swelling bunches of grapes, then gave up and walked away. Yes! Del gave a little fist pump. The neglected hillside was beginning to look cared for again.

Del looked over to where Ken was loading the tools and leftover wire into his ute. If it wasn't for Ken, the vineyard would be nowhere near finished. He'd been a huge help, spending his weekend taking down the sagging netting and using a post lifter to remove the rusted star pickets. Then he'd rammed in the shiny new galvanised ones with a post driver. He'd done a great job, saving Del days of work and earning her friendship and respect. She was starting to suspect that he was sweet on Darby, however, and she wasn't sure what to think about that. It smacked too much of him trying to take her father's place.

Ken was a good person – quiet, hardworking and polite – but he didn't offer much by way of conversation. But there was one issue he was vocal about – the Mount Morton mine expansion, or, more precisely, his opposition to it. Del had heard plenty on the topic during their two days working together. She could understand why. Ken might raise cattle now, but as a young man he'd been a coalminer. Now he suffered from the early stages of black lung disease. And when she'd asked what she could do to thank him for his help, he had something very specific in mind.

'Come to a meeting of the progress association with me and your mum tonight. That young feller from Sydney is giving a talk.'

'Vince?'

'That's the one. He's going to give us some tips for stopping the damn mine. And you must be sick of sitting around at home most nights.'

Ken was right. She was growing very bored in the evenings, with only her mother for company. Playing Scrabble, watching one of two regional free-to-air television stations that had reception or reading alone in her bedroom. What a contrast to her old life. Her nights with Nick. Romantic weekend trips to Sydney or to the coast. The challenge of researching articles and the adrenaline rush of meeting deadlines. Never ever finding herself at a loose end.

Darby always invited Del along when she went into Berrimilla for a pub meal, but so far Del had declined. Her early ambivalence towards Ken had been holding her back. But she had to admit that he'd made a real effort to help and befriend her.

'I know how you said you don't want to get involved,' said Ken. 'But what would it hurt to come and listen tonight, eh?'

'Nothing,' she said, pleased at the thought of seeing Vince again, in spite of herself. 'Of course I'll come.'

The corners of his pale blue eyes crinkled with pleasure. 'I'll pick you girls up at seven o'clock sharp.' A shadow passed over the sun and he glanced at the sky. Dark clouds were rolling in from the west. 'And tell Darby she'd best lock her poddy lambs in the shed tonight. The weather's turning.'

Del followed Ken and Darby into the town's century-old Mechanics Institute Hall. When she was a child, her Brownie troop used to meet there and she hadn't been inside since. Not much had changed. The same tongue-and-groove tallowwood floors. The same high sash windows that never let in much light. The same cedar beams under the corrugated iron roof. Even the same wall-mounted electric fans.

No sign of insulation. As Del remembered, the place was freezing in winter and an oven in summer.

A trestle table along one wall held an urn, cups and saucers, and the petition against the mine expansion. Several people were already signing it. Chairs had been set up facing the stage – an eclectic mix of modern stackable plastic ones, padded vinyl ones that had seen better days, and a few of the original timber hall chairs. They found a seat towards the back. Del gave a quick intake of breath as she recognised the initials carved in the back of the chair in front; her own initials, scratched using the tip of a compass. Past and present existed side by side in Berrimilla. She turned towards the door. People were still streaming in. A good turnout. Soon it would be standing room only.

A microphone and overhead projector had been set up on the stage, and there was Vince, talking to a dark-haired young woman in a long flowery dress. Was that his girlfriend? Del looked away, annoyed that she'd even asked herself the question. When she looked back, the girl had left the stage and was sitting beside a man holding a baby. She took the child and bounced it on her knee. Not Vince's girlfriend after all.

'There's a bigger crowd than I thought there'd be,' whispered Darby, looking pleased. She pointed across the room. 'The Coopers are here, and Tony Palmer. I thought they were in favour of the mine. Tony hoped his boy might get a job there.'

Ken snorted. 'He's dreaming. That lad wouldn't know a hard day's work if it hit him on the head. Fancies himself a rock guitarist, he does. I hear he plans a move to Sydney when school finishes to join a band. Everybody seems to know except his father.'

Vince stepped over to the microphone and held up his hand. The murmur of voices in the hall quietened. 'I know many of you here see me as an outsider, with no business interfering in your community affairs. But the truth is, I have a very personal stake in stopping this mine expansion.' A dramatic pause allowed people's curiosity to mount.

'Eight years ago, the government approved an open-cut coalmine not far from my grandfather's Queensland farm.'

Vince put up a photo on the overhead projector. It showed a picturesque farmhouse, surrounded by vineyards and rolling green hills.

'Growing up, I spent nearly every school holidays at that farm.' He put up a shot of a laughing, dark-haired boy swinging on a rope hung over a river. 'For a city kid, it was a slice of pure paradise.

'Then the mine came. At first, Grandpa was pleased. The company said it would invest in the community – create jobs, sponsor sporting teams, rebuild the church. It said the mine would be the best thing that ever happened to their little town. Well, it wasn't. They lied about everything: about the social impact, about the health impact, about the jobs. Coal dust poisoned Grandpa's crops and his stock's drinking water.'

More photos appeared on the projector, one after another. Grapevines coated in soot. An inky dark dam. Grey sheets hanging on a line. Dead lambs. Del's heart ached, and a dismayed murmur travelled around the room.

'The reality was polluted creeks and bore water. Twenty-four-seven noise. An epidemic of asthma. And as for the jobs bonanza? Most went to fly-in, fly-out workers. People began leaving the town in droves. Grandpa had lost my grandmother to cancer the year before. Now he also lost his friends, and the community he'd lived in for seventy years. It broke his heart. He tried to sell, but nobody wanted to buy the land.'

Vince put up a picture of a 'For Sale' sign beside a farm gate.

'My grandfather was a proud person. He'd devoted his life to that farm, and now it was worthless.'

A photo of a twinkle-eyed old man with a leathery face smiled from the screen. Vince scrubbed a hand across his eyes. Were those tears?

'I found his body hanging in the shearing shed.'

A collective gasp rose from the audience, and for a while nobody spoke. Vince turned off the projector and stepped down from the stage, visibly upset. Several people in the front row stood and offered their condolences.

Ken whispered something to Darby, then went forward to address the crowd. 'I'm sure we'd all like to thank Vince for that powerful presentation.' The hall resounded with the sound of applause. 'And since we have him here, are there any questions?'

Dozens of hands went up. Ken clapped Vince on the back and encouraged him to return to the stage. It seemed everybody had a query.

Del sat very still, stunned by Vince's talk. It had been an impressive performance. He could have simply delivered a string of statistics and Greenpeace talking points. Instead, he'd won over the townsfolk by opening up about his personal tragedy. She couldn't help thinking about Nick, and the coincidence that both men had lost loved ones to suicide.

Vince had regained his composure and was answering questions in a calm, authoritative manner. People were nodding in agreement as he spoke, even the Coopers. He'd single-handedly pulled off a public relations coup in the Berrimilla Hall that night. Del imagined him repeating his success in other town halls around Kingfisher Valley, imagined him visiting homes and community groups to tell his heart-felt story.

Del didn't know the full circumstances of Vince's experience. It may have happened years ago, before mines required strict social and environmental assessments. There wasn't necessarily any correlation with Berrimilla's situation. But his account had nonetheless struck a chord with the townsfolk.

She almost felt sorry for Nick in his publicity push for the mine. He may have the might of Westcorp behind him, but there was no doubt about it – Vince Gambino would prove to be a formidable opponent.

CHAPTER 23

Nick stowed away the last of his gear and looked around the humble room. It was number twenty-seven of more than two hundred similar portable units, known as dongas. Each contained a single bed, a bathroom, an air conditioner, a desk, a cupboard, a television, a microwave and a fridge. Basic, but it would do.

Earlier that day he'd explored the rest of Mount Morton Village, a place Nick had not visited before. It was located a few kilometres north of the Kingfisher Valley town of Gidgee Creek and provided live-in accommodation for mine workers. The village boasted a modern camp kitchen and a dining hall where buffet-style meals were served free of charge around the clock. There were laundries, a gym, a swimming pool, barbeque areas, a recreation hall and a general store. There was even a bar called the Wet Mess that opened for two or three hours twice a day after the mine workers' staggered twelve-hour shifts finished. Air quality monitors were positioned around the site.

Nick had opted to live with the miners to gain an understanding of how they felt about their jobs, and how the general community felt about them and the mine. Although some workers were locals, a substantial number came from farther afield. These were the DIDOs – drive-in, drive-out miners. It was a common employment arrangement for Hunter region mines. Many were bussed in from hundreds of kilometres away, living on site for rostered shifts, usually two weeks on and one week off.

Nick hadn't thought much about it before, but now he wondered how the locals felt about so many out-of-towners working at the mine, when regional unemployment was high. He'd been employed by his father all his working life, but he'd never had much to do with the practical side of the business. He'd graduated with a Master of Business Administration from Sydney University. As Westcorp's managing director, his job mainly involved big-picture stuff. Developing company policies, overseeing audits and providing financial projections for the board of directors. He was looking forward to discovering more about the nitty gritty of mining operations.

Nick had spent the afternoon literally at the coalface, talking to workers. Most said that the mine was viewed positively, but a surprising number said that people had growing concerns about coal, citing climate change and ecological damage as their main worries. That was a turnaround from five years ago when Carson had opened an additional mine in the east. Back then, studies showed that new economic opportunities were all that mattered to the locals. This time around it would be more important than ever for Nick to spruik Westcorp's dedication to environmental management and rehabilitation.

Nick had asked the camp kitchen for a takeaway dinner pack of beef curry and rice. He slipped it into the microwave in his donga, put a sixpack of Heineken in the fridge and helped himself to a stubby. Ugh – warm beer, but he drank it anyway. Then he leafed through the folder his assistant, Pam, had prepared for him.

A lot of research had gone into the information contained therein. The main concerns of the good folk of Kingfisher Valley were listed by level of importance from one to twenty. Pam had created her ranking by examining issues raised in local papers, by following and sometimes joining local social media groups and by conducting online surveys that offered participants discounts at local businesses.

The number one concern was the cost of living, followed by health care, the economy and the environment. Employment came in at number five, just ahead of housing and education. Nick had expected jobs to be at the top of the list, but he supposed that cost of living and the economy were all tied up with jobs. And the mine expansion would employ an additional five hundred people. That carrot should prove to be an easy sell.

Nick turned to the section in the folder titled 'Opposition'. There seemed to be two main players. A local residents' association had started a petition asking the government to deny the permit for expansion. That wouldn't come to anything. An environmental impact statement was well underway, along with the customary dust and noise management plans. And on top of that, Carson had a private handshake agreement with the premier, who gave a fast-track approval process the nod. That might not be strictly aboveboard, but it was the way of these things. Nick saw nothing wrong with it, providing Westcorp complied with all the necessary legal require-ments. For as long as he could remember, Carson had been coming to gentlemen's agreements with various politicians.

In addition to the residents' group, an activist was causing trouble by conducting town meetings and stirring up feelings against the mine – a man by the name of Vince Gambino. He wasn't a local and didn't seem to have an organisation backing him, although he claimed to be partly funded by Greenpeace. Nick almost felt sorry for him. A lone wolf wouldn't stand a chance once the Westcorp publicity machine swung into action. Perhaps he'd arrange to talk with the man, to convince him of the mine's environmental credentials. That might be the quickest and easiest way to neutralise him.

Nick closed the folder and tried his curry. Not bad. He then selected the very first of his mother's diaries from the shelf by the bed. He lay down on the donga's hard, single mattress and began to read. Suddenly Natalie was a young woman again and he was two years old.

It was after midnight when Nick finally stopped reading. He'd finished the sixpack, but the rest of his curry dinner remained forgotten on the desk. He closed the third journal, the one where he was four and Natalie confessed her first suspicions about Carson's infidelity.

He's on a business trip to Sydney again. It's lonely here in this big old house with just a child for company. Not that I don't love Nick – I absolutely adore him – but I adore Carson too and miss my lover and best friend. When he's home, life is wonderful, and I feel foolish for doubting him. There could never be a more caring and devoted husband. But when he's gone, my mind plays tricks. I go through his pockets and find theatre ticket stubs – always two. The faint scent of a woman's fragrance lingers in the weave of his jacket ...

Were her fears genuine? Or was Nick witnessing, through her own words, the beginning of his mother's mental illness?

He turned off the light and lay back, his thoughts racing. The early diaries offered him a fascinating window into his past. For the first few years his parents had shared a happy marriage, that much was clear. Carson kept his focus on his family, always surprising Natalie and little Nick with presents and unexpected trips to exciting places. Hayman Island. Fiji. Disneyland.

And it was intriguing to gain a picture of Bobby, Carson's older brother who'd died when Nick was five. Nick had no memory of his uncle. Until now, Bobby had been a shadowy figure, linked only to the tragic car accident that had killed him and Nick's grandparents. But through his mother's diary entries, the man was coming to life.

Natalie, Bobby and Carson had been close. Bobby was the best man at their wedding, and she wrote about him often. She wrote about the fun the three of them had on a holiday together, about how they shared their hopes and dreams and plans for the future. She'd pasted an envelope in the back of the diary containing postcards that Bobby had sent her from a trip to France. He was, without doubt, one of his mother's closest confidants and friends.

But it was apparent that Bobby and Carson had very different personalities. Even as a young man, Carson was filled with ambition, keen to develop and expand his father's mining empire. Bobby, on the other hand, seemed uninterested in the family business. Natalie wrote that he was a keen birdwatcher and naturalist who'd wanted to study biology at university. But he was the oldest son, which meant the full weight of parental expectation fell on him. So, Robert Henry Shaw was being groomed for the managing directorship of Westcorp, although his heart wasn't in it.

Bobby says that extraordinary fossils are often seen in the coalface. Mostly they're destroyed because his father, Hugo, insists that the mining work must go on. Bobby is livid at the waste. He showed me some spectacular examples of ferns he collected from the slag heaps at Disappointment Creek.

And Natalie devoted a lot of time to Carson's outrage at being denied the top job.

Carson complains that Bobby doesn't even want to be managing director. And it's true – he doesn't. Carson's envy is poisoning their relationship. It upsets me to see the growing tension between them. I blame Hugo and his ridiculous, old-fashioned ideas. Why should the oldest son inherit the family business, when the second son is far better suited? It's making them all miserable and tearing the brothers apart.

This was fascinating stuff. Nick had no idea that Uncle Bobby had originally been anointed to run the company. The only reason Carson was in charge was because Bobby had died. Nick imagined how conflicted Dad must have felt after the fatal car crash that killed his family. It was because of that tragedy that Carson became head of

Westcorp, a position that meant the world to him, a position that defined him. How often had Carson said that his work was his life? Nick had always admired him for his commitment and ambition. It came as a shock to think that, if not for a vicious twist of fate, Carson might have never held that position at all.

CHAPTER 24

Del watched with satisfaction as the flock of tiny sheep wandered along the rows of grapevines. They'd already made terrific headway clearing out the weeds. Ken was helping her set up an irrigation system, together with a little tank that would add fertiliser to the water-saving drippers. In a few more weeks the vineyard would look as neat and well-loved as she'd always hoped it would.

It was late spring, and big bunches of grapes were swelling in the sun. The sight filled her with pride. Up until now, Del hadn't been sure there would even be a harvest. Her care and attention might have come too late in the season, and pests and disease could easily have claimed the crop. But looking at the young fruit, her fears were allayed. She closed her eyes and imagined her father standing beside her, heard him chuckle the way he did when he was pleased with something – a bittersweet moment.

Well, if she was going to have a harvest in autumn, she'd better figure out what to do with it. She had no wine-making equipment and wouldn't know what to do with it if she did. It would take time to learn the vintner's craft. She'd need to approach a local winery to see if they'd buy her first crop of grapes. Del was confident they would; shiraz and pinot noir varieties were in demand and fetching good prices. But she'd need to build facilities and learn how to process the second year's harvest herself. The added value for wine versus grapes at the farm gate was substantial. A dollar's worth of grapes could be turned into ten dollars' worth of bottled wine. And, in any case, she was impatient to produce a homemade vintage for her father's sake. The day she slapped that Bluebird Shiraz label on her first bottle would be one of the happiest days of her life.

Del leaned on the vineyard gate and laughed as two of her sheep, Sooty and Sweep, held ramming matches. They eyed each other and backed up, all the while pawing the ground and tossing their hornless heads. Babydolls were a naturally polled breed. Del had got to know the new sheep during the days she'd spent pruning and training the grapevines. She'd named her favourites. There was Ma, who saw herself as the leader and protector of the flock. If Tiny wandered too close, Ma would stamp her front feet and run at him. It was funny to see the tiny ewe, barely sixty centimetres tall, scare off the towering wolfhound. Then there were the three amigos – Flopsy, Mopsy and Topsy. They always grazed together. In defiance of conventional flocking wisdom, the sisters set themselves apart from the mob. When the other sheep went one way, as often as not the independent triplets went the other.

For all their fierce posturing, Sooty and Sweep were only five-month-old ram lambs. Del hoped they'd be mature enough to join with the ewes by April, which was apparently when Babydoll sheep came into season. Darby's crossbred Merinos would happily accept being mated any time from October on, but Del had learned that wasn't the case with British heritage sheep. They were autumn breeders, brought into oestrus by declining daylight hours.

What a lot there was to learn: winemaking, the vineyards, the Babydolls. Del planned to undertake a crash course in all of it. And the StarNet satellite dish arriving that afternoon was key to doing just that. Fast and reliable internet would be a dream. She couldn't wait for tonight to dive into some solid research. Del checked her watch.

Two o'clock. Time to get back to the house; the delivery driver would be here soon.

When she arrived home, Vince was on the porch, lounging in one of the old cane chairs. Del grinned. She couldn't help it – she was glad to see him.

He rose slowly and languorously like a cat, unfolding his long legs until he stood straight-backed and smiling. Sunshine glinted off his earring. With his long dark hair, olive complexion and eyes the colour of rich molasses, he was a very different man from Nick. A flash of insight made her wonder if that was why she liked him.

'Have you come for a second go at changing my mind about your campaign?' she said.

He raised an eyebrow, asking the question. 'I could sure use your help. Maybe you could get a piece about me published in the local paper? You must still have connections.'

That was true. Celia would welcome a freelance article from Del. Her backstabbing former editor had sent several emails over the past few weeks. Some full of apologies. Some offering Del her job back. Some trying to enlist Del's help in writing a follow-up exposé of Carson based on new information. What a nerve.

Del washed her hands under the tap beside the verandah, then gestured for Vince to go inside. 'Are your boots clean?' she called. He paused, inspected the soles of his shoes, then pushed open the flywire door. Del followed him inside.

The dynamic between the two of them was different without Darby in the room. They sat at the kitchen table, taking each other in, exchanging small smiles and silently making a connection.

Del broke eye contact first. She stood up and walked to the kettle. 'Tea?'

'I could go a beer if you have one.'

She grabbed two of Ken's stubbies from the refrigerator.

When Del had first met Vince, he'd been wearing a threadbare green jumper. She recalled it well, right down to the Sea Shepherd

Conservation Society pin on his chest. Seems she'd been paying attention. Today he wore a blue farmer's shirt with rolled up sleeves. Part of a tattoo showed on his tanned forearm. It resembled the spokes of a wheel. She tried not to look.

Vince took a gulp of beer and took off his shirt. Del pushed her chair back, startled. He didn't seem to notice how disconcerted she was. His tanned torso was well-muscled and almost entirely hairless. Vince pointed to the tattoo. 'It's Buddhist – the eight-spoke Dharma wheel symbolising the Noble Eightfold Path.'

Del stared at the beautiful tattoo. With it fully revealed, she could appreciate the intricacy of its design: the two-tone spokes shaded yellow and gold, the red jewel-studded rim of the wheel and the swirling tri-coloured centre.

He flexed his bicep, which seemed to show the wheel off to greater effect. 'I suppose you think it's some kind of hippy claptrap.'

'Oh no,' she said, wanting to touch the symbol on his arm. 'It's beautiful. I studied Buddhism during my first year at uni. The Eightfold Path leads to enlightenment, right? Let's see if I remember. To follow it you need right understanding, right thought, right speech, right action, right livelihood, right effort, right mindfulness and … ' She thought hard for a moment. 'Right concentration.'

Vince gave a round of applause, seeming impressed. 'And where do you think you stand along that road to enlightenment?'

Del grinned. 'A damn sight further along than when I was a journalist. Just so you know, I'm well and truly done with that. Now, put your shirt back on before my mother walks in.'

Vince returned her grin and did as she asked.

The dogs started barking. Del looked out the window to see a van struggling up the steep driveway.

'StarNet!' She rushed outside.

The po-faced driver climbed from the cab. 'Why on earth you folks want to live way out here in the sticks is beyond me,' he grumbled. 'Do you know how long it took me to get here? And I got lost. The GPS tried to kill me. Kept wanting to send me over cliffs.'

Vince unsuccessfully tried to stifle a laugh. Del frowned at him.

The poor delivery man seemed so thoroughly miserable that she thought he might cry.

'Some navigation systems mistake fire trails and surveyed roads for actual roads,' she said. 'It depends on the brand. On the way back, use Google Maps instead. It's much more reliable.'

Her advice was met with a grumpy *harrumph* and a curt, 'Sign here.'

She signed the delivery docket while the man opened the back of the van. He extracted a cardboard carton, which didn't look large enough to hold a satellite dish. After depositing it on the porch, he drove away without a word.

'What's in the box?' asked Vince.

Del took the penknife from her belt and slit open the carton. It was her satellite dish all right, but so much smaller than she'd expected. The NBN dishes she'd seen were twice as big. Oh well – size wasn't everything. 'It's supposed to deliver super-fast internet.'

'How does it work?' asked Vince.

'Apparently, you just plug it in.'

Del fetched an extension cord and her laptop. The dish came with a tripod stand and Vince helped set it up temporarily on the drive.

'That can't be right,' said Del. 'It's angled sideways, not pointing at the stars at all.'

She tried to turn the dish, but it wouldn't budge. They plugged it in anyway and waited. For a while nothing happened. Then the dish suddenly moved. It gradually raised its face to the sky, adjusting position every few seconds until it settled on a particular angle. The movements were endearingly lifelike.

'It's searching for low-orbit satellites to communicate with.' For some reason Del was whispering, as if talking too loudly might disturb the dish's concentration. 'Apparently, there are thousands of them up there, spinning around the world, and StarNet are launching more every day.'

Vince looked solemnly at the little dish as it once again changed angles. 'ET phone home.'

Del giggled and punched him playfully on the shoulder. 'Stop it.'

Tiny wandered over to inspect the little dish and promptly lifted his leg on it.

'No!' yelled Del, shooing him away.

Vince didn't even try to smother his laughter this time. 'You can't very well leave that thing sitting on the ground. Shouldn't it go on the roof or something?'

Del searched in the box. 'Here's the modem, and this must be the roof mounting kit.' She pulled out a piece of pipe and some brackets. 'Ken's going to put it up, but he can't do it until the weekend.'

'Show me.' Vince took the mounting kit from her and inspected it. 'Don't worry,' he said with a satisfied nod. 'I'll do it.'

'I couldn't expect—'

Vince held up his hand as if the matter was settled. 'Just find me a ladder.'

It turned out that Vince was a capable handyman. In no time he'd attached the mounting kit to the corrugated iron roof and was ready to attach the dish. She couldn't help admiring the straightness of his back and the breadth of his shoulders as he came down the ladder.

'Shouldn't we give ET a test run before he gets a home on the roof?' he said.

Del plugged the modem into the extension cord, opened her laptop and clicked on the StarNet symbol that appeared on her desktop. 'Five bars!' she said, excitedly. 'I've actually got five bars! I've never had more than two here before, and half the time I couldn't connect at all.'

On an impulse she threw her arms around Vince's neck. His mouth swooped down to steal a kiss. Del's own lips responded to him for a few delicious moments before she pulled away.

Vince ran a hand over his red bandanna. 'Was I out of line?'

Del felt light-headed, so much so that at first it was hard to answer him.

'There's something I haven't told you,' she said at last. 'I've sworn off men.'

Vince's bold gaze and half-smile seemed to say, *you could have fooled me*. 'I suppose there's a story behind that decision.'

'One I won't be telling you.'

'Fair enough.' His eyes caught and held hers. 'Let me know if you change your mind.'

CHAPTER 25

Having fast and reliable internet was a game changer for Del. Each evening she immersed herself in research. She wanted to know all there was to know about her new agricultural endeavours. For grape growing she learned about soils, topography, vine vigour, yields and fruit composition. For winemaking she learned about the equipment she'd need: fermenters, barrels, pumps, a hydrometer, tubing, bottles and bottling equipment. She learned about the process: crushing, soaking, fermenting, racking, ageing and filtering. Del wanted to have a firm theoretical grasp before she had to be hands on.

She pored over sheep pedigrees and stud books, identifying the best breeding lines and genetic combinations within her flock. She joined the Australian Stud Sheep Breeders Association and the separate Babydoll societies, finding a warm welcome from other members and a wealth of useful information about the adorable, rare breed.

Del compared business models and accounting plans, never getting to sleep before the early hours of the morning. But fast internet did more than provide her with information to get her new ventures off the ground. It ended her isolation from the outside world.

During the three months since she'd been back at the farm, Del had avoided exposure to anything beyond sleepy little Berrimilla. Her radio was tuned to a country music station that played songs of heartache and lost love. When Darby sat down to watch the seven o'clock evening news on television, Del left the room. She hadn't opened a newspaper once, not even the copies of the *Winga Gazette* that lay on the kitchen dresser. When Darby had finished with them, Del used them as weed mats in the vegetable garden.

Del had needed that time to regroup and come to terms with the new direction her life was so unexpectedly taking. It wasn't easy letting go of her dream career, so she'd avoided anything that could possibly remind her of her love of journalism.

Del's father had been a fan of the Serenity Prayer and had often quoted it to her. 'God, grant me the serenity to accept the things I cannot change, courage to change the things I can, and wisdom to know the difference.'

Well, Del couldn't change what had happened, so she'd better learn to accept it. And in the meantime, she'd expand her horizons and take an interest in the outside world again.

One evening she began scrolling through the national headlines online. It was the usual stuff. Floods up north. A man attacked by a shark on the west coast. A state minister resigning after assault allegations were made against him. She paused her scrolling, thinking of Carson. He was also an elected official who'd resigned after allegations were made against him. Del couldn't help herself. She googled his name.

A multitude of results came up. The first one described Carson Shaw as a mining magnate, businessman and popular mayor of the Central Ranges in NSW. That was out of date. Carson had apparently resigned months ago.

The next few results were more pleasing. They referred to Carson as the former mayor who'd resigned under a dark cloud of suspicion. Although he denied it and was quoted as saying, 'I'm retiring from my mayoral role to spend more time with my family.' Del snorted. Yeah, sure.

She kept scrolling. What? Carson had withdrawn the threat of a lawsuit against Celia and the *Winga Gazette*. *What would Nick make of that?* she wondered. It was as good as Carson admitting his guilt.

She kept scrolling. News about Natalie's death and the funeral. Her feature article on the Shaw family came up. Del hurried past that one. Suddenly, she caught her breath. A picture of Nick appeared on the screen – a recent corporate photo. Maybe it was the fault of an unflattering filter, but his slicked-back hair was a nondescript brown colour, rather than its actual sandy-red, and his eyes appeared to be dullish grey instead of green. He wore a suit and tie and his expression was stern. It was a terrible likeness, and not the Nick she knew at all.

The article read, 'Mr Nick Shaw, managing director of Westcorp Mining and Pastoral Pty Ltd, is spearheading the ninety-five-million-dollar Mount Morton Optimisation Project.'

Optimisation Project? Weasel words. It was a huge mine-expansion program. According to Vince, it would eat up a thousand hectares of land and extract an additional sixty-five million tonnes of coal.

Del read on. 'At a press conference on Monday, Mr Shaw promised the people of Kingfisher Valley a bright future, with job opportunities and investment in the region set to soar. He said the optimisation plan would be approved through the NSW government's fast-track assessment process.'

Del shook her head in disbelief, although she didn't know why she was surprised. The truth was that she'd never shown an interest in Nick's work. She'd switch off when he droned on about audits or policies or board meetings. Nick had learned not to talk about his job and Del had liked it that way.

Now she wished that she'd paid attention. Did the Berrimilla Progress Association know the expansion was set to be fast-tracked? Did Vince? That particular assessment process was dodgy as all hell. Last year Del broke a story about a chemical manufacturer polluting a town water supply. The plant lacked even the most basic safeguards, yet it had sailed through the same fast-track program that Nick now proposed for Mount Morton.

'The special arrangement is designed to cut green tape,' the minister had told her in an interview. Cut it? More like remove it all together. For the first time, a worm of worry squirmed in Del's belly. Were Vince and her mother right? Did the mine really pose a clear and present danger to Berrimilla?

Del had faith in Nick. She couldn't imagine such a fine man being involved in anything deceitful or detrimental to her beautiful Kingfisher Valley. But Carson? She didn't trust him one bit, and Nick had a gaping blind spot where his father was concerned. Del looked once more at Nick's picture on the screen and then scrolled away from it. Vince had asked her to assist with publicity for his campaign. She almost wished that she could.

Carson gazed dismissively around Nick's little donga. 'I can't fathom why you're staying here. What about the accommodation I arranged? A guest chalet at our McClellan Vale estate. It's where the others are.'

'Good for them,' said Nick. 'But that's a forty-minute drive away. I want to live and work here. Immerse myself in the local community.'

Carson looked nonplussed. 'It's not method acting, son. I've sent you an entire team of people to do the grunt work. You have an important job.'

'I know, so let me do it my way.'

A sudden weariness crossed Carson's face, making him look older than his sixty years. 'Very well, but if you think I'm having lunch at that camp kitchen, you're mistaken.' He gestured towards the door. 'Let's go for a proper feed.'

Carson had driven up from Winga that morning to brief Nick on the progress of the government approval process. They could have consulted via Zoom, but Nick had encouraged Carson to come in person. For one thing, Nick thought it would be good to get him out of the house. He'd barely left Westbrook since his wife's death.

But there was another reason that Nick wanted a face-to-face meeting with his father. It was time to find out why he'd changed his mind about suing the *Winga Gazette*. If there was any truth to the allegations printed in the paper, Nick had to know.

They went for lunch in the beer garden of the Royal Hotel at Gidgee Creek, the closest town to the mine. Not only did Nick want to sample the local fare, but he wanted to sound out the publican. Nobody had their ear to the ground like the owner of a country pub.

Nick got more than he bargained for from Gavin, the gregarious publican. It didn't take much to get him started either. Nick didn't tell the man who he and Carson really were, which, considering the circumstances, was probably just as well. All he did was ask what people thought about Mount Morton, and Gavin bent his ear for ten minutes, airing his grievances while supposedly taking their order.

'I remember when that mine first opened fifteen years ago. We thought it would be good for the town, inject some new capital and jobs, bring in some new people. But those blokes are no use to us. That bloody village of theirs is self-contained. They hardly come into town at all. I renovated my rooms upstairs for boarders, but no takers. And I can count on the fingers of one hand the number of local lads who've found work at the mine. Most are knocked back 'cause they don't have the skills. I suppose that's true. Folks around here are mainly farmers. But back in the day, we were promised training. We were promised that new families would move here – players for our sporting teams and kids for our school. Instead, all we get is coal dust and bloody DIDOs.'

Carson *harrumphed* loudly and waved the menu. 'I'll have the pepper steak. Make it rare – and don't take all day.'

'In a minute, mate.' Gavin kept talking, 'I grew up in Kalgoorlie. Now there's a proper mining town for you. That was in the day of the eight-hour shift, of course. None of this twelve-hour shit, leaving the miners too buggered to do anything but sleep. We all lived, worked and played in the one community. I told that Vince feller the same thing at the meeting last night.'

Vince, the Greenpeace guy? Nick wanted to know more, but one glance at Carson's red face and flared nostrils showed he was about to blow a fuse. So, perhaps it was for the best when a group of customers came in, demanding Gavin's attention. But Nick made a mental note to be back for a drink at the bar tomorrow – this time without his father in tow.

'What an insufferable man,' muttered Carson.

Nick took a swig of beer and watched a vein throb at his father's temple. 'He makes some good points, though. If we want to win hearts and minds, we have to take the locals with us.'

Carson snorted. 'Hearts and minds. What a load of rot. You realise you're simply going through the motions with this community campaign, don't you? The new mine's a foregone conclusion.'

Nick's fingers closed a little tighter on his glass. He loved his father, he really did, but did Carson have to undermine him like that? Suggest that his work wasn't meaningful? Carson was wrong, of course. Nepotism could only take the expansion so far. Nick still had to secure the required environmental and social assessments before any official approval could be finalised.

Nick's indignation spurred him to broach a second, more personal matter. 'Level with me, Dad. Why aren't you suing Celia?'

The sudden change of subject caught Carson off guard, and Nick's world shifted as something flashed in his father's eyes. It showed for the briefest moment, but it was unmistakable, nonetheless. An expression that Nick had prayed to never see there. Guilt.

And then it struck him. He'd lost Del over a lie.

CHAPTER 26

'I should have come home when you scattered Dad's ashes,' Del said to her mother one morning over breakfast. She'd always felt guilty about that. She should have helped perform that final service for her father. But instead she'd left town straight after the funeral. 'I wish I'd been there.'

'You still can be,' said Darby, helping herself to homemade blackberry jam.

Del tipped her head to the side, puzzled. 'But you—'

'Your father's ashes are in the bedroom on a shelf by the window – so he can see the garden.' She topped up her tea from the pot, then paused to look at Del. Her lips pressed together in a sad smile. 'It didn't seem right to have a send-off without you.'

'I don't understand. Whose ashes are under the tree by the memorial plaque?'

'Rocky's.'

'Dad's kelpie?'

'Allan loved that dog more than life itself. They were soulmates. Rocky seemed like a fitting stand-in for your father.'

Darby left the kitchen and returned with a blue enamelled urn. She passed it to Del.

'Thank you for waiting.' Del held it in shaky hands, surprised by its weight. 'Maybe that's why I can't move past Dad's death,' she whispered. 'He needs to be set free, and I know just the place.'

Del put some cutlery and paper napkins into the woven wicker basket. She wasn't much use in the kitchen, and preparing a picnic would normally be her mother's department. However, the nature of today's outing had sent Darby into an emotional tailspin, so Del had stepped up to the plate.

She'd made scotch eggs, coleslaw and chicken sandwiches. The sausage rolls and chocolate brownies came from the bakery. She'd also made a thermos of hot tea and had found a bottle of Dad's favourite Shiraz at Berrimilla's licensed general store.

'You get in the car, Mum.' It was clear from Darby's flushed face and red eyes that she'd been crying. 'I'll be there in a minute.'

Darby gave her daughter a grateful smile and went outside.

Del checked that they had everything: the picnic blanket and the basket stocked with food, insect repellent, the thermos, the wine – and Dad's ashes.

They parked the car by the distinctive, twin-trunked sassafras along Rakali Road. Del hadn't visited her father's favourite fishing spot since she was a teenager, but she remembered the way there as if it was yesterday.

Oddly enough, Tiny seemed to know where he was going too, unerringly following the overgrown forest path leading down to the cascades. It wound through a forest unchanged for thousands of years. Time stood still here. No bulldozers or axe men had touched this remote corner of the river.

The track skirted a towering black booyong. Del paused to admire its massive buttress roots, like great grey elephant limbs. They stretched two metres up the trunk and snaked along the ground, anchoring the rainforest tree to the topsoil. It was already ancient –

an old man of the forest with a mossy green beard – growing as it was meant to grow. Unchallenged. Reaching for heaven.

They emerged from deep shade and stepped onto the sunny river bank. Del gasped as a shock of recognition hit her. Four small waterfalls spilled from the cliff face, silver streams breaking into rainbows of spray on the rocks below. This part of the river was as familiar to Del as her father's face.

Darby put a hand to her heart and gazed around the little glade. She paled, all the colour draining from her face, and Del put a steadying hand on her arm. 'It's all right Mum. We can do this together.'

The Kingfisher River formed the western boundary of Cobbee Basin, a vast tract of wilderness and a rare example of an old-growth subtropical rainforest. Del's mind was crowded with precious memories of four seasons spent there. Autumn, and she and Dad were collecting purple Davidson's plums for Mum to make jam. Winter, and she was a little girl being carried on his shoulders to keep her out of the mud. Summer, and she was twelve, running on ahead of him to take a dip in the plunge pool below the cascades – an ideal natural swimming hole. Spring, and she was eighteen, sitting beside him on the sunny river bank, holding a fishing line but not bothering about the fish. An excuse to while away a few hours together. A quiet time to philosophise – to share hopes and dreams with her father. Tears brimmed in her eyes. This was finally goodbye.

Del reverently lifted the urn, the wine and two glasses from her backpack. She stood with her mother on a broad rock above the river, and together they tipped the precious ashes into the swift running water. She prayed for a sign, hoping for the azure flash of a kingfisher. Dad's bluebirds were once common around the falls. But she had to be content with a tiny reed warbler, singing his heart out from atop a pile of bleached driftwood. A fitting enough requiem for the solemn occasion.

'Here's to you, Dad.' She and Darby clinked glasses, but even as Del said the words, a rogue thought crept in – one she'd been determined to ward off on today of all days. If it wasn't for her mother, Dad might still be alive. Del pushed the thought away.

Darby began crying softly.

'Mum, do you want to say something?'

Darby wiped her eyes and raised her glass. 'Here's to a loving father, a wonderful husband and the best man I'll ever know. I miss you every day, my darling.'

After a few minutes of private reflection, they climbed down from their vantage point. Del spread the blanket on a sunny patch of river sand where they'd often picnicked when she was a child. The connection to her father was powerful there. She imagined that if she spun around fast enough, she'd catch a glimpse of him strolling towards her with a fishing rod in hand and a smile in his blue eyes, the sun catching in the handful of silver strands in his short blond hair. It was a bittersweet moment.

'Where's Tiny?' asked Darby. 'I packed him a lamb bone.'

Del glanced around. The big wolfhound was nowhere to be seen. 'Wait here,' she said. 'I'll find him.'

She didn't know which direction to take, but something drew her upstream. Del found Tiny playing in the river below the rapids. The clumsy pup was pouncing after little fish in the shallows. He looked up when he saw her, uttering a series of joyful yips and thrashing his tail in welcome.

And then she heard it – that familiar, high-pitched call from a nearby stand of pink-flowering corkwoods. Del held her breath as a bright blue bird darted from the treetops. Then another, and another. Del laughed aloud as a swarm of azure kingfishers skimmed the river. Brilliant blue wings. Snow-white cheeks. Gleaming golden breasts. Colours so vivid they looked freshly painted. There must have been ten of them. Del had never seen so many together before. She gave silent thanks to the universe for celebrating her father's life with such a dazzling display of nature's beauty.

Tiny finally tired of his game and came trotting back. Del hugged his shaggy neck, grateful to the wayward dog for leading her to this place. As Del turned to go she saw something white, half-obscured by scrub on the opposite bank. Too large for a mudlark. Too large even for a cockatoo. A trick of the light? She moved closer, rock-hopping across the river until she could see what it was. A sign, freshly planted in the earth.

Mount Morton Mine Offset Area.
Trespassers will be Prosecuted.

That couldn't be. Del had never questioned the status of Cobbee Basin. She'd always assumed it was a national park. It formed part of a significant songline for the Wonnarua people and was crisscrossed with hiking and bridle trails. She and her father had spent many happy days there, camping and fishing along the river, trail riding and spotting rare birds: speckled warblers, powerful owls and the elusive regent honeyeater. The basin was a well-kept secret among local fish- ermen, campers and twitchers – treasured and enjoyed since time immemorial. So how could trespassers now be prosecuted?

Del gazed up at the distant peak of Mount Morton looming over the basin. She felt a chill. Did Westcorp have a claim on land this far west of the mine? Could this ancient place, brimming with bluebirds and memories, be at risk? She patted Tiny and took one last look at the river. No kingfishers flew there now. The magic had slipped off the day.

Del didn't tell her mother about what she'd seen until that evening. After dinner she poured them both large sherries and beckoned Darby out to the cane chairs on the verandah.

'Your Dad and I used to do this,' said Darby. 'Sit out here to watch the twilight. Do you remember?'

'Of course.' Del tasted her drink and made a face. 'Why else would I be drinking sherry? I hate the stuff.'

They sat for a while in companionable silence, listening to the evening birdsong chorus.

'Did you see any bluebirds today?' her mother asked.

Was Darby a mind reader? Del told her the story. 'Tiny led me to the spot. Ten kingfishers, maybe more, darting everywhere. Have you ever seen such a thing?'

'I have.' A slow smile spread over Darby's face as she sipped her sherry. 'Many years ago, when I first moved here. A crown of king-fishers – that's the collective noun. Back then the river ran wilder and higher. It brimmed with fish and frogs and caddis flies – all the food the bluebirds could ever want. It used to be alive with kingfishers from the headwaters down. Your dad said they could raise three broods a year, and the fledglings stayed with their families for months. But you never see a concentration like that any more.' She put a hand on Del's arm. 'Unless it's a sign from heaven.'

Del tried to imagine a time when today's magical scene at the rapids was commonplace. 'There's something else. I saw a sign on the opposite bank near the rapids. It claimed Cobbee Basin belongs to Westcorp.'

Darby's sigh held all the sadness of the ages.

'I don't understand. Isn't it a national park?'

Darby shook her head. 'I wish. It's a state park or, more precisely, a state conservation area. The *conservation* part of the name is a complete joke, an oxymoron. The government allows exploration and mining in such reserves.'

Del took some time to digest that unwelcome piece of informa-tion. 'What's an offset area? It was on the sign.'

'That's also a joke,' said Darby. 'Get me another sherry and I'll explain.'

Del went inside, re-emerged with the bottle and poured them both another drink.

Darby took a sip of sherry before explaining, 'A biodiversity offset allows environmental damage in one area to be offset by protecting another area. So, if the Mount Morton expansion destroys five thousand hectares of forest, it can claim Cobbee Basin as an offset. It's also meant to serve as a buffer between Berrimilla and the mine.'

'Well, that's a good thing, right?'

'Wrong,' said Darby. 'The protection declaration isn't worth the paper it's written on. Our state government regularly hands out approvals for mining in offset areas. The mine would need to apply for one, but with the premier and Carson Shaw as thick as thieves ... ' She shrugged.

Del looked askance at her mother, thinking back to what Celia had said about Carson and his mistress, Stacey Turner. *Stacey told me Carson pushed dodgy mining approvals through Council. No environmental impact studies. No threatened species assessments. Stacey turned a blind eye.* And that was just at the local level. Just how far and how high did the corruption go?

'Why didn't you tell me this before, Mum?'

Darby sputtered into her drink in protest. 'How many times have you said you're not interested in our campaign?' She couldn't hide the frustration in her voice. 'Whenever Ken and I talk about it, you leave the room. For Chrissake, Del, you won't even sign a simple petition to support us. I don't get it.'

What could she say? Of course Darby didn't get it. She didn't know her daughter had been engaged to Westbrook's new managing director, however briefly. She didn't know Del had promised herself not to cause Nick any more trouble.

But if Cobbee Basin was in danger? If the mine expansion threatened her father's special place, his special birds? Then all bets were off. Nick was a big boy. He could look after himself.

CHAPTER 27

Monday morning, and Nick sat in the demountable timber-yard office opposite Kevin Hubbard, sawmill owner and president of the Lockerton Football Club. A document wallet containing glossy Westcorp publicity material lay open on the desk in front of him.

Kevin eyed the brochures suspiciously and shook his head. 'A few of us went to one of those town hall meetings. Got the good oil on how your fucking mine expansions work, my word we did.'

Nick stifled a groan. Damn Vince Gambino and his slide shows! Wherever Nick went and whoever he talked to, that bloody man had been there first.

Nick tried again. 'I'm afraid Mr Gambino is running a misinformation campaign. What are the objections to Westcorp holding an evening information session at your clubrooms to set the record straight?'

Kevin crossed his arms and frowned.

'We'll put on a slap-up barbeque,' said Nick. 'Giveaways and discount vouchers. Games for the kids and free booze. Along with a short presentation by Westcorp outlining the opportunities offered to your community by the Mount Morton Optimisation Project.'

Kevin held up his hand. 'Nah, mate. We—'

'I haven't finished. Westcorp plans to announce a generous three-year sponsorship for your football club. The players and their families deserve to know.'

'A sponsorship.'

'That's right.'

Kevin pondered this offer for a while. 'And we only get the sponsorship if we host this shindig of yours.'

'Well, no. It's not a condition of our support. Westcorp simply wants to announce it there.'

Kevin's face cracked into a grin and he offered his arm. 'That's mighty kind of you lot.'

This is more like it, thought Nick as he shook Kevin's hand. 'Someone from Westcorp will be in touch to organise a time and date for the barbeque.'

Kevin's smile fled. 'Not happening, mate. Have you heard that young bloke Vince's story? Found his grandfather hanging in the shearing shed. Expanding the local mine destroyed that poor old feller's farm and broke his heart. Shocking, it was.' He rubbed his eyes.

Unbelievable. Was Kevin tearing up?

'I've already signed the petition that's going 'round, along with most of our players and supporters. It'd be bloody hypocritical of us to hold a Westcorp barbeque, considering.'

Oh, great. The club would take the sponsorship money but oppose the mine. The worst possible outcome.

Kevin didn't even have the decency to look apologetic. 'Who did you say you were again?'

'Nick Shaw. Managing director of Westcorp Mining.'

Kevin raised his brows and whistled. 'So … You're one of the bigwigs. I suppose our little town should be flattered.'

I'm actually *the* bigwig, thought Nick. So, what was he doing wasting his time like this? He'd genuinely wanted to help the people of Kingfisher Valley. Under Carson, Westcorp had taken a top-down, dictatorial approach to public relations. Nick had looked forward to bringing a more modern, consultative approach to the whole winning hearts and minds thing. But after two weeks on the job he had to concede that it wasn't working. Well, how could it, when bloody Vince Gambino already held community hearts in his hand?

These people had no idea what side their bread was buttered on. It was astonishing, really. On the surface, Kingfisher Valley wasn't a good fit for an environmental campaign. Its people were farmers and loggers and labourers. Small business owners and tradies.

Yet, for each person who welcomed Nick's promise of jobs and growth, there were three more who didn't believe anything he had to say. They looked at him like he'd killed Gambino's grandfather himself. Well, he'd had enough. From now on, his aides could take on the thankless task of community liaison.

It irked him to think that Dad had been right all along. Nick had more important things to do, and he could do them back at Winga. These important tasks weren't entirely business related. Wrapping up the new mine's social and environmental assessments. Managing the approval process. And confronting Carson over his lies.

For Nick no longer suspected that his father had been unfaithful. He knew. The diaries, Carson's reluctance to sue – that damning flash of guilt on his face in the Gidgee Creek Hotel beer garden. The evidence was in. It was time for some answers.

But there was something he wanted to do before he went home. Nick had seen a flyer in a shop window announcing a 'Go Home, Westcorp' town meeting tonight. He wanted to see for himself how Vince Gambino was single-handedly turning the valley against him.

Nick arrived early and sat in his car outside the little Dandalee RSL hall. It was a modest weatherboard building, but well-maintained with a fresh coat of cream paint and a rather grand statue of a World War I digger standing with his rifle on a plinth out the front.

There were already a few people there, and more were arriving all the time. A good turnout, considering Dandalee boasted just two hundred and twenty-seven official residents. Another ute arrived. At this rate the entire population of the small town would soon be here.

Nick got out of his car and went inside, curious to lay eyes upon this Vince Gambino character. That must be him, there at the front of the hall – a tall, good-looking man, with tattoos, an earring and long dark hair tied back by a red bandanna. A bit of a rebel, by the look of him. Not the type that Nick imagined salt-of-the-earth country folk would warm to.

Nick took a seat to the side, trying to appear inconspicuous. It was a cold night, and he raised the collar on his coat to help hide his face. It would be embarrassing to be recognised.

Vince stood at a wobbly folding table that had seen better days. A stack of printed A4 sheets of paper sat at one end, along with that goddamned petition that seemed to be everywhere. Vince was fiddling with an antiquated overhead projector. Clearly, he didn't have money backing him, not with that sort of outdated technology. Nick compared this amateurish offering with his own presentations. The giveaways and glossy brochures. The interactive whiteboards and slick computer projection systems. Chalk and cheese. And yet, the hall was almost full. This guy could pull a crowd. Nick went forward to collect a flyer and resumed his seat.

A young, blonde woman with her back to him was setting up an old-fashioned, pull-up projector screen on a tripod. She was having trouble, not being quite tall enough to hook the top part to the stand.

An elderly man went to help. 'Here, let me do that, love.'

The girl swung around to thank him. Nick let out a swift breath and he felt a tug inside his chest. It was Del. Del, the woman he'd loved – and still loved. Del with the lovely smile, the clever hazel eyes and the fearless determination to tell the truth. The woman he'd planned to marry, planned to spend his whole life with. What in the world was she doing here?

Del stepped over to Vince and offered him the gorgeous smile that Nick knew so well. She lightly touched his arm – a familiar, affectionate gesture that tore at Nick's heart. Then she turned to face the audience, and the surprises kept coming.

'I'm Del Fisher and I'd like to thank you all for coming along tonight. Some of you may know that I come from the Fisher family who pioneered the settlement of Kingfisher Valley.' There were a few approving nods.

Nick almost fell off his chair. Did she? How extraordinary. Del had always been a closed book, refusing to talk about her roots, except in the most general of terms. Nick knew she was born in the mountains, but not where. He knew she'd loved her father fiercely, and that he'd died, but he didn't know the details. He knew she was estranged from her mother, but he didn't know the circumstances behind the rift.

'Before I hand you over to Vince, I'd just like to say that at first I was sceptical of his claims, just as many of you here tonight might be. I thought that the Mount Morton mine expansion could be good for Kingfisher Valley, bringing jobs and an injection of funds and new people for our community.' She paused dramatically. 'I don't think that any more. I think the mine will reduce land values, threaten Cobbee Basin and pollute our air and water. I think the promised jobs will overwhelmingly go to drive-in, drive-out workers. And I think that we should all oppose this mine.'

Clapping and a few *hear, hears* greeted Del's declaration.

Nick gaped stunned and confused. He scrubbed his palms over his face. It made no sense. Del wasn't an activist. Her journalist training had taught her to steer clear of such causes, making her a model of impartiality. When local dogs were being poisoned, she'd investigated their owners just as thoroughly as any disgruntled neighbours. When some Winga locals opposed a wind farm, she'd written an article devoting an equal amount of space to the pro-turbine group as she did to the irate residents.

Nick had never met a more neutral person than Del Fisher. She didn't hold a strong view on anything as far as he could tell. Hell, he didn't even know which way she voted! And yet here she was, siding against him and spouting the same misinformation as Vince Gambino. It was hard to believe. Nick felt a pulse of anger as bile rose in his throat. Hadn't this woman caused him enough heartache? His first instinct was to storm out. Even looking at the back of Del's head where she now sat in the front row made his blood boil.

Vince turned out the main lights and started his slide show. He was talking about his grandfather, and his grandfather's farm and how much it had meant to him – building a connection with his rural audience. Nick was barely listening so he turned on his phone to record Vince's spiel. He couldn't concentrate on it now. He was thinking about Del and how she'd dropped her bombshell article and then vanished without a trace. He was thinking about the pain she'd caused his mother. His beautiful mother, now dead. And though he knew how unfair it was, he blamed Del for exposing Carson. How he would have loved to go back to a time when he trusted and believed his father.

When the talk was finished, Del suddenly turned. And as if her gaze was guided by radar, she stared straight at him.

CHAPTER 28

D el didn't know why she turned around. A feeling, perhaps. Gut instinct. A vague idea that throughout the talk she was being watched. In the dim hall it was hard to see, yet something drew her gaze unerringly to a man sitting in the shadows. Did she know him? An overwhelming sense of familiarity caused her to stand and make her way to where he sat.

Someone turned the lights back on and she gasped aloud. 'Nick?' So, he'd come to find her. A gush of love left her weak. Did he believe that she wasn't responsible for the fateful article? Had Celia told him the truth?

Del took him in – the set of his chin, the strength in his face, his thick hair gleaming dark reddish-gold under the dim hall lights. Her eyes lingered on his arm, now out of the cast. This was the man she'd fallen in love with, and him being here seemed too good to be true.

Del took Nick's hand and tugged him to the back of the hall while a question-and-answer session got underway.

'It's so good to see you,' she whispered. 'How did you know I'd be here?'

Del waited for his response, longing to hear his voice, anticipating that special smile that would melt her heart. But something was wrong. Nick remained stony-faced. He didn't speak to her or look at her.

'Nick, what's wrong?'

He strode out the door. Del chased after him and found him on the porch. And when his eyes at last met hers, she saw only surprise in them, not love.

Then the truth hit home. Nick hadn't come for her – of course he hadn't. He couldn't have possibly known that she'd be there tonight. It had been a last-minute decision on her part.

No, Nick was there to spy, to observe Vince's presentation and look for weaknesses. It was simply a case of *know your enemy*. Nick was Carson's man, after all. A naive child who hero-worshipped his bastard of a father and ignored reality. How had she fallen in love with someone like that?

'You shouldn't be here,' said Del, struggling with her disappointment.

'Neither should you,' said Nick. 'Why on earth are you giving that moron the time of day?'

'Vince is no moron.' Del's eyes blazed with anger. 'He's onto your father. He sees him for the lying, cheating, double-dealing crook that he is. Unlike you, so gullible that you'll make every excuse in the book for Carson to avoid facing the truth.'

Nick took a step back. He'd never seen Del display such passion and outrage before, and the worst thing was that she was right. Carson had lied to him and Mum for years. Even when Nick suspected it to be true, he'd been slow to accept it. Loath to believe that he'd been misled about his father's character for the whole of his life. It was indeed a final humiliation for this truth to be confirmed to him by Del. But that didn't excuse her falling for Gambino's hippy nonsense.

'Yes,' said Nick. 'Carson lied to me.' He pointed to Vince. 'But he's lying too. The mine extension is my project. I'm following every social and environmental protocol in the book. It will be a real boon for

Kingfisher Valley, and you have no right to tell these people other-wise. How much do you know about this Gambino bloke anyway?'

'You say Vince is lying,' said Del. 'I suppose my mother is lying too, is she?'

'Your mother? I'm confused. I thought you were estranged from your mother.'

'Not any longer.' Del jabbed a finger at his chest. 'And just as well. Otherwise I'd never have known what you're planning. I used to camp at Cobbee Basin with my father. People love that place and you sure as hell better leave it alone.'

'What are you talking about?' said Nick, raising his voice. 'That's a designated offset area, completely protected.'

'Did your father tell you that? Well, there's no problem then.' Del's words dripped with sarcasm. 'Carson is a man of his word, right?'

Nick couldn't believe what he was hearing. Yes, Carson had been an unfaithful husband. But that had nothing to do with how he conducted business. By impugning Carson like that, Del was impugning Nick as well. 'Leave my father out of it. Haven't you done enough damage to me and my family?'

The argument was growing louder. People were staring as they exited the hall.

Vince excused himself from answering questions and came over, concern written on his annoyingly handsome face. 'Are you okay, Del?'

Nick turned on him. 'What's it to you?' He heard the belligerence in his voice, but didn't care. He focused all his shock and frustration – and, yes, jealousy – on Vince.

'Calm down, mate.' Vince exchanged a glance with Del, then took her arm in a familiar way and tried to steer her from the porch

Nick saw red. He shoved Vince hard. Del pushed between them and glared at Nick as Vince held up his hands and backed away.

A frowning middle-aged man came forward. 'We'll have no fighting here.' A murmur of assent rose from the crowd gathering round. 'Mr Shaw, isn't it?'

Nick nodded, wishing that he hadn't been recognised. The bush telegraph travelled quickly. In a few days' time everyone would know that he'd gatecrashed the meeting and tried to pick a fight with Gambino.

'I'd ask you to leave, sir,' said the frowning man. 'You're not welcome here.'

A few cheers went up. Nick took a last look at Del. She had that stubborn set to her chin that he knew so well. He turned his back and left.

Nick started his car, cheeks burning with impotent anger. How humiliating. To be turfed out of Gambino's stupid meeting with the full approval of everyone there – including Del.

He thought of the bold way Gambino had taken hold of Del's arm, and his knuckles showed white on the steering wheel. Despite their argument, Nick had been profoundly moved to see Del again. His love for her had come powering back, a love he'd desperately tried to push aside ever since the publication of that damned article. Yet, now he believed that the printed allegations were true. Did that change anything? Of course it did.

He should have listened to her that day when she'd come to him at the cottage. She'd told him she didn't write the allegations. He shouldn't have questioned it. She'd told him they were true. He should have believed her.

Nick's thoughts turned to why Del had been at the hall in the first place. She'd always been secretive about her childhood, entreating him not to delve into her past. And, of course, he'd honoured her wishes. But not any more. He intended to find out everything he could about why she'd turned up at the little Dandalee hall that evening, and why she was in the company of Vince Gambino.

Were Del and that man an item? Had she moved on so quickly? There was so much he didn't know. Well, if she had moved on, it qualified as a rebound relationship, and rebound relationships never lasted. There was one thing Nick was absolutely sure of. He didn't trust Vince Gambino with his good looks and his earring and his homespun appeal.

Nick accelerated down the deserted road. He needed to discover more about the man. He'd put his research team onto it last week when he realised that Gambino was becoming a real problem. They hadn't come up with much so far. Apparently, his name didn't show up on Google prior to last year, which was odd, because he claimed to have been a graphic designer before volunteering for Greenpeace. Surely there'd be something about the man on the net. Had his people missed it? Had they underestimated the importance of a lone activist, with barely any funding, talking to handfuls of people at country halls? Maybe they had, but Nick wouldn't.

All his life he'd been a trusting person, determined to give others the benefit of the doubt. But Carson's dishonesty had handed Nick a life-changing serve of disillusionment. Perhaps he was paranoid now. Perhaps he'd gone from one extreme to the other. Who knew? But if Del was interested in Gambino, Nick needed to be sure that the man was exactly who he said he was.

It might be too late for him and Del, but whatever happened, he wanted her to be safe and happy.

CHAPTER 29

Del stood on the hall porch, gazing into the darkness. She wore her warmest coat, but she still shivered. Whether from cold or shock, she couldn't tell.

If only she'd taken her own car. Del wanted nothing more than to go home and process her feelings, awash as she was with conflicting emotions. It had all happened so quickly. Discovering Nick. The elation when she thought he was there for her. The aching disappointment when she realised that he wasn't. Their argument and Nick's hostility towards Vince.

She ran through it all again in her mind, slowly this time, while she waited for Vince to wrap up the meeting. Hang on. During the argument she'd glossed over something Nick said – something important. *Carson lied to me.* That's what he'd said.

How painful it would have been for Nick to finally accept that, let alone confess it to her. Del's heart went out to him. Under other circumstances his admission might have opened the door for them. If Nick was willing, they might have taken tentative steps towards repairing their relationship. But not while he was championing the mine expansion.

The last few people were leaving the hall. The night had been another success. Nearly everybody had signed the petition. Vince emerged from the building in conversation with an elderly woman, but he seemed distracted and kept glancing across the porch at Del. After a minute or two the woman patted his hand, wished him good luck and said goodbye.

Vince hurried over to Del. She gave him a nervous smile, although why she was nervous, Del didn't know. The silence yawned between them. His eyes asked for an explanation. She supposed she owed him one but was not inclined to give it.

Vince finally broke the silence. 'You know that jerk?'

Del bristled, but stayed silent. Nick was many things, but a jerk wasn't one of them.

He tried again. 'Nick Shaw is a friend of yours, and you didn't think to mention it. Why was he here, Del? Did you ask him? Are you a Westcorp spy?'

Now he'd gone too far. 'Don't be ridiculous. I had no idea he'd be here. I was as surprised as you were.'

Vince's frown softened, and his face creased with amusement. 'I very much doubt that.'

'Oh, stop it,' Del scolded. 'Nick and I dated for a while, okay? It's no big deal.'

'No big deal, eh?' Vince raised his brows. 'Well, it is to me. I thought we were, you know ... ' He brushed a strand of hair from her eyes. 'I thought we were coming to an understanding. And now I find that you've been – how can I put this?' He paused. 'You've been sleeping with the enemy.'

How dare he! It was none of Vince's business who she slept with.

'Take me home,' she yelled, shoving his hand away from her face

There was that amused smile again. Del wanted to slap him.

'Wait while I get my gear.' Vince turned and went back into the hall.

Del sighed and followed him inside. Helping pack up would get her home quicker.

Vince stowed the rolled-up projector screen in the back of the ute. 'There, that's the last of it.'

Del climbed into the passenger seat without a word. The Dandalee RSL Hall was forty minutes away from Kingfisher Farm. She wasn't looking forward to the drive.

Just as she'd suspected, Vince intended to take advantage of his captive audience. He began asking questions. 'So, tell me about the jerk?'

She gritted her teeth, but didn't answer.

Undeterred, Vince went on. 'I'm right, aren't I? About us getting closer?'

Don't bite, she told herself.

'You did kiss me, after all—'

'Okay, yes, we're getting closer. And that was you kissing me, by the way.'

'A fair call,' Vince conceded. 'But you kissed me back.'

And she had. The truth was that Del found everything about Vince irresistible. His good looks and charisma. His counterculture edginess. His tattoos and bee earring. But it was much more than physical attraction. She was drawn to the passion he held for his cause. Vince had given up a career to fight for what he believed in. To fight for a land and people that he wasn't even connected to. Del hadn't come across that sort of selflessness before. It held a strong allure. And despite swearing off men, she was falling for him.

Yet when she'd recognised Nick that evening, her old feelings had returned with a vengeance. She'd argued with him, but not because she didn't care. It was because she cared so much. And now Del found herself sunk in a pit of confusion.

Nothing would stop her fighting for Kingfisher Valley – a fight that was growing legs. Del had put the petition, which she'd once been so dismissive of, online. It now boasted thousands of signatures – enough to present to Parliament and hopefully sway the premier. Tony Marshall, a local solicitor, was preparing a case for the Land and Environment Court on behalf of the Berrimilla Progress Association. Momentum was building.

But equally, Del couldn't ignore her feelings for Nick. True, they were on opposite sides of this issue. But there was more to life than opposing the mine. She was burning to know how Nick had been convinced of Carson's lies. And what exactly did Nick believe his father had lied about? Knowing Carson, there were sure to be more buried secrets somewhere.

She hated that their first encounter since Natalie's death had been so combative. Del wished that she could go back in time a few hours and redo their meeting. She wished that she'd kept a lid on her disappointment and anger, and simply let Nick talk. Because that was what she desperately wanted – to talk with him.

'A penny for them,' said Vince, startling her.

She'd argued with Vince, too. Del tried to see tonight's event from his point of view. It was only natural he'd be thrown by a top Westcorp Mining executive turning up at the meeting.

'Sorry for yelling at you,' she said. 'But I really had no idea that Nick was coming tonight.'

Vince glanced across at her. 'And I'm sorry for that *sleeping with the enemy* crack. It was unforgivable. I know it's no excuse, but I was bloody well knocked for six when the jerk arrived.'

Del bit her tongue and this time kept her temper in check. Defending Nick to a man like Vince would be impossible.

'So, if he didn't come to see you, that means he came to see me. Our little get-togethers must be having some impact.'

Our little get-togethers. Considering this was only Del's second one, and the first where she'd actually spoken out about the mine, it was overly generous to include her in the credit.

'You know they are,' she said. 'Your town hall meetings have turned public opinion against the mine. That's an amazing achievement, considering all that Nick's promising: the jobs, the sponsorships, the giveaways—'

'The bribes, you mean.'

'Well, yes. You could call them that.'

'I don't get it,' said Vince, sounding genuinely confused. 'You're fighting to stop Mount Morton. So is your family – your whole town. And yet you used to date Westcorp's managing director?'

It sounded improbable, even to Del. 'That was a lifetime ago.'

And it was, although measured by real time it hadn't even been four months. Four months that felt like four years. In that other life she'd been an ambitious professional woman, a star reporter with a high-profile new job at a major Sydney daily. She'd been looking forward to designer clothes, fabulous holidays and a handsome salary with all the perks. She'd been engaged to a wealthy and influential man – the region's most eligible bachelor – and was soon to join a prominent family worth millions. Yet she'd been estranged from her own widowed mother. If Del was honest, back then she'd only been concerned with herself. Too busy to look after anybody or anything else, not even a pet.

Contrast that with her new life. Del was single again, and she spent her days on a quad bike, spraying weeds, cleaning slimy troughs and spreading fertiliser. Pruning vines and feeding out hay. Fixing pumps and rounding up wayward cows and sheep. She wore dirty jeans and lived on savings. She slept in her old bed at her mother's house, owned a shaggy rescue dog and was campaigning to save an old-growth forest. Her former colleagues, Celia Bloom in particular, would barely recognise her. Hell, she barely recognised herself.

She was a different person now. Not as wealthy or successful, at least by her previous standards, but oddly enough she liked herself more. And if the truth were known, her father would have liked this new Del more too. For eight years she'd grieved for him, but grieving wasn't honouring. By mending fences with Darby, restoring his vines and protecting Cobbee Basin, Del was truly honouring her father. The realisation made her smile.

CHAPTER 30

Nick drove back to the village in a daze. He collected his few things, and carefully packed the diaries. Then he headed for Westbrook. The four-hour drive meant he'd arrive well after midnight, but there was no way he was going to wait until morning. He needed answers from Carson, and he needed them now.

The sky was clear when Nick left Mount Morton, but he was soon driving into a storm. Normally he broke up the long trip by stopping halfway, but on this occasion he drove straight through. Drowsiness wouldn't be a factor tonight. He doubted he'd ever sleep again.

It was after two in the morning when Nick arrived at Westbrook. He unpacked quickly at the cottage, leaving the diaries in the car until the rain eased. Then he drove up to the main house. All was in darkness, as it should be at that hour. But there was something out of the ordinary – a blue car parked in the driveway.

Nick didn't recognise it, so he braved the rain for a closer look. An early-model Honda Accord station wagon with dented panels, a My Little Pony figurine dangling from the mirror and a 'Honk if you think I'm sexy' bumper sticker. Did Carson have a house guest? It didn't look like the sort of vehicle that would belong to one of his friends. So, what was it doing here in the middle of the night?

Nick let himself in, turned on the lights and climbed the stairs to the master suite. Strange to think that the last time he'd done that his mother had been alive. He could sometimes feel her in the house, but not tonight.

Nick's mind was awhirl with the questions he meant to ask his father, and how he planned to ask them. First, he'd rouse Carson, demand that they talk, and give him time to properly wake up. Then he'd take him downstairs, make some strong coffee, and begin the interrogation. When had his father's infidelities started? How many times? Did he realise that Mum had known?

Nick opened the door to his parents' bedroom. His father was snoring. Nick switched on the light and stared at the bed, open-mouthed. Carson wasn't alone. A woman lay asleep beside him, her long red hair spread out on the pillow. She wore a sparkly dog collar and appeared to be naked under the covers.

The woman woke more quickly than Carson did, sitting up and pulling the sheet over her large, freckled breasts. She stared at Nick with wide, frightened eyes and he was struck by how young she was. Twenty-five years old at most.

A pair of jeans, lace knickers and a skimpy top lay on the chair where Mum used to sit and brush her hair. Nick tossed them to the girl. 'Get out.' He turned his back to allow her some dignity. In less than a minute she'd fled the room.

Carson took longer to wake up, blinking and looking groggy. At first, he didn't seem to notice Nick standing by the door.

'Really? She's young enough to be your granddaughter,' said Nick, his voice hoarse with barely controlled fury. 'And in Mum's bed?'

Nick waited for his father to sit up, half expecting him to bellow and curse the way he usually did when he was on the defensive. But instead he had the good grace to be ashamed, unable to look his son in the eye. His chin actually trembled. It should tremble. Carson deserved to be filled with abject shame.

Yet despite this undeniable truth, it still shocked Nick to see his father so humbled. Had he seen it before? He knew the answer before he'd asked himself the question. Of course he hadn't. Until the last few months, Carson had been like a god to him. The all-loving, ever-benevolent, unassailably perfect father. The rock of his childhood, the safe port in the storm whenever Mum descended into the depths of depression.

But Nick's view of the world was crumbling like foundations built on shifting sands. He'd read his mother's diaries. He'd been privy to her fears, her disappointments – her suspicions. The thought that Carson's cheating might have driven her to her death was the bitterest of pills.

'Get up,' said Nick, with undisguised contempt. 'And meet me downstairs. There's a lot we need to talk about.'

Carson sat at the kitchen table with hunched shoulders. Nick made coffee, and placed one mug in front of his father and sat down oppo-site him. He could smell whisky on Carson's breath.

'That girl,' said Nick. 'You're taking a risk. Haven't you given these women enough ammunition to use against you?'

Carson stared into his mug, as if he might find the answer there. 'Mandy won't talk,' he mumbled. 'I pay her too well.'

Nick stared, seeing him as if for the first time. The man seated before him was barely recognisable as his father. The lens of truth, free of its former filters, cast Carson in a very different light. He looked washed out, older, shrunken – his clothes a size too big for him.

'Is that what you did with the woman in that article? Stacey Turner? Paid her off?'

He gave a derisive snort. 'She was only after the money. My lawyers have offered her enough to keep her quiet. She's signed a non-disclosure clause. If she whispers another word to anyone it will cost her a fortune.'

'So, you got to her.' Nick found it difficult to talk through his disgust. 'I know Stacey wasn't the first. How many, Dad? And how could you have done that to Mum?'

'Hold on, son. Your mother never knew. I would never have hurt her like that.'

'Wrong, Dad. She knew. It's all there in her diaries.'

Carson paled. 'What are you talking about? Nat's diaries are sealed up in the guest wing.'

'Wrong again. I have them, and I can promise you that Mum knew about your cheating for years. I think it's what caused her depression.'

Carson's face crumpled as he rubbed his eyes with a shaky hand. Nick studied him for any sign of dissembling, but found none. Carson's shock and dismay seemed entirely genuine.

'You're an arrogant bastard, aren't you?' said Nick. 'Pretending all this time to be the perfect husband and father. Congratulating yourself on getting away with your dirty games.' Nick almost choked on his words. *Keep it together*, he told himself, fighting back tears. 'Have you any idea, Dad, how much I used to trust and respect you?'

'You have to forgive me.' Carson might have meant it as a command, but his voice was wavering. 'I kept my affairs away from you. I never thought you'd be harmed.'

'And Mum?'

'I thought I'd kept them away from her too. You, of all people, must know how much I loved her.'

'I always thought you did. But I was wrong. Betraying Mum and keeping her in the dark wasn't love. Letting her drown in suspicions was more like torture.'

Carson shook his head, as if he didn't understand what he was hearing. 'She never said a word. Are you certain that she knew?'

'Oh, she knew. It started twenty-four years ago, right, when I was six? A young Westcorp publicist. You bought her expensive jewellery. Mum found the receipts. Two of everything. One for Mum, one for the other woman. Not very imaginative, Dad.'

From the horrified look on his father's face, Nick knew he'd hit home.

'About those diaries,' Carson said. 'Your mother never wanted anyone to read them, not even me. I'll open up the guest wing so you can put them back.'

'Oh, right,' said Nick through a clenched jaw. 'Because you care so much about what Mum wanted. Well, let me tell you what she didn't want. She didn't want a lying husband who slept with other women and took advantage of the people who worked for him.'

Carson had the good sense not to speak.

'Here's what's going to happen. You're going to write a letter to Mum confessing every indiscretion that you've ever made and apologising for them.'

'What's the point of—'

'It's the principle, Dad. And then you'll hold a press conference admitting that you were unfaithful during your marriage and expressing deep regret for the hurt you've caused.'

'Don't be ridiculous, Nick. I'm head of a multi-million-dollar corporation. My reputation—'

'It's a bit late to worry about your reputation, Dad. You as good as confirmed Stacey Turner's allegations when you resigned as mayor and backed down from suing the *Gazette*. Everybody thinks you did it anyway. Owning up to it publicly will probably bring you credit, if anything.'

'And if I don't?'

'I'll hold the press conference myself.'

'So, you're threatening me?' Some of Carson's customary bluster was returning. 'I could fire you – disinherit you.'

'You could.' Nick tipped his head from one side to the other, as if he was weighing up Carson's words. 'But I wouldn't give two hoots. And if you don't do what I ask, I'll resign anyway.'

Nick leaned closer, looking deep into his father's anxious blue eyes, the eyes he'd loved for so long.

'Help me out here, Dad. I don't want this to be the end for us, but you don't get a free pass. I can't forgive you unless you atone in some major way for what you've done.'

And there it finally was – comprehension on Carson's face. 'All right, son. I'll do it.'

Nick exhaled, unaware that he'd been holding his breath. Maybe they could salvage their relationship after all. 'Okay, Dad. But there better not be anything else that you're not telling me.'

CHAPTER 31

Del pushed in the back door, dirty and tired, with Tiny at her heels. She'd been working in the vineyard, installing the final section of drip irrigators by herself. It had taken all day and she still wasn't finished. Ken had been suffering from shortness of breath that week and Del had told him to go home. Yet another reason to stand against the mine – black lung disease could be fatal.

It was almost summer and she still hadn't secured a firm buyer for her grapes. The wineries that she'd approached were being cagey, waiting to see how good the local harvest would be before committing to the purchase. The long-range weather forecast was a favourable one for vintners. If it proved accurate and there was a glut of grapes, she might not be able to sell them at all. It was a depressing thought.

Del glanced at the wall clock. She hadn't realised how late it was. One thing she missed about her job was having weekends off. It was Friday. At the *Gazette*, Saturdays and Sundays were usually hers to do whatever she wanted. But working for herself meant no discernible break between work and play. No doubt she'd be testing the dripper installation in the morning.

Del checked on the lasagne her mum had made, though the timer said it still had twenty more minutes to go before it would be ready.

Darby must have heard the oven door and sang out from the lounge room. 'Leave it alone, love. It will only take longer.'

'But I'm starving.'

'Make yourself a cuppa while you wait, then. There's a fresh pot.'

Del took her mug of tea into the lounge room where Darby was turning on the evening news.

And there on the television was Carson Shaw holding a press conference.

'There has been a lot of interest in the reason for my recent resignation as mayor of the beautiful Central Ranges,' he began. 'Some have speculated that it was prompted by the allegations of sexual misconduct levelled against me. As an individual, I have a right to privacy like anyone else. But I am also a public figure, and I understand that people deserve answers.'

Carson took a breath and glanced to the side, as if checking with someone.

'I'm here to confirm Ms Stacey Turner's story. We shared a consensual sexual relationship for a period of six months some years ago while she was employed by the Central Ranges Council. This is something that I deeply regret, as I was both mayor and a married man. I do however reject the accusation that this relationship was in any way abusive. Ms Turner herself has since withdrawn that claim, and I have accepted her retraction.

'Let me take this opportunity to apologise to Ms Turner if I caused her any emotional distress. I apologise to members of our community who understandably feel let down. But most importantly, I want to apologise to my late wife, Natalie, and to my son, Nicholas. You deserved a better man as a husband and father. Thank you. I won't be taking questions.'

Darby gave a derisive snort. 'Well, how do you like that? The man simply issues an apology and carries on with his life. He'll probably even get kudos for his honesty. Meanwhile, the women he's taken advantage of are left to pick up the pieces.'

Del was fascinated by Darby's reaction. 'So, what – you believe Carson is a serial offender?'

'Well, yes, if the rumours are anything to go by. That press conference was no more than a public relations exercise meant to draw a line under Carson's misconduct. Show's over, nothing more to see here, folks. Trouble is, the average punter is so gullible, they'll believe him.'

Del sipped her tea, lost in thought. Was Darby right? Would the admission work to Carson's advantage? She couldn't think of any other reason why he'd fess up, even in such a limited way.

The oven timer beeped and Darby turned off the television. 'Set the table will you, love?'

But Del was disappearing into her bedroom.

'Where are you going?' asked Darby. 'Don't you want any dinner? I thought you were hungry.'

It had been a hectic time for Del since she'd chosen to support Vince and the campaign against the mine. Her old bedroom was now transformed into an operations centre. The whitewashed Queen Anne desk that she'd loved so much as a teenager now overflowed with notebooks and flyers. A combined printer and scanner sat on a corner shelf. The fairy lights and posters of boy bands had been replaced with wall-mounted cork boards. One held a regional map, with red pins marking where Vince had conducted his talks, and green pins marking where he was yet to speak.

Scribbled on a whiteboard were the names of potential locations for future talks. Nursing homes, craft clubs, libraries and even book groups. Several primary schools had expressed interest in a presentation suitable for kids. Vince had become a local celebrity, and everyone wanted in on the act.

Del was also busy helping Tony research his case for the Land and Environment Court. And she was writing again, although not under her own name. That was still a bridge too far. 'Use my name, if you like,' Darby had offered. 'Although I still don't understand what's wrong with yours.'

Del interviewed farmers worried about water quality. She interviewed old-timers about their early memories of Kingfisher Valley. With Ken's help, she'd founded the Cobbee Basin Protection Society, which was growing exponentially. Acting as her own photographer, she'd started covering Vince's talks and wrote freelance articles about the growing opposition to the Mount Morton mine expansion.

Yet apart from a few 'Letters to the Editor', Del – writing as Darby – hadn't had much luck submitting to papers or online news sites. Many residents of the Central Ranges depended on coalmines in one way or another. No one denied that the transition to renewable energy was coming. Yet many still saw coal as king, and editors steered away from controversial topics. It looked like she'd need to use her old network of contacts in the newspaper world to get her pieces published more widely.

So, the idea of approaching Celia Bloom had already been germinating. Good God, if anyone owed Del a favour, Celia did. However, up until now, Del hadn't quite found the courage to contact her. But Carson's press conference changed everything. Del didn't want the world to *draw a line under Carson's misconduct*, as Darby had put it. He hadn't merely conducted one brief, misguided affair with a consenting staffer. Del had read the heart-breaking testimonials of the many women that Carson had allegedly abused over decades. Celia had also said that Carson was being investigated by ICAC and had asked for Del's help to break the story.

Del had said no. Of course she had – back then it was all about protecting Nick and making up for the heartbreak that she'd unwittingly caused him. But as she'd previously told herself, Nick was a big boy. His eyes had already been opened, although only a slit perhaps. Del was convinced that Nick knew just a fraction of his father's wrongdoings.

Del wanted Carson to pay for whatever he'd done, so it was time to forgive her former boss. In a weird way, Del owed her. She'd never have gone bush if Celia hadn't pulled her outrageous stunt. She wouldn't be restoring Dad's vines or repairing her relationship with Darby. Now she needed to discover everything Celia knew about Carson, and hope that, by a strange quirk of fate, she might be able to protect Kingfisher Valley at the same time.

A knock came at the bedroom door. 'Vince is here, love,' Darby called. 'I've asked him to stay for dinner. Can he come in?'

Vince strolled into the room with his magnetism at full throttle. Her desk lamp cast him in mysterious degrees of light and shade. Del went a little weak, feeling like a girl again. No *boy* had ever set foot in that room while it was hers. She'd left home long before lovers were a thing in her life. And it was disconcerting to see this charismatic man in her previously private space.

Vince gazed around with a half-smile. Del became acutely aware of what hadn't changed in her childhood room. The soft toys still piled atop the wardrobe. The giant dolphin stickers cavorting on the walls. The doona cover, with its mishmash of punk-rock images – faded chains, bones, bats, safety pins, skulls and mohawks. Stencil outlines of Johnny Rotten and Sid Vicious.

'It's my old bedroom … ' Del murmured shyly.

'I kind of guessed.' There was that enigmatic smile again. 'You had a big bed for a little girl.'

Del felt her cheeks redden. She wanted to say that when Dad became ill he needed a special hospital bed and she'd inherited her parents' old four-poster. But she couldn't find her voice. Vince's sheer physicality was overwhelming.

An undeniable sexual chemistry had been building between them, even more tangible during the past two weeks. Vince was a charming man. He made the normally serious Del laugh, and she loved spending time with him. They flirted with each other, joked around and had exchanged some sexy banter. They'd even kissed once.

Del wasn't sure what had stopped her from acting on her desire. Maybe it was because they lacked opportunity. She wasn't particularly tempted by the sagging two-man tent that Vince set up each night on the leeward side of his ute. But maybe it was something deeper. Despite the strong attraction between them, Del sensed that some part of Vince was still closed off from her. Although his personal story was touching hearts all over the valley, he was reluctant to discuss his life or his past with her. Why was he holding back? If she was going to embark on a new romantic relationship with a man, she wanted all of him.

Vince sat down on her bed. He lazily traced the outline of Johnny Rotten's profile with his forefinger. Del watched, mesmerised. The air between them seemed to pulse with energy. The charged atmosphere made her nervous and excited all at once. Vince looked astonishingly handsome, with his liquid amber eyes, shining blue-black hair and that golden bee earring catching the light. Del swallowed hard, fighting the urge to kiss his chiselled face. It didn't seem right in her childhood bedroom. How she wished she had her own place.

Vince patted the spot on the bed beside him and the moment passed. That small, patronising action had annoyed her. Did she need his invitation to sit on her own bed? Or was she inventing excuses? Del sat on the desk chair instead.

Vince gave a dramatic disappointed sigh, then made a wide gesture with his arm, indicating the corkboards, the whiteboard, the laptop and the reams of notes spilling from the desk. 'It looks like a war room. I didn't realise you were taking my cause quite so seriously.'

'Your cause?' Again, Del bristled. 'It's my cause too, and Darby's and Ken's. The cause belongs to anyone who cares about Kingfisher Valley.'

'Fair point,' Vince said, his tone conciliatory. 'Why don't you fill me in, then?'

Del explained what she was doing and the progress she'd made so far. She hadn't shared most of this information with him before, believing he was far too busy with his own efforts to bother with hers.

'And best of all,' Del said, 'A local solicitor is working with me pro bono to present a case to the Land and Environment Court. We're asking for an injunction to prevent Mount Morton proceeding. We'll be ready to file next week.'

Vince stared, open-mouthed. 'Why didn't you tell me?'

Del experienced a delicious flush of pride. 'I wanted to surprise you. I was going to wait and hopefully present the injunction as a fait accompli. Tony says we have a good chance of success. But since you're here, I couldn't resist sharing the news.'

But instead of looking pleased, Vince's face clouded over. 'I can't believe you've been doing all this stuff behind my back.'

What a strange response. They were fighting for the same thing, weren't they? What did it matter who did what?

Darby knocked. 'Come on you two. The lasagne's getting cold.'

'I've let the cat out of the bag,' Del told her mother over dinner. 'Vince knows about Tony and our plans for an injunction.

'About time, too,' said Darby with a proud smile. 'Isn't it marvellous news?'

Vince nodded and took a big mouthful of lasagne.

The conversation turned to Carson and his shocking press conference. They all agreed it had been a self-serving farce, though Vince didn't contribute much to the discussion. In fact, he remained strangely subdued during the meal. Del had expected him to be as excited as she was about the upcoming court hearing. Instead, he'd barely said a word. Why? Surely Vince wasn't actually pissed off about her acting independently. He'd been surprised, that's all.

Or maybe he'd meant to make a move on her in the bedroom, and he was upset that she'd fobbed him off. Well, what did he expect? The timing was all wrong with Darby just outside the door.

What they needed was a place to themselves – somewhere to explore their feelings away from prying eyes. Someplace more comfortable than a tiny tent. Because Del did have feelings for Vince. She caught his glance and a familiar shiver pulsed through her, making her skin prickle.

'Mum, you said your friend is looking for a house-sitter next week. How about Vince?'

'Why, yes, he'd be perfect.' Darby beamed at him. 'And Hermit Hill is central to the whole valley. What do you say, Vince?'

He was texting on his phone and didn't seem to hear.

'Vince, I said would you be up for some house-sitting? The weather's turning cold next week and you'll be far cosier in a house than in a tent.'

He stood up and slipped his phone in his pocket 'Yes, sure. But right now I have to split. Something's come up.'

'Anything I should know about?' asked Del.

'Thanks for dinner.' Vince gave Darby a peck on the cheek. 'Best lasagne ever.' He gave a brief wave and backed out the door.

Darby looked at her daughter with raised brows. 'What was up with our Vince today? He didn't seem himself.'

'Yes, he did seem distracted,' Del said as she cleared the table. 'Nothing wrong with his appetite though. He went back for seconds.'

Del went outside in time to see Vince's white ute speed off, tail-lights like glowing embers fading into the night. What an intriguing man. Well, if Vince was serious about moving forward with her, next week would be the perfect time. They'd have a charming old miners cottage to themselves for a whole week: pressed metal ceilings, open fires and a wood-fired range. Del couldn't wait.

CHAPTER 32

Nick was packing to leave. After a few days back at Westbrook, he'd realised he could no longer live with his father. Even the cottage was too close. So he planned to move back to Kingfisher Valley, to Westcorp's McClellan Vale estate, until he wound up his current job. Then he'd buy a place of his own. Del had often urged him to, but he'd always felt so comfortable at Westbrook. So completely at home. Not any longer. It was time to grow up. It's not like he could feel his mother there any more, not since that day he found his father in bed with that woman He would have Mum's diaries, and in a way, wherever the diaries were, his mother was too.

Last week, Carson had done as Nick asked. He'd publicly confessed to his infidelity, albeit under duress. But far from it being an atonement, Carson had received a huge boost in public opinion. Nick had predicted that it might happen, that people might respect his father for coming forward. But he hadn't predicted that Carson would embrace his newfound popularity like a convicted murderer embracing God.

The *Gazette*'s 'Letters to the Editor' were full of praise. Talkback radio callers said how refreshing it was to see a politician show accountability. Social media posts expressed renewed sympathy about Natalie's death, and even used her to make excuses for Carson.

Our former mayor has lived a life plagued with tragedy. As a young man he lost his parents and his only brother in a car crash. He lovingly stood by his wife for more than two decades, supporting her through frequent bouts of depression. Through her years of hospitalisations and treatments. Raising their son almost as a single father. However wrong it was for him to stray (something that he has bravely admitted to) it's perhaps understandable that he has sought some comfort elsewhere at times.

'I might have a crack at becoming mayor again,' Carson had announced that morning at breakfast.

Nick had wanted to slap him. But fair was fair. Carson had done as he'd been asked: called the press conference, made the public admission. Nick would try to let it go. But forgiveness wasn't on the cards – not yet. Maybe never.

Right now, Nick had a more immediate problem to solve – Vince Gambino. The man's support was surging, despite Westcorp's efforts to ward him off. Nick had even tried Carson's go-to strategy of bribing the bloke to leave. Thank God he hadn't shared the details of that failed plan with his father.

'Standard procedure when paying someone off,' Carson always said, 'is to get it in writing, make it look legitimate and include a savage non-disclosure clause.'

But Nick thought he knew better, believing that Gambino would never go for a paper trail. He'd approached the man after one of those damned talks, this time at the Goonaroo Library. Hundreds of people had turned up to hear Gambino spout his hogwash.

'I know you think that you're doing the right thing,' Nick had told him. 'And I admire that. But you're wrong.' He'd handed over the fat envelope stuffed with cash. 'Consider this a donation. There are plenty of genuine environmental causes out there. Spend it on one of those.'

The treacherous bastard had smiled, took the money and then kept right on campaigning. It seemed that he'd spent a portion of his ill-gotten gains on 'Go Home, Westcorp' signs. According to Nick's team back on the ground, they'd sprung up everywhere – along roads, in the middle of intersections, outside houses and farms.

Kids could exchange empty cans and bottles for anti-mine bumper stickers, posters and decals. Gambino kept boxes of the paraphernalia in his banged-up old ute, along with complimentary treat bags of Caramello Koalas and jelly beans. It was a popular program, and apparently there were always queues of kids lined up at his campsite. Soon there was hardly a car, a truck, a school bag or a shop window in the valley that wasn't plastered with anti-mine propaganda. Gambino could write the book on running a successful grassroots campaign.

One way or another, the guy had to be stopped. So, a few days ago Nick had set the full force of Westcorp's research department onto digging up some dirt on the man. It wasn't how Nick normally rolled. That's why he'd been putting it off. But now the time had well and truly arrived. All was fair in love and war – and this was both. It infuriated Nick to think that Del was on the other side of the issue. How he'd love to discredit Gambino in her eyes. Nick said goodbye to Carson and set off for Kingfisher Valley.

Hours later, Nick pulled up to the grand cast-iron gates of Westcorp's McClellan Vale Wine Estate. Located at the end of a long private road, the nineteenth-century stone winery and Victorian era manor house was nestled in the foothills of Yenga National Park. A dozen luxury chalets were dotted around the manicured grounds.

Nick parked at the house and went to reception.

'Good afternoon, Mr Shaw.' The pretty young woman gave him a dazzling smile. 'I'm Melanie. Will you be staying here with us in the main residence, or would you prefer a chalet?'

'A chalet, please.'

She organised him a key card, but held it tantalisingly on her side of the desk. 'You're in number ten. Dinner is available at our restaurant from six o'clock.' She flicked her blonde curls and looked deep into his eyes. 'I'm available tonight if you'd like a private winery tour.'

'No, thanks.' He held out his hand for the card.

Her smile faded and she pushed it across to him. As he turned to go she called him back. 'There's a parcel for you, Mr Shaw.'

She handed over a thick brown package. It was from his research team. Maybe he'd finally catch a break when it came to that bloody Gambino character.

Nick spread the material from the dossier over the oaken desktop of his plush chalet office, relishing the chance to take it all in. He poured himself a whisky and took a big swig. It was taking him some time to appreciate the significance of what was before him. The game was over, and he'd won.

Nick picked up the smiling old man's picture again. Kissed it and took another gulp of whisky. No doubt about it. This was the same photo that Gambino had been dragging around the valley for weeks. The photo of his poor dead grandfather. Except this old man wasn't his grandfather. He wasn't even dead. He was alive and well and living in San Vito Lo Capo, Sicily. Gambino had lifted his profile pic from Instagram.

There was more – much more. None of the photos used in the presentations were genuine. The farmhouse surrounded by green hills and vineyards wasn't in Queensland. It was in Tasmania. The sooty sheets on the line were in Malawi and the grapevines coated in coal dust were in India. It was also impossible to identify any rural Queensland town adversely affected by a coal mine that fitted Gambino's description.

Both his grandmothers were alive. He had two living grandfathers, and neither of them were farmers. One was a retired gasfitter who lived in Perth, and the other was a carpenter in Rome. Vince Gambino had been born thirty-one years ago as Bernard Bonucci. He was raised

in Melbourne and his parents still lived there. He'd gone to Preston
High School and studied advertising at Latrobe University. Last year
he'd changed his name to Vincent Gambino – the name of his
favourite football player, apparently. Nick raised a glass to toast his
researchers. Damn, those guys were good.

Nick felt like dancing. Well, why not? First thing tomorrow he'd
hold a press conference and expose Gambino for the fraud that he
was. What a coup that would be! When the good folk of Kingfisher
Valley discovered that Gambino was lying to them? That he was
manipulating them with fictitious sob stories in order to achieve the
result he wanted? The man wouldn't be able to show his face
anywhere in the valley without being lynched.

Nick was about to pour himself another drink when he suddenly
put the whisky bottle down. There was one thing he could think of
that would be better than humiliating Gambino in the eyes of the
world. And that was humiliating him in Del's eyes. And some minor
snooping had turned up the address of her mother's farm.

He checked the time. Five-thirty and the farm was only an hour's
drive away. Nick toyed with the idea of calling Del first, because he
finally had her correct number. He'd discovered the reason why he
hadn't been able to get through to her earlier. It wasn't that she'd
blocked him. The number listed under her name in the new phone
that Carson had given him was one digit out. It had taken him weeks
to realise the error, and by then it was too late. He and Del were
finished. Carson had apologised, arguing that it was an easy mistake
to make. Nick wasn't so sure.

He decided against ringing Del. She'd probably tell him not to
come, or at least ask him why he wanted to. And how could he
adequately explain Gambino's deception over the phone? Del needed
to explore the fascinating dossier for herself. She needed to see the
smiling old grandfather who wasn't really dead, and then see the same
photo on a Sicilian man's Instagram page. She needed to read the bio
prepared by Nick's researchers, marvel at the screenshots of Bernard
Bonucci's archived Facebook page and run down the rabbit hole of
advanced reverse-image search techniques. He imagined the expres-

sion on Del's beautiful face when the penny finally dropped: the disbelief, the astonishment and anger. He didn't want to hurt her, but she needed to know the truth.

A knock came at the door – an unwelcome intrusion into his triumphant daydreams. It was Melanie, the pretty receptionist, holding a wicker basket of food and wine. And there was that dazzling smile again. Nick stared at her, uncomprehendingly.

'I noticed that you haven't booked for dinner. So ... ' She touched a hand to her ample cleavage, then smoothed her hair. 'I thought you might enjoy a hamper of our very best local produce.'

She held out the basket and he took it, absentmindedly.

'You know ... Nick. Can I call you Nick?' She took a step closer. 'I'm still available for that private tour tonight if—'

Nick shut the door and took a quick look through the basket: olives, cheese, macadamias, berries and chocolate. He removed the two bottles of French champagne – Del might regard them as a tad too celebratory. But everything else could stay. Nick smiled. The hamper would make a perfect gift for Del's mother. First impressions counted, after all, and he intended to make the very best of impressions on Del's rediscovered family.

Holding that happy thought, Nick went for a shower. The dossier on Gambino was a game changer. He hadn't felt this good for months. And the possibility of seeing Del again was the absolute icing on the cake.

CHAPTER 33

D el was feeding out lucerne to the Babydolls when her phone rang.

'How about helping me move in?' said Vince.

She laughed. 'What, you can't carry a sleeping bag inside by yourself?'

'It's not just the sleeping bag,' said Vince, indignantly. 'I have a backpack too.'

Del threw her sheep the last biscuit of hay. 'Will you cook me dinner?'

'Absolutely. I think I have a can of baked beans somewhere. Can you bring a loaf of bread?'

Del grinned and felt a familiar flutter in her stomach. Tonight she and Vince would finally be alone together. Not at some campground with half-a-dozen kids lined up for lollies and bumper stickers. Not stealing a few minutes behind a town hall after a talk. But alone in a charming, renovated miners cottage with a country kitchen and cosy sunroom. A cottage with proper bedrooms.

Over the last week, Del's relationship with Vince had cranked up fifty notches. She didn't have to wonder about where she stood with him any more. After that lasagne night at the farm, Vince had returned the following morning with all trace of his sullen mood gone.

'What got into you last night?' she'd asked him. 'You barely said a word.'

'Sorry. Something private came up, but it's sorted now.' He'd trained his amber eyes on her. 'I didn't properly thank you for all the extra work you've done on the campaign. But do me a favour will you? Keep me in the loop from now on, eh?'

'Deal.' She'd reached out to shake his hand. Instead, he'd pulled her to him, kissing her with such delicious thoroughness that her head spun.

'I'm crazy about you,' Vince said hoarsely when the kiss ended. 'It's like I'm sixteen again. Let's see where this thing goes, eh?'

And sixteen was just about how old Del felt when she was with him – her passion as intense as any high-school crush.

After that, they were constantly hungry for each other: holding hands, exchanging long looks and falling into impassioned kissing sessions whenever they got the chance. Vince was like a drug. The more time she spent with him, the more time she wanted. There was no denying her building desire – or his. It wasn't love – well, not yet anyway, although she was drawn to his selflessness and the zeal he felt for his cause. But it was most definitely lust.

Del found herself watching Vince unawares. His strong, well-muscled body moved with an easy grace that made a dizzying current race through her. She loved his smooth olive skin, his aquiline nose and high cheekbones. She loved his velvet-edged voice and deep-timbred laugh, his tattoos and his bee earring. She even loved Vince's hands – large and hard, with knuckles that he cracked absentmindedly when he was thinking. She imagined them running over her skin.

Del was ready to take things to the next level. But it left her conflicted. She still had unresolved feelings for Nick, feelings that had burst back to life when she'd seen him at the Dandalee hall. She'd spent sleepless nights wondering what to do. Regretting that their first meeting after so long had been acrimonious. Wanting to put things right.

And Del had come to a decision. She'd meet Nick and make her peace with him. He deserved some closure as much as she did. He was the man she'd loved for years, the man she'd planned to spend her life with. And at the same time, she'd try to get the answers she needed about Carson and find out what Nick knew.

But that could wait. Tonight, she'd devote herself to Vince and the delicious possibilities that their fledgling relationship had to offer.

The sun was dipping below the mountains when Nick reached his destination. The damn GPS had taken him the wrong way, trying to send him down a fire trail it had mistaken for a road. A faded sign beside the rusty gate read 'Kingfisher Farm'. That made him smile. Del loved kingfishers.

As he was closing the gate behind him, three barking dogs came pelting down the steep driveway. Hope leaped in Nick's heart as he recognised the tall grey one. Del's rescued stray, minus the leg cast. Did that mean Del was here? He was about to find out.

When Nick reached the house, his hope faded away. Two vehicles were parked there – neither of them Del's. They both had 'Go Home, Westcorp' bumper stickers. He got out of the car cautiously, wary of the dogs who were milling around and barking. But their wagging tails allayed his concerns.

A solid, grey-haired man came around the side of the house and shushed the dogs.

'I'm Ken Tucker. Can I help you?'

'Good to meet you, Ken. I'm looking for Del,' said Nick. 'Is she here?'

Ken took in Nick's late-model Audi, then looked him up and down. 'And who's asking?'

Nick stepped forward and offered his hand. 'Nick Shaw.' Ken ignored his outstretched arm. 'Del and I are old friends.'

'Nick Shaw – you're that bloke from Westcorp, right?' Ken didn't try to hide the expression of contempt on his face. He spat on the ground. 'Turn that fancy car of yours around and fuck off. You're not welcome.'

'Now look here ... '

A middle-aged woman emerged from the house. Del's mother. She wore a kitchen apron over jeans and was plump, with a lined, sun-reddened face and silvering hair. But the resemblance to her daughter was undeniable. It was there in the shape of her face and her clever eyes.

She wiped her hands on the apron and came over. 'What's going on, Ken?'

Nick side-stepped the man and shook the woman's hand. 'Good to meet you, Mrs Fisher.'

'Please, call me Darby.'

'I was wondering ... Is Del here?'

Darby shot Ken a questioning look. He cracked his knuckles and jerked his head in Nick's direction. 'This bloke is Nick Shaw from Westcorp. Reckons he's a friend of Del's.'

Darby frowned. 'You're the man behind the mine expansion? Well, if you're here to change our minds, you're wasting your time.'

'I'm not here in a professional capacity,' said Nick. 'I just want to see Del.'

'Well, I doubt that she wants to see you. Del's working her butt off trying to stop you and your filthy mine.' Darby called the dogs over to her. 'How do you know my daughter? I can't imagine her not telling me something like that.'

Really? Nick wanted to say. *I know for a fact that, until recently, your daughter told you absolutely nothing for eight years. Otherwise you'd know that we'd been in love and planning to marry.*

Instead, he merely said, 'Believe me, Darby. Del and I are close acquaintances. If she's not here now, I'd appreciate you telling me when she might be back.'

'Del is staying with a friend,' said Darby, stiffly. 'And if you're such a close acquaintance, why don't you just ring her and ask her yourself?'

'Now clear off,' said Ken. 'And don't come back.'

Nick sighed and got back in his car. So, Del was staying with a friend. He could well imagine who that friend might be and it made his blood boil. He looked ruefully at the luxury hamper sitting on the back seat. So much for making a good first impression. But Darby had been right about one thing. *Why don't you just ring her and ask her yourself?*

Why indeed? Del had to know what a snake in the grass Gambino was, and she had to know now. He found her number in his phone and dialled it.

CHAPTER 34

Del pondered the mysteries of life. Now she and Vince finally had a temporary place of their own and perfect privacy, she'd gone all shy. On the drive over Del had imagined them tearing each other's clothes off the minute she stepped inside, barely reaching the bedroom before they were in the throes of passion. But when Vince offered her a bunch of flowers picked from the garden on her arrival, she hadn't even kissed him. Instead she'd accepted them with almost formal thanks and fussed about in the cupboards for a vase.

And so much for baked beans. Vince had served up an excellent chicken parma, complete with chips, salad and a cheap but quaffable shiraz – a meal worthy of any country pub. Afterwards, they sat together on a chintz-covered couch on the porch. Drinking wine. Dousing themselves with Aeroguard and watching the sunset. Rose Cottage sat above a huge, willow-ringed dam. Gnats danced in little clouds against the sky and the mozzies were voracious.

They made small talk, listened to the froggy chorus tuning up and watched Tiny chase rabbits in the darkening garden. Del felt oddly stiff and awkward.

'We file the injunction in the Environment Court tomorrow,' she said. 'How do you rate our chances?'

'We'll walk it in.' Vince put a gentle hand on her thigh. She flinched – although she hadn't meant to – and he withdrew it. Del couldn't help thinking that her hesitance had something to do with Nick. Was she really over him enough to do this? She hadn't been with anyone else for years. To do so would draw a line under the most important relationship of her life. The sad finality of that was a genuine passion killer. She swigged her wine. Why the hell wouldn't that damn man get out of her head? Del had no doubt that Vince was picking up on her ambivalence.

Del took Vince's hand. 'This is crazy,' she said. 'Let's go to bed.'

In the pale porch light, she studied his face and saw a slow, hungry smile spread across his classic features. Vince stood up, tugged her to her feet and swung her into the circle of his arms. He kissed her hair, her cheek, her eyes – then his lips found hers. But for once she didn't shiver with desire. There were no jangling insides or delicious prickles along her skin. The kiss was a dud.

Very slowly, Vince let her go and raised his brows. Those gorgeous bedroom eyes asked her what was wrong. Oh dear. Del could hardly say she'd just realised that she wasn't over Nick. Or could she? Maybe honesty was the best policy. And then her phone rang.

Vince kicked at a verandah post. 'For Chrissake, Del, couldn't you turn the bloody thing off for once? Don't answer it.'

She almost didn't, but his irritation had fuelled some of her own. Who was he to tell her what to do? She'd been a journalist for so many years that being without her phone was like missing a limb.

Del picked it up to see who was calling. Nick? He'd always had good timing. She took the call and walked into the twilight garden.

'Hello, Del.' Nick's voice – familiar as a kingfisher's cry. Del had heard it almost every day for years. He'd made all those morning calls even before they were officially together, right from when they'd first started dating. How many times had she been annoyed by them, when she was rushing off to work or trying to meet a deadline? But she was suddenly grateful for those thousands of calls. They'd said commitment. They'd said love.

Nick asked, 'Is Vince there?'

Silence from Del.

'I have to see you.'

'Why?'

'I'll tell you when I get there.'

Del knew his voice so well, but she'd never heard such urgency in his tone. 'When you get here?' she asked. 'How do you know how to get here?'

A pause. 'I don't. Will you tell me?'

Del gazed into the dusk, searching her soul for the answer. Maybe this was the closure she needed. A chance to clear up the unanswered questions plaguing her. Get Nick out of her system once and for all. It was the only way she'd be able to move forward with Vince or anybody else. Tonight was proof of that.

'Rose Cottage, 178 Stringybark Road, Hermit Hill.' It was only a whisper. Del could picture Nick punching the address into his GPS.

'Soon,' he said. 'I'll see you soon.'

Del didn't return to the house immediately. Instead she whistled for Tiny and wandered along a leafy path beside the dam. The last, faint light of day still lingered, as if reluctant to give way to the darkness. Tiny sensed her turmoil and for once stayed close, occasionally pushing his cold nose into her hand. What a comfort he was. She couldn't imagine life without the clumsy hound. Yes, Tiny was the reason why she hadn't been able to meet Nick on the day that Celia had published the fateful article. But he was also the reason why Del had returned to her roots and reconnected with her mother. If not for Tiny, she'd be living the high life in Sydney. It still amazed her that she didn't want that any more.

Del, lost in thought, didn't realise how far she'd walked. When she turned around, it was too dark to see, though Rose Cottage shone like a beacon on the hill above the path. She slowly headed back, guided by Tiny's warm shoulder against her leg. As she strolled towards the cottage, she planned the questions she wanted to ask Nick. What exactly had Carson told him? Was Nick responsible for Carson's surprise press conference? And most important of all – did Nick still believe that she was behind the initial allegations?

Soon she'd also have to deal with the tricky matter of how to tell Vince about Nick's visit. She imagined saying to him, 'Oh, by the way, I know this is supposed to be our first romantic evening together, but I invited my ex and your sworn enemy over for a chat. You know, the man spearheading the Mount Morton mine expansion that you and I are implacably opposed to.' It sounded outrageous even to her.

Tiny whined and licked her arm. They were almost back at the house. And as Del opened the garden gate, twin beams of light split the night, momentarily blinding her. Tiny started barking. The car swung around and Del stared at it, blinking as her eyes adjusted. Nick had arrived.

Del hurried up the last few metres of the path to Rose Cottage. Before she'd even reached the porch, she heard shouting. Why hadn't she come back earlier? Leaving Nick and Vince alone together was a recipe for disaster. Tiny began barking again. The pair of them raced around to the front of the house, where the porch light showed Nick brandishing a manila folder in Vince's face.

Seeing Nick again caused a visceral reaction in Del, as if dozens of butterflies had taken flight in her belly. He seemed taller than she remembered, bolder and more sure of himself. She'd never seen such determination or resolve on his handsome face. His green eyes flashed with an inner fire – utterly compelling, utterly irresistible.

At first the men didn't notice Del. They were too heavily involved in a yelling match. Only when Tiny leaped forward and grabbed Vince's trouser leg in his jaws did they turn around. Del's heart turned over when Nick's gaze met hers, and she felt a powerful pull of attraction. The strength of that response took her by surprise.

'Tiny, leave off.' The dog gave the pants a final shake and trotted over to sit beside Del.

Vince glared at her. 'What the fuck is this jerk doing here?' He stood with his legs planted wide, nostrils flared. The cold, flinty expression in his eyes made Del take a step back.

'Apparently Nick has something to tell me,' she said. 'Something that can't wait.'

'Bloody oath, I do.' Nick waved the folder wildly. 'Gambino's a lying fraud. His grandfather didn't hang himself in a shearing shed. His grandfather isn't even dead – neither of them are. There's no Queensland town with an asthma epidemic, no polluted bores, no ruined family farm.' He jabbed a forefinger at Vince. 'This scum made the whole thing up.'

Del looked in confusion from one to the other, waiting for either man to say something that made sense. Time seemed to stand still.

'Vince – why is Nick saying this?' She waited. 'And why aren't you denying it?'

Nick smacked Vince on the chest with the folder. 'Yes, go on. Tell her why you're not denying it?'

Vince shoved Nick back, but he still didn't speak. His expression grew hard and resentful.

A cold stone settled in the pit of Del's stomach. 'Vince?'

'Okay, okay,' He ran his hand over his hair. 'So, I exaggerated a bit.'

'A bit?' said Nick with a mocking laugh. 'His sob story is complete bullshit!' Nick offered Del the manila folder with a triumphant smile. 'A comprehensive dossier on your Mr Vince Gambino, AKA Bernard Bonucci. Everything he's told you is a lie.'

Del snatched the folder from him and marched inside. Tiny, Nick and Vince trailed after her. She stood at the kitchen table and began leafing through the folder.

'You know that I've won, right?' Nick said to Vince in a low voice. 'You've taken the people of Kingfisher Valley for fools. They'll never believe—'

'Will you shut up!' Del yelled. Tiny growled in agreement.

She picked up the old man's photo and thrust it at Vince. 'Is this your dead grandfather?'

He had the good grace to hang his head in shame.

Nick, on the other hand, looked jubilant. 'I told you—'

'Nick, I said shut up!'

Nobody spoke as Del leafed through the documents in the folder for a few more minutes.

'Did you ask your research department to dig up dirt on Vince?' she said at last, turning to Nick.

'Not dirt,' said Nick. 'Facts. I asked them to dig up facts.'

'And where's the dossier on me?'

Nick looked confused. 'There isn't one. Of course there isn't.' He pointed to Vince, a look of utter contempt on his face. 'I thought you'd want to know what a fucking fraud your friend here is.'

Del glared at Vince. 'What were you thinking? You've just guaranteed we lose.' She threw the folder at him. 'Your bloody lies have handed Kingfisher Valley to Westcorp on a plate.'

'So I overreached,' said Vince. 'But it's not a fair fight. The jerk has a billion-dollar company behind him, and I'm here handing out homemade flyers and posters? What was I supposed to do?'

'You were supposed to tell the truth,' said Del, feeling the prick of tears.

'I did,' said Vince. 'Coalmines have caused all of the things that I talk about at my presentations. In West Australian coal regions, doctors report a big increase in asthma. Groundwater and creeks are polluted all around the Black Thunder mine in Queensland. In Brolga, they can't drink their tank water and half the town have left. At Denton, they dumped slag heaps in the biodiversity offset area.'

'Well, why not say that?' said Del. 'Why all the bullshit?'

Vince looked bereft. 'I thought that rolling all the negative impacts into my own personal story would make it an easier sell.'

'Oh, it did.' Del wiped tears from her eyes. 'The whole valley fell for it hook, line and sinker. And now nobody will believe a word you say.'

'She's right, mate,' said Nick. 'You'd better pack your bags and leave before you're run out of town.'

'Don't you dare say that to him!' Del rounded on Nick, who was looking insufferably smug. 'At least Vince was trying to do something good. He just went about it the wrong way. But you? You've used the power of Westcorp's research department to discredit our entire campaign – not just the dodgy bits.' She was crying properly now, tasting salt on her tongue. 'And now my beautiful Kingfisher Valley is at risk all over again. Cobbee Basin's rare rainforests are in the firing line.'

'Del, no. Cobbee Basin is protected—'

'How stupid do you think I am?' Del unleashed all her anger and disappointment on Nick. 'I'm an investigator at heart, remember? I've done my research. I know just how many offset areas have been polluted or cleared or even added to open cuts in this state. Your fucking father just clicks his fingers and some New South Wales politician rolls over.'

'It's not like that,' Nick protested. 'There are proper procedures and safeguards . . .'

'Can you hear yourself? For fuck's sake, Nick. Grow up. You have no idea what your father and his damned corporation are capable of. When will you open your eyes?'

Tiny jumped up, paws on her shoulders, and licked the tears from her face. Del kissed his nose then pushed him down and grabbed her overnight bag from the corner of the kitchen.

'You two deserve each other.' Del cast one last disgusted look at the two men, whistled Tiny and marched into the night.

CHAPTER 35

Nick stood by Rose Cottage's kitchen sink and stared out the window, fighting the urge to go after Del. No, she was too upset right now. She needed time to process what she'd learned – to come to terms with Gambino's duplicity. Then they'd talk. Then she'd listen. So, instead, he reluctantly watched Del load Tiny and her bag into the back seat of her car and drive away.

He gazed into the night for a long time after she left. He should have been over the moon with relief and happiness. He'd saved Del from making a terrible mistake – exposed Gambino for the liar he was. Del would never trust the man again. And he'd neutralised the grassroots campaign that was threatening the multi-million-dollar Mount Morton Optimisation Project.

But instead he only felt a powerful and unaccountable sense of unease. Del's final words haunted him. *Grow up. You have no idea what your father and his damned corporation are capable of.* Could that be true? Nick had imagined that he was finally wise to Carson and all of his faults. Good lord, it had been a steep and painful learning curve. Seeing the father that he'd loved and trusted for the lying, unfaithful husband that he'd truly been. Accepting that Carson's serial philandering might well have been responsible for Natalie's decades-long battle with depression – a battle that she'd tragically lost.

Gambino tapped him on the shoulder, shaking him from his reverie. 'Hey, jerk – want a drink?'

Nick swung around. Gambino was waving a bottle of Glenfiddich scotch, easily recognisable by its distinctive golden-stag logo.

'Sure,' said Nick. He'd already won. Why not celebrate?

They sat at the kitchen table, coming to a temporary truce over the promise of a fine drop. Gambino poured them both a generous serve and they sat back in their chairs, eyeing each other, half hostile and half curious. Nick raised his glass and took a sip. Smooth as silk. He idly wondered how a bum like Gambino had got his hands on such an expensive bottle of whisky. Pilfered from a cupboard, most likely. The pretty cottage clearly didn't belong to him.

Nick had meant to be magnanimous. Gambino was on the ropes and he was the conquering hero. It would be churlish to gloat. But he couldn't help himself.

'What were you thinking, man? Did you think we wouldn't find out?

Gambino gave a defeated shrug. 'So, I made a mistake. I'll leave town in the morning.'

Nick knew he should stop, but in his mind's eye he pictured Gambino kissing Del, making love to her. It made him see red. 'I still can't fathom how stupid you were.'

Gambino poured himself another generous drink and then put the whisky bottle under the table. 'Give it a rest, mate. Why don't you climb into that luxury car of yours, go back to that luxury chalet and let this peasant loser get on with getting blind drunk?'

It seemed fair. Nick was about to drain his glass and leave when a disturbing thought hit him. 'Go back to that chalet,' he repeated. 'Why did you say that?'

Gambino rolled his eyes. 'What the fuck are you talking about?'

'Why did you say I should go back to my luxury chalet?'

Gambino frowned. 'Well, a bloke like you?' he said. 'It makes sense you'd be living in the lap of luxury.'

'But a chalet,' said Nick. 'It's an unusual word to use, don't you think? Kingfisher Valley is hardly a ski field.'

Gambino buried his face in his hands. When he looked up again, he seemed oddly pleased with himself. 'I should have kept my mouth shut.'

'I said, how did you know where I'm staying? I never told Del.'

Gambino sighed, then glanced dramatically from left to right, as if he thought someone might be listening. He leaned forward and whispered, 'Carson thought you needed some help.'

'What?' For a moment Nick couldn't draw breath. His lungs seemed to have shrivelled and his throat was tight. He swallowed hard, shoved his chair back from the table and stood up. 'Fuck me. You're from Westcorp.'

Gambino shrugged matter-of-factly. 'We win by controlling every outcome, Nicky-boy, and we do that by playing both sides. You should know that.' He grinned at Nick's gaping mouth. 'But then, you're not the sharpest tool in the shed, are you? Not like your father. That's why he kept you in the dark on this. But he trusted me. He gave me carte blanche to tell my bullshit story, then send you that dossier so you could "expose" me. But it's over now. I've made your job easy. These people will be putty in your hands once they learn that I lied to them.'

Nick shook his head in disbelief. 'You really are a piece of work, aren't you? So, what about Del's heart? Was that all play-acting too?'

Gambino's smile had a malicious twist. 'The delectable Del Fisher? She posed me quite a problem, working so hard on the campaign. All that activism behind my back. But fortunately, I found out what she was doing in time. You know that injunction against the mine that Del and her friends are filing tomorrow?'

The surprises just kept coming. Nick knew nothing about an injunction.

Vince continued, 'Well, it doesn't stand a chance.'

'How could you know that?'

'Your old man, Nicky-boy. He's wangled a tame judge on the bench. Didn't he tell you?'

Nick sat dumbstruck. Half an hour ago, Del had told him to grow up, to open his eyes. She'd told him that he had no idea what his father was capable of. And she'd been right. Carson had toyed with him and the entire Kingfisher Valley community. Played them all for fools. That alone was unforgivable. But if Carson had a judge in his pocket? That was criminal corruption at the very highest level.

'Shame about Del,' Gambino said with a wicked grin. 'You should have turned up tomorrow. I was on a promise tonight.'

Nick swung his right arm back, braced his feet and sent his fist crashing into Gambino's smarmy face. The force of the blow tipped the chair over and sent the bastard sprawling. Gambino sat up slowly, moaning and feeling his nose.

'Take a message to my father, will you, Vinny-boy?' Nick threw the rest of his whisky in Gambino's face. 'Tell him I quit.'

Nick jumped in his car and drove away. After a minute or two he veered onto the verge, parked beneath a stand of beech trees and shoved the door open. He took off at a run down the road, pushing himself to the limits of endurance, careless of stumbling in the dark. He climbed a paddock fence and tore up the grassy slope, startling a mob of cattle that galloped away, tossing their horns and snorting.

He ran until his lungs were burning and his legs trembled, ran until he reached the top of the hill. Then he let out a great, primal howl. He screamed his misery to the silver moon. Screamed his pain and grief. What an idiot he'd been. Always covering for Carson. Tying himself in knots to make excuses for him. Trying so hard to love Carson despite all he knew.

Nick thumped his skull into a tree trunk, trying to knock some sense into himself. Del was right. It was time to grow up. Time to stop being a little boy who hero-worshipped his father. Time to be a man who knew the difference between right and wrong – to accept that for some reason his father had no moral compass at all. It scared him to think what else Carson might be capable of.

Nick sank down at the base of the tree and wept. It was a long time before the shuddering sobs subsided. His mouth was dry as dust and he felt cold all over – so cold that he thought he might never be warm again. The scene with Vince in the kitchen was playing on a continuous loop in his head. Each time Nick relived it, some new repercussion presented itself to him.

What if Del was right about the mine expansion? All the proper assessments and approvals had been sought. He'd overseen them himself. It should all be aboveboard. But then again, what did he know? With Carson as the grand puppetmaster, apparently nothing was as it seemed. He'd need to reinterpret everything in the light of this new knowledge.

When Nick felt calm enough to drive, he returned to the car and headed for his chalet at McClellan Vale. Not that he planned on staying long. In the morning he'd find alternative accommodation. But first he'd see Del. He'd camp outside the house at Kingfisher Farm if he had to.

His phone rang. Carson's ring tone – Wagner's 'Flight of the Valkyries'. *Let it ring*, Nick thought bitterly. It would be the last time Nick would hear it. When he got home, he'd block the number and remove the contact from his phone.

CHAPTER 36

Del fluffed her pillow and pulled the covers up higher. Normally she was up at seven, in time for one of Darby's breakfast cookups. But not today. Today she planned to stay in bed.

Tiny scratched at the door again. Del let him in, only just beating him back to the bed. 'Move over, you big lug.'

Del pulled the pillow over her head. How on earth was she going to tell Darby about what Vince had done? How would she tell Ken and the others in the Berrimilla Progress Association? How could she bear to?

Del wondered what Nick would do this morning to discredit their grassroots campaign. Hold a press conference? Go on regional television? Talk on the radio? All three? How long would it take him to spread the news about Vince's deception? Del felt heartsick. It would devastate a lot of good people.

Darby knocked at the door. 'Del, you have to see this!' She burst in with a copy of the morning paper. 'Look at the front page. It says that Vince is a fraud. That his grandfather never even had a farm.'

Del groaned and sat up wearily. So, Nick's offensive had already begun.

'Why don't you seem surprised?' Darby peered at her daughter more closely. 'Whatever happened last night? When you came in you looked like you'd been crying.'

Del turned away from her mother. Darby deserved an answer, but Del couldn't bring herself to speak. That explanation was just too painful.

She took her phone from the nightstand and turned it on. A dozen missed calls from Nick and three texts.

I have to see you. Will be there soon.

Followed by, *Gambino works for Westcorp.*

And then, *I swear I didn't know.*

What? Del stared at the texts. Vince worked for Westcorp? Impossible. The man had single-handedly united the whole valley against the corporation. But then again, Nick wouldn't lie about something so important. The fact was that Nick wouldn't lie at all. So, Del forced herself to think the proposition through and try it on for size.

Yes, Vince had turned Kingfisher Valley against Westcorp. But by faking his moving personal story, he'd now achieved the opposite result. Public opinion would swing firmly back in favour of the mine. Shit. She'd badly underestimated how far Carson would go to get what he wanted. The depths of his deviousness were unimaginable.

Thank God Nick wasn't a part of it. The man she'd loved for years had his faults – the main one being his faith in his father. But she knew him to be an honest, loyal and trustworthy person. A man of his word. A very different kind of man from Vince Gambino. Good grief – if Nick hadn't turned up when he did last night, she might well have slept with the bastard. It made her sick to think of it.

'What's wrong?' said a wide-eyed Darby. 'You look like you've seen a ghost.'

Del tried to gather her scattered thoughts. 'I'll explain later,' she told her mother. 'But right now I'm expecting a visitor. So if you don't mind, I need to get dressed.'

She ushered Darby and Tiny from the room and tugged a comb through her hair. At the very least she owed Nick a hearing. As she buttoned her jeans, she heard shouts coming from the front of the house. Was that Ken's voice? His car had been parked at the house when she got in last evening. He must have stayed the night. Del pushed that disagreeable thought aside.

She hurried outside to find Nick and Ken arguing on the porch. Darby was urging them to calm down, but neither man was listening to her.

'Stop it, Ken!' yelled Del. 'I want to talk to Nick.'

Ken, his face like thunder, stalked away.

Darby hovered on the porch and cast an anxious look at Del. 'Are you sure, love? You're sure you want to talk to that man? Do you know who he is?'

'Yes,' she said, feeling rather guilty. Darby didn't know that Del had been engaged to *that man*. Darby knew almost nothing about the last eight years of her daughter's life. Del intended to remedy that, and soon. But right now, she needed to hear what Nick had to say.

'Mum, would you excuse us, please?'

Darby wrung her hands together and then went inside.

Nick gazed at Del, his expression eager and unsure all at once. He looked very handsome standing there. The morning sun highlighted the copper tones of his hair, and his sombre expression gave him a compelling gravitas. He might be trying to push through the Mount Morton expansion, but, as she'd told herself once before, there was more to life than opposing the mine. She would hear what he had to say.

'Hello, Del.'

She glanced back at the house to see Darby and Ken peering through the window. 'Let's go for a walk.'

They headed up the hill, with Tiny and the collies leading the way.

'That article in this morning's *Gazette*,' said Nick. 'It didn't come from me. I had nothing to do with it.'

Del stopped and stared at him. 'You expect me to believe that?' The absurdity of their situation hit her. 'How the tables have turned,' she said with a hollow laugh. 'I recall a time when I tried to convince you of something similar.'

'Del, listen ... '

But she had already marched away.

When they reached the vineyard, Del stopped and indicated a log bench beneath a blue gum. Ken had put it there so she could sit in the shade and watch her Babydolls.

Nick took in the lush vines with their bunches of grapes plumping in the early summer sun. 'Your mum has a vineyard?'

'No,' said Del. 'I have a vineyard. Now tell me what's so important.'

They sat down on the log and Nick told her his extraordinary news. 'My father has outdone himself this time. He had me spruiking the mine, and Gambino opposing it. Then Gambino sent me that dossier so I would expose him for a fraud and discredit the entire anti-mine movement.'

'You're kidding me!' Del searched his face for any trace of deceit, not quite knowing what to look for. Nick had never lied to her before. 'You mean Vince sent you that folder himself?'

'He told me straight up. Bragged about it even. I reckon Gambino's responsible for that press release in today's paper as well. He probably had a media push ready to go,' said Nick, bitterly. 'Apparently, Dad doesn't trust me with something as important as coordinating his misinformation campaign.'

Del blinked at him stupidly. Surely not. She'd believed in Vince, admired him, confided in him. She'd told him about the direction of her campaign. And all along he'd been spying on her – deceiving her and all of the people who trusted him. Vince was indeed the lowest of the low.

Nick hung his head, the very picture of shame and dejection, and Del's heart went out to him. Nick would understand her shock and confusion all too well. He'd endured a far harsher betrayal than she had. He'd been fighting for years to maintain his faith in Carson, despite his father's faults. Del wished that she could have somehow spared him the pain of this latest treachery. Yes, he'd been stubborn – wilfully ignorant, even – where his father was concerned. But she loved his loyalty – a quality that the double-dealing Vince Gambino had no concept of.

Del put a tentative hand on Nick's shoulder. 'What will you do?'

He looked up and covered her hand with his own. 'I'll tell you what I won't do. I won't believe another word my fucking father says.'

Del's heart softened further. 'It must have been hard facing up to what he'd done. Carson, I mean. Sending Vince in behind your back.'

Nick smiled ruefully. 'You don't know the half of it.'

'Then tell me.'

For a few moments his mouth moved silently, as if he couldn't bear to utter the words. 'That injunction your group is filing in the Environment Court today? It will fail.'

'How can you know—'

'Gambino says the judge is in Dad's pocket.'

Del couldn't bring herself to speak. They'd been so hopeful of success, and now this? She already suspected Carson of bribing politicians. Or maybe he blackmailed them or struck some other kind of Faustian deal. But if Carson was bringing undue influence to bear on the judiciary? That might be the biggest scandal the state had ever seen.

'I'm as stunned as you are,' said Nick. 'How could I have kept my head in the sand for so long?'

Del had the good grace not to say I told you so.

'You want to hear more? It wasn't just Stacey Turner. Dad slept with women right throughout his marriage. He may well have been the one to drive my mother to suicide.'

This did not come as a surprise to Del. She thought back to the heartbreaking testimonials that Celia had shown her. Even if only half of them were true, it meant that Carson hadn't just slept around. He'd routinely used his power and position to coerce unwilling women into sex. Some of them had been mere girls. But she wouldn't confront Nick with this ugly truth – not yet anyway. He had enough on his plate. She only had to take one look at his ashen face to see that his world was crumbling.

Del lightly rubbed his back, a familiar gesture. 'You made Carson do that mea culpa press conference, right?'

'I wanted him to take some personal responsibility for once. And I thought it might be a way of making it up to Mum. But that was a phony apology, and it only worked to Dad's advantage. He really is the Teflon man. No mud ever sticks.'

Del could see the pain Nick was in, but she still had to ask. 'So that feature in the *Gazette* … Do you still believe that I was behind the allegations against your father?'

'Of course not.' He shot her a sideways glance. 'But if you were, you'd deserve a medal. If not for that article, I'd still be swallowing Dad's lies.'

Del hadn't thought that she could despise Carson any more than she already did. But looking at Nick's stricken face, at the hurt in his eyes? How could a father do that to his own son?

'I'm sorry this happened.'

Nick turned to her, a look of astonishment on his face. 'You're sorry? After everything my family and I have put you through?'

He reached for her hand, and after a moment's hesitation she let him take it. Too much water had passed under the bridge between them. Too many painful misunderstandings. Yet, perhaps they could still be friends, if nothing else.

'Tell me, Del.' His voice brimmed with feeling. 'How can I make amends?'

CHAPTER 37

'I don't understand.' Darby pointed to Nick, who was standing in the corner of the kitchen. 'Why on earth would you go anywhere with him?'

Del put her laptop bag down and checked that she'd packed the cord. 'I'll explain properly when I get back. But first, sit down, Mum. Nick has something to say. You too, Ken.'

They all took seats at the kitchen table. Darby and Ken stared uncertainly at Nick. Del sat beside him as he provided a potted version of what he'd told her. That Vince was a fraud who worked for Westcorp. That their application for an injunction would fail. Del couldn't bear seeing the shock and disappointment on their faces.

'This might sound strange,' said Nick. 'But until today I didn't know who my father was.' He glanced at Del, who smiled in encouragement. 'He's a terrible person, and I won't work for him any longer.'

Ken furrowed his forehead, his brows knitting together. 'So, what … Are you saying that you're on our side now?'

Del held her breath. Nick was hurt and angry with his father. Angry enough to pack in his job. But that could be a knee jerk reaction that he'd regret in a day or two. Was he really ready to change sides and fight against Westcorp?'

'Yes, that's exactly what I'm saying,' said Nick, and Del was thrilled to hear the determination in his voice. 'Dad has got away with his lies and manipulations for too long. He's hurt too many people.' Nick smiled at Del. 'That's why I need your daughter to come with me, Mrs Fisher. My dad needs to be stopped – and I'm hoping that Del can help me stop him.'

Del kissed Darby goodbye. 'Don't worry, Mum. Nick's a good man.'

Darby frowned. 'How can you know that?'

'He's an old friend. I'll explain when I get back.'

And she would. She'd tell Darby all about the life she'd lived for the past eight years: her engagement to Nick, winning her dream job at the *Sydney Morning Herald*, Celia's inexplicable treachery and Carson's decades of sexual predation. It would be cathartic – an emotional cleansing.

And once she'd done all that, she'd talk to Darby about Dad. The manner of his death remained the elephant in the room. She and Mum were coexisting peacefully enough, working together on the farm and campaigning against the mine. But their relationship remained fragile. It felt like they were tentatively crossing a lake covered in thin ice and they were both afraid to fall in. Well, it was about time they dived down.

Del hopped in Nick's car, waved to Darby and Ken, and they set off to … Well, she didn't really know. All she knew was that Nick had something he wanted to show her. He'd been tight-lipped on the details. 'I can't tell you,' he'd said mysteriously when she pressed him. 'And it might mean nothing. You'll need to see for yourself.'

'How has Carson reacted to you quitting?'

Nick snorted. 'He doesn't believe it. He sent me an email saying, "Come home when you've finished your temper tantrum."'

'He's a real piece of work,' said Del, shaking her head.

'You're not kidding. When I was in the hospital, I tried ringing you non-stop. Turns out Dad had put the wrong number in the phone he gave me. Just one digit out. I didn't notice. Who knows people's phone numbers any more?'

'What a bastard!' said Del. It felt good to be able to vent her feelings about Carson without Nick springing to his defence.

'And he put a block on my phone so that you couldn't ring me. I thought it strange that I didn't hear from you. I would have thought it even stranger if I'd remembered our engagement. But when that bridge knocked me on the head, I lost some time.'

Del looked at him aghast. 'You mean you don't remember asking me to marry you?'

'Oh, I do now. Receiving your letter and the ring in the post jogged my memory. I can't tell you what a surprise it was.'

They drove on in silence, while Del tried to process Nick's startling news. Ten minutes later, she received a phone call from Tony Marshall, the pro bono lawyer who'd filed the injunction against the mine.

'You were right,' said Del when Tony hung up. 'The judge ruled against us. He said that despite respecting and understanding our concerns, the expansion should proceed because Westcorp had addressed all relevant social, environmental and air quality concerns.'

'That's not true,' said Nick. 'The final reports haven't even been made. I don't know why I've worked so hard to prepare Westcorp's case according to the rules. Looks like they'll be rubberstamped no matter what. You know, I've always known how Dad operated, but I thought there was at least some legitimacy to his success. I never thought of it as corruption. I thought it was normal for the wheels of big business to spin inside the wheels of state.'

'You were brought up with it,' said Del. 'And you trusted your father. It's only natural that you couldn't see the wood for the trees.'

'Well, I see it now,' he said. 'And I have you to thank for that.'

His words gave Del a warm glow, but the problem of how to stop the mine remained.

'We can't give up now,' she said. 'But Tony says we can't lodge an appeal once the expansion wins its final approval.'

'That's true,' said Nick. 'The rules are rigged. No legal right exists to challenge the expansion once it's approved, and I'm afraid that approval is a forgone conclusion.'

'So, you're saying it's hopeless?' asked Del.

It took Nick a while to answer. 'It's a long shot,' he said, 'but there just might be a way. There might be a way to stop Carson dead in his rotten, corrupt tracks.'

'Here we are.' They drove through the imposing entrance of the McClellan Vale estate. The Westcorp logo – a stylised pick held by a fist – was emblazoned in gold on the gates. Del stared out the window, impressed by the lush green vista. Hectares of vines clothed the low hills, stretching as far as the eye could see. One day Kingfisher Farm would look like that.

Nick parked beside a villa nestled within a pretty fernery.

'Come on in.' Nick looked grim. 'This place belongs to Westcorp. Tomorrow I'll find somewhere else to stay.'

Del grabbed her laptop and followed him inside.

'Would you like coffee or something to eat?' He headed for the fridge in the open-plan kitchen. 'I have cold cuts and sourdough—'

'Nick, what did you want to show me?'

He heaved a great sigh. Whatever this was, Nick was finding it hard. He disappeared into what she guessed was the bedroom. Soon he emerged with an old moleskin notebook and placed it reverently on a coffee table. One page was flagged with a yellow post-it note.

'My mother's diary – well, one of them.'

'Oh, Nick. What a treasure trove of wonderful memories.'

'A treasure trove, but I promise you – not all the memories are wonderful.'

Del sat on the couch and reached for the diary. 'May I?'

'Please.' Nick sat down beside her. His physical presence sent a familiar prickle up her spine.

Del opened the moleskin. The author had a beautiful copperplate hand, and each entry was headed with a day and date. She turned to the page flagged with the post it-note. 'This is from ten years ago.'

'Go on, read it.'
Del read the marked entry.

Well, I'm back in this infernal hospital. I tried phoning my mother today, but she wouldn't take my call. My father has also deserted me. It seems they don't want to be associated with their crazy daughter. And I think I am indeed crazy. My thoughts are scattered and disorganised. I can't concentrate enough to read a book. I sleep all day and wake up more weary than before. I wonder if it's the drugs. I take so many pills that there's no room left in my stomach for food. But the specialist says that I need them, and I trust him. Carson would never allow the doctors to harm me.

My only friend in this awful place is a figment of my imagination. Yet Bobby seems so real. We talk in my mind, but I don't tell anyone because I know he's really dead. It was because of him that I'm here again. Bobby sent me a letter. It was from him, I know, because I recognised the writing. He begged me to tell the world that he's alive. I told Carson about it. He was distressed, saying it meant my depression had returned. He asked to see the letter. I said that it had frightened me so much that I'd burned it. And it had frightened me. Receiving letters from dead people is surely a sign of insanity. I know now that I must have imagined it. Even so, I will never go to the place where I hid that letter for fear I will actually find it. Then my descent into madness and delusion will be complete.

'Your poor mother!' Del had read the page twice before looking up. 'And Bobby is your uncle?'

Nick nodded. 'He apparently died in that car crash twenty-five years ago; the one that killed my grandparents.'

'Apparently?'

'I know Carson now – I know what he's capable of. He was desperate to run Westcorp. When his father died the entire corporation went to Bobby as the eldest son. But after Bobby's death, Carson got the lot.'

Del let the awful implication of his words sink in. 'What are you saying? That Carson killed his brother in order to inherit Westcorp?'

'Maybe. Or maybe Mum was right and Uncle Bobby is still alive somewhere. Or maybe Mum was simply delusional all along. But whatever the truth is, however heinous, I need to know.' His eyes bored into hers like twin laser beams. 'I have no right to ask,' he said. 'But here goes anyway. Will you help me, Del? Will you help me discover the truth?'

CHAPTER 38

Del stared at Nick, assessing him. Trying to judge if he was ready for this. 'I'll help you,' she said at last. 'But first, tell me – what does your gut say about Carson?'

Nick looked grim. 'The ground has shifted beneath my feet so many times that I don't know what to think any more. I do know that Carson is beyond ruthless. Look what we've discovered already. He bribes and cheats and deceives. Gaslights his wife. Double-crosses me. Who knows what else?'

Del couldn't look at him.

Nick narrowed his eyes. 'What is it?'

She stood up and walked to the window.

Nick followed her. 'Del, tell me. There's only ever been truth between us.'

Yes, only truth. The lies that had torn them apart belonged to other people. So, she finally told him about Celia and the dozens of testimonials from women that Carson had victimised.

Nick ran his fingers through his hair when Del finished speaking. Tears glistened in his eyes, and it broke Del's heart to see them. After everything that had happened, Carson still had the power to hurt his son.

She hugged Nick's stiff shoulders and rubbed the familiar hollow of his back. It felt so natural. Del closed her eyes and suddenly they could have been back in his cottage at Westbrook. She sighed, softly. If only they could time travel to before everything had changed, back to that night under the stars when Nick had presented her with the beautiful blue tulip and the ring hidden inside it.

Nick rubbed his eyes with the heels of his hand.

'Come and sit down,' she said. 'And make me one of your marvellous brews. I've missed them.' But what she really wanted to say was *I've missed you.*

Half an hour later they were sitting at the beautiful ash dining table laden with steaming mugs of coffee and a tin of shortbreads that Del had found on the sideboard.

'If we're going to do this,' she said, 'you must convince Carson that you've forgiven him. Can you do that?'

Nick's face fell.

'You look like you're about to face the executioner,' she said with the softest smile.

'Well, how do you expect me to suck up to Dad after everything that's happened?'

Del shrugged. 'Do you want me to help you or not?'

'Of course. You're the hot-shot investigative journalist.'

'Was,' she corrected. 'Past tense. But we need to buy ourselves some time. Apologise to Carson and resume work on the mine approvals. Lull him into a false sense of security. And try to slow down the assessments while you're at it.' She dipped a biscuit in her coffee. 'Can you do that?'

A pulse started in his cheek, the way it did when he was agitated. 'Yes, all right. I can do that.'

'Good. Now tell me, is there anything else in your mother's diaries that I should know about?'

Nick took a sip of coffee, leaving a milky moustache on his upper lip. Del wanted to gently wipe it away.

'Mum thought he was shagging other women,' he said. 'She was right enough there.'

'Anything else?'

Nick's face briefly sank into his hands before he pulled himself together. 'Mum thought Carson might have had someone special. You know, a favourite. A mistress. Someone that he'd been seeing on and off for years.'

'Did she ever mention a name?'

'You're kidding me, right? Mum never knew names. Most of the time she thought she was imagining things, being paranoid.'

'Okay ... and when did Natalie think it might have started with this favourite?'

'A long time ago. At least fifteen years. Maybe more. I'll go through the diaries tonight and find out for you.'

The cogs in Del's head were spinning. A long-term mistress? 'Come on.' She stood up and tugged Nick's hand. 'We're going to Winga.'

Celia beckoned them into her office. It felt surprisingly good to be back at the *Gazette*. Warmly greeting former colleagues. Soaking in the excitement and energy of the newsroom for one last time.

'It's good to see you two back together,' said Celia.

Del shook her head. 'We're not actually ... '

She glanced at Nick for some support. 'No,' he agreed, awkwardly. 'We're not ... '

Celia shrugged, clearly uninterested. 'How can I help you? Are you after your old job, Del? We'd love to have you back.'

'First,' said Del, 'you can confirm for Nick's benefit that you altered my article to include the accusations against his father.'

Celia gave her a tight-lipped smile. 'I did no such thing.'

'Are you sure about that?' Nobody could doubt the veiled threat behind Del's tone. 'Because if you don't tell Nick the truth, I'll make it public that you've been having a longstanding affair with Carson Shaw. And that it began well before your beloved Greg started showing symptoms of Huntington's. How do you think he'll feel when he hears that his devoted wife has been shagging the mayor for years behind his back?'

Celia went white. 'That's a damned lie!'

'We both know that it isn't.' Del leaned forward in her chair. 'You said yourself that I'm the best newshound around. I have plenty of proof.'

Silence yawned between them. And as the tension became unbearable, Celia's expression gradually morphed from one of defiance to one of defeat. 'This will destroy Greg,' she said simply.

'Well, you should have thought about that before you decided to mess with me. I can assure you that it's not nice to be on the receiving end of a public humiliation. One that will break your partner's heart and kill the trust between you?'

'Enough!' Celia shoved back her chair and stood up.

Del tipped her chin towards Nick. 'Haven't you got something to tell my friend here?'

Celia hesitated for a moment before resuming her seat and taking a very deep breath. 'It's true, Nick. I inserted those allegations about Carson into Del's article. She knew nothing about it. They were all true, mind.'

'And why did you do that?' Del asked. 'Why not publish them under your own name?'

Celia gave her a wry smile. 'Isn't it obvious? Carson is a vengeful man. At the very least he would have told Greg about our affair.' Celia held up the palm of her hand like a stop sign. 'Don't look at me like that. My husband is a good person and I love him. Not the way that I loved Carson. Not with a wild, heart-in-your-mouth kind of passion. But it's love, nonetheless, and I don't want Greg hurt.'

'Tell me,' said Del, with barely controlled venom. 'What was behind your timing? Why expose Carson when you did? You sat on his crimes for years.'

Celia's mask of self-control slipped. Her face crumpled, her chin trembled and a single tear ran down her rouged cheek. 'You know, it's a relief to get all this off my chest,' she said in a voice thick with emotion. 'Carson dumped me.' The tears flowed in earnest now. 'I loved that man. He always came to me with his problems, not to Natalie.' Celia snorted. 'She was such a fragile flower. I was more of a wife to him than she ever was.'

Del could feel Nick tense beside him and she put a calming hand on his arm.

'I tolerated his other women, his stupid dalliances.' Celia shook her head. 'I knew they meant nothing. Just sops to his rather large ego. But he always came back to me. He loved *me*.' She smiled through her tears. 'What Carson and I shared was extraordinary – a spiritual bond.' She stood, arms spread wide in a dramatic gesture, and looked skywards. 'A heavenly match. Something that would last forever.'

'But it didn't.'

'No.' Celia slumped back in her chair and sniffed back a few final tears. The hardness was returning to her face. 'Carson broke it off by text. We'd been together for twenty years, and he broke it off by text. It tore out my heart.' The old defiance had returned. 'Did that bastard really think that I'd let him get away with it? And then when I found out the truth about what he'd done to those poor women, the sexual assaults, the exploitation … He deserved every consequence of that article and much more.' She shot Del a questioning glance. 'I ask you – what would you have done?'

The air hung heavy with the gravity of Celia's confession.

'You're a damned coward.' Del spat the words. 'Letting me take the fall.'

'It was a risk,' said Celia. 'I worried that Carson would blame me anyway. He'd just ditched me in the most callous way possible. It might have occurred to him that I'd exact a little vengeance of my own. But no. The arrogant prick was blinded by self-belief, convinced that I'd remain unfailingly loyal to him no matter what he did.'

Del squeezed Nick's hand. 'Can you give us a few moments alone, Celia?'

Celia pasted on a smile and went to the window. She studied her reflection in the glass and dabbed at her face with a tissue. 'My mascara is running.'

'Please, Celia?'

She turned on her high heels and left the office.

They waited until the door slammed shut before turning to each other.

'How soundproof is this office?' asked Nick.

'Fairly soundproof if we speak softly,' said Del. 'I should know. I've tried to eavesdrop often enough.'

'How did you know that Celia was Dad's long-term mistress?' whispered Nick.

Del checked to see if her old boss was loitering near the door. 'I didn't.'

'Shit!' Nick broke out in a grin as Del's words sank in. 'That was some bluff.'

'More of an educated guess,' said Del. 'But it struck gold, and that's the main thing. Now we have Celia over a barrel, she'll give us whatever we want.'

'And what do we want?'

'Anything on Carson that we might be able to use. Copies of the testimonials made against him by various women. Stuff on the ICAC investigation.'

'ICAC investigation?'

'Apparently Carson is a person of interest. And I want to know more about this Bobby business and that letter your mother mentioned in her diary. Celia's been cosying up to Carson for years. She might know something.'

Nick gave his head a slight shake and laughed. 'My God, you're good.'

Del inclined her head. 'Why, thank you. Now, let's get Celia back and put her through the wringer.'

CHAPTER 39

I t was after six o'clock before they left Celia. It had been a
productive afternoon. They had a stack of files with them, along
with two memory sticks and an audio recording of their conversation.
Del was making sense of them as best she could in the car while Nick
drove, but it was hard to concentrate. She couldn't wait to get home
and make a closer examination of the material.

Del looked up from her reading. 'Hang on. You missed the turn-
off.'

'What do you mean?'

Del swivelled in her seat and looked out the rear window. 'The
road to Berrimilla was back there.'

'Berrimilla?' Nick sounded surprised. 'I thought—'

'What – you thought we'd just go back to your place?'

'Well, why not? You said we had a lot of work to do.'

'No, I said I had a lot of work to do. What you need to do is reconnect with Carson and slow down those assessments. See if you can
delay the final approval of the mine expansion.'

Nick braked to let a mob of stray sheep get off the road and then
pulled over. 'Why don't I simply make it public that Gambino was

working for Carson? It will stymie the social impact assessment. The whole valley will turn against Westcorp again.'

'Do you have any proof that Vince worked for Carson?'

Nick ran his hands around the steering wheel, then slowly shook his head.

'My God, Nick, will you never learn?' Del hadn't meant to sound quite so harsh. 'Carson will demonise you. I can see the copy now. "In a vindictive final act, Westcorp's former managing director Nick Shaw – who was sacked on Wednesday for incompetence – is peddling unsubstantiated rumours designed to damage his father's stellar corporate reputation."'

His shoulders fell, but he kept eye contact with Del.

She continued, 'And if we're to find a way to stop Carson, he needs to trust you.'

Nick closed his eyes and pressed a hand to his temple like he was getting a headache.

Del softened her tone. 'It will be hard pretending to your father, I understand that. You're instinctively an honest person. But I need some time, Nick. A few days to go through what we have from Celia. Then we'll decide how to proceed.'

'Okay. I can do this.' Nick took hold of her hand and his voice grew husky. 'Wouldn't it make sense for you to work from my place?' He lightly stroked her wrist, making it tingle. 'It would help us to, um … communicate more effectively.'

There it was. An invitation to Nick's bed, at the very least. And at most, an invitation to resume their relationship. She recalled the bleak weeks after Celia published that damned article. Back then, Del would have given anything to be sitting somewhere with Nick's fingers trailing up her inner arm. It hurt to think that time had passed.

Del withdrew her hand. 'Take me home to Kingfisher Farm.'

He reached for her fingers again and she shook him away. 'We can't go back, Nick. I'm not the same person that you fell in love with.'

'That's not true.'

'Don't tell me what's true or not!' Del snapped. Her words came out in a rush. 'The person you loved was shallow and selfish. Don't you remember what a conceited bitch I was? Back then it was all about me. It was about how big a story I could break. How big a splash I could make. How many people I could impress. God knows why you loved me at all.' She nodded emphatically, wagging a finger at him, and her voice rose a few octaves. 'I feel it showed very poor judgement.'

Del couldn't breathe. She shoved the door open and jumped out, leaning against the car and dragging some air into her lungs. Dusk was falling. A family of kookaburras commenced their rollicking evening chorus. They seemed to be laughing directly at her.

Nick came to stand beside her. The kookaburras' call swelled in volume, echoing around the hills, echoing around her brain so that she could barely think. Then it stopped abruptly. The sudden silence magnified the emptiness she felt.

Nick put his hands in his pockets and kicked at the leaf litter. 'Kookaburras are kingfishers, you know. The world's largest king-fishers.'

Del couldn't help a small smile. 'You always did know the right thing to say at the right time.'

Nick inclined his head in acknowledgement. 'You forgot to say that I also make great coffee and have perfect taste in women.'

The setting sun bathed Nick's face in an attractive rosy glow. She liked looking at him – liked his stubbly cheeks and his neat widow's peak.

'Tell me, sweetheart,' said Nick.

'I'm not your sweetheart.'

'No.' He ran his hand through his hair. 'If you're not the woman I was ready to marry a few short months ago, then who are you?'

Del crossed her arms. 'I'm a woman who wants to breed the best Babydoll sheep in the country. Who wants to make the best wine this side of the Murray River. Who wants to go for early morning walks with her dog and watch the sunrise. And who wants to preserve Cobbee Basin for her children, if she's lucky enough to have any. It's a remarkable place, Nick. I'll take you to see it the first chance we get.'

'Truly?'

'Truly.'

'And you don't want to be a reporter?'

'No. Now, does that sound like the woman you wanted to marry?'

'I thought you weren't sure about kids?'

Del shrugged. 'A person can change their mind.'

'And you really want to make wine?'

'More than anything.' She opened the car door. 'Now take me home, Nick. Take me home to my sheep and my vines and my dog.'

It was almost midnight when they arrived back at Kingfisher Farm. The barking dogs heralded their arrival, and despite the lateness of the hour, Darby was waiting on the porch.

Del had snoozed for much of the trip. She was grumpy and groggy with sleep as she began gathering up her things.

'What now?' asked Nick.

'I told you.' Del rummaged through her bag, checking that she had the memory sticks and her phone. 'Apologise to Carson. Reconnect. I'll go through the stuff we have from Celia. In the meantime, do what you can to slow down the mine assessment process.'

'When will I see you?'

'I don't know.' Del stopped stacking folders and turned to him. Even in the dim light of the dashboard she could see how crestfallen he was. 'You're trying to regain Carson's trust. How will it look if we're seen together? As far as he's concerned, I'm public enemy number one.'

Nick sighed and got out to help her carry her things.

Del put a hand on his arm. 'I can't thank you enough for your help, Nick. I know, well, you've always been so devoted to your father ... '

His smile was heart-meltingly warm. 'You're not the only one who's changed.'

Darby hurried over, calling, 'I've been so worried!' And she looked it. Mum seemed to have developed a few extra frown lines on her face since that morning.

Del couldn't see Ken's car, and she suddenly wished that she'd been kinder about him staying over. Darby could have used his support tonight. The fallout from Vince and his lies was all over the local bulletins. The Progress Association's campaign would have taken a hit. Add in the news of the failed injunction, and it meant her mother's day had been truly terrible.

Del imagined Darby, with only the dogs and her disappointment to keep her company, waiting alone as darkness fell. Wondering where her daughter was, what she'd been doing and why on Earth she'd spent the day with Westcorp's managing director. Del owed her an explanation, but she was bone weary. It would have to wait until morning.

CHAPTER 40

The next morning Del allowed herself the luxury of a lie-in. At first light, when Tiny whined to go out, she let him outside and went back to bed, hoping to grab forty more winks. Yet sleep eluded her. She could hear her mother in the kitchen – the kettle whistling and plates clinking. No doubt Darby was desperate for the explanation that Del had promised her.

Del stretched and yawned, then reached for her earphones and mobile. There were two hours of recordings from yesterday to go through, but she particularly wanted to replay the part where Celia talked about Bobby. Ostensibly, Celia had said nothing significant, but Del couldn't help feeling that she'd missed something.

Del sat up, ran her fingers through her tangled hair, and then skimmed through the recording until she found the section of audio she was looking for. Celia said that Carson sometimes talked about Bobby, and always with great fondness. He talked about how close they were as children and how devastated he was when Bobby died. And he talked about how his brother was never happy being heir to Westcorp's top job.

'According to Carson, Bobby hated working for Westcorp. Bobby was a hippy at heart. He'd come home from the office, change from his suit into overalls, smoke some weed and disappear into his organic vegetable patch. He loved birdwatching and fossil collecting and nature photography. Bobby said that if he had his way, he'd close down the mines. But he didn't dare tell his father, Hugo, how unhappy he was. Hugo had a hold over his sons. They would never go against him.'

Del paused the recording. *Well, well*, she thought. Domineering fathers ran in the family. She clicked through to where she'd asked Celia if Carson was capable of killing his brother.

'Oh no. Carson loved Bobby. He missed him terribly, even after all that time. Sometimes he talked as if his brother was still here. We'd be watching a film or listening to some music and he'd say, "Bobby would like this."'

Del pressed pause, rewound to listen to the grab a few more times, then rang Nick.

'This is a lovely sur—'

'Listen, Nick. Yesterday, Celia said your uncle Bobby hated working for Westcorp. Does anything in Natalie's diaries confirm that?'

'Well, yes. Mum wrote that Bobby wasn't cut out for the job. He wanted to study biology and become a naturalist, but my grandad wouldn't have it.'

'Do you remember what Carson told Celia?' said Del. 'He said that his brother would close down the mines if he could. Does that tally with the picture Natalie painted of Bobby?'

'It does, yes.'

'Listen, Nick. Did Natalie ever talk to you about Bobby in the present tense?'

'No, I don't think so.'

'Think hard. Take your time.'

The clock on the wall ticked out the seconds. When Nick finally spoke, his voice was thick with emotion. 'On that last morning, Mum came to see me at the cottage. She was distraught about the allegations made against Carson. Crying and hysterical and utterly humiliated.'

'Nick?' Del could hear the pain behind his words and wished she was there with him. 'I need you to go on.' This was so hard on him. Damn Celia and her coward's vengeance.

'Out of the blue, Mum said, "I want to see Bobby." But she was confused, Del. Not making any sense. I reminded her that Bobby had passed, but she'd lost track of reality.'

Del was in full investigative mode. 'What happened then?'

'Mum started searching through my kitchen cupboards looking for some letter.'

'A letter.'

'Yes.'

Del's mind was working overtime. 'Nick, have you spoken to Carson yet?'

'Give me a break. It's seven-thirty in the morning.'

'Who cares? Call him now, Nick. Apologise. Say you weren't serious about resigning. Say you're coming home to Westbrook today to mend fences.'

Two hours later Del emerged from her room. Darby was kneading a batch of scone dough in the kitchen and listening to a country music station. She usually listened to local talkback radio, but that was no doubt too painful today. Reports of Vince Gambino's fake story and the failed injunction were all over the news.

Darby looked up. Del hated seeing such sadness and defeat in her mother's face. Darby tried to smile but it didn't reach her eyes. The three dogs were gathered around her feet in a circle of sympathy.

'Sit down, Mum. Let's talk ... '

Del told Darby about the last eight years of her life, starting with her graduation from Sydney University with a master's degree in journalism.

'I'm so proud of you, darling.' Darby wiped her floury hands on the front of her apron, took it off and hung it on a wall hook. 'I'd have loved to share that special day.'

Del would have loved that too. But when she tried to picture her mother in the crowd, it only made her think of how her dad should also have been there.

'I became friends with Nick Shaw at uni. We bonded in a bar one night while moaning about the trials of being only children.' She smiled at the memory. 'We met again three years later when I began working at the *Winga Gazette*.'

Darby was staring, open-mouthed. Del hesitated, knowing what a shock this next revelation would be for her mother, wondering how to put it. No point pussyfooting around, she told herself. Might as well just say it. 'We started dating, fell in love and planned to marry.'

Darby blinked slowly and sank down on a kitchen chair. 'You and Nick Shaw?' She seemed dazed. 'You mean Westcorp's Nick Shaw. The man who came here yesterday?'

'Yes, Mum.'

'Were you ever going to tell me?'

Del called Tiny over for moral support. 'Well, it's a moot point. We broke up months ago.' Tiny put a paw on her lap. 'Now can I finish, please?'

Del told Darby about winning her dream job at the *Sydney Morning Herald*, about Celia Bloom's treachery, Natalie's suicide and Carson's decades of sexual predation. 'He's a monster, Mum. Carson Shaw takes advantage of everybody he meets, even the people closest to him. Nick understands that now.' She reached across the table and covered Darby's hand with her own. 'He's on our side.'

Darby just sat there, dumbfounded. Del was pretty dumbfounded herself. She'd hoped that opening up to her mother would bring a sense of relief. But instead it had made her feel vulnerable, frozen – unsure if she'd done the right thing. It wasn't until the collies made a grab for the dough on the bench that Del moved. She shooed the dogs outside.

'I'll put the scones in the oven, shall I? And make us a pot of tea.'

Darby was so stunned that she didn't even complain when Del

formed rough rounds with her fingers instead of using a cutter and forgot to glaze them with milk. 'There.' She slid the tray of misshapen scones into the oven. 'How long will they take? Fifteen minutes? Twenty?' Del set the timer and sat back down.

'So, you and Nick.' Darby's voice was little more than a whisper. 'Are you two getting back together?'

'No, Mum. But we *are* going to stop Carson from hurting anyone else. And we *are* going to stop the mine. Nick's working to delay the assessments to buy us some time.'

'My poor darling.' Tears glistened under Darby's eyes. 'I wish I'd known all this. I wish I could have been there for you.'

'It doesn't matter, Mum.'

'Of course it matters.' Del couldn't meet her mother's gaze. 'You still blame me for your dad's death, don't you?'

There it was. She admired Darby for having the courage to say it out loud. But Del wasn't ready to dive into that fraught issue today. The kitchen had become an emotional pressure cooker and she was already overwhelmed.

The dogs started barking and the strand of tension in the room snapped. Del breathed a sigh of relief. A visitor would provide just the circuit breaker she needed.

'Yoo-hoo. Is anybody home?' Kim Khan pushed open the door, with a pet carrier in one hand and a bottle of champagne in the other. 'Surprise!'

Del had never been so happy to see anyone in her life. Darby wasn't so thrilled. She frowned, clearly unhappy for their talk to be interrupted.

'Morning, Del. Morning, Mrs Fisher. I have a present for you guys.'

Kim put the carrier on the table and unzipped the top. Two snowy-white heads popped out.

Darby's frown instantly vanished. 'Oh my God.' She lifted a puppy and cradled it in her arms. 'They're adorable!'

And they were. Del couldn't imagine anything cuter than these baby Maremmas. The second pup climbed from the carrier, tail wagging madly. With its shiny black nose, floppy ears and soft woolly coat it looked like a cross between a tiny lamb and a teddy bear.

'These are the livestock guardian dogs I was telling you about, Mum.'

'What? These itty-bitty little things?'

'They're brother and sister,' said Kim. 'You can name them if you like.' She took the pup from Darby and put it back in the carrier. 'And they're not pets. They need to go down to the shed and be raised with the sheep.'

Darby picked up the other puppy and gazed into its dark, soulful eyes. 'You look like a Kimba to me.' She snuggled it close. 'They're too little. They couldn't be more than eight weeks old.'

'That's the perfect time for them to bond – with sheep, not people.' Kim tried to take the puppy, but instead Darby gathered up Kimba's brother as well and disappeared with them into the lounge room.'

'Good luck prying those pups off Mum,' laughed Del. 'But seriously, Kim – you're a lifesaver. Things were getting a bit intense in here.'

Kim popped the champagne cork. 'Glasses?'

Del looked at the wall clock. 'Ten o'clock. Not too early?'

'It's never too early for warm champers.' Kim poured three glasses. 'Time to toast the new members of your family. And after that, you'd better explain what I just walked in on'

CHAPTER 41

Nick drove through the gates of Westbrook with a sinking heart. He dreaded the ordeal ahead. Betraying his father would be the hardest thing he'd ever done.

Carson was waiting for Nick on the stone steps of the homestead. He sang out when he saw his son, waving and smiling. Nick's mouth went dry. It was a bittersweet moment. Up until today, Nick had lived to see that smile. He'd basked in its approval as a boy and strived to earn it as a man. It was a precious thing. But now Carson's smile sent shivers of shame up Nick's spine. He'd never lied to his father before now.

'Hello, Dad.'

Carson came down the steps, his gait slow and a little stiff. His knee must be bothering him again. Nick had only been away for a few weeks, but his father seemed frailer than he remembered. Carson stumbled a little on the last step, and Nick's protective instinct kicked in. *What a hypocrite*, Nick thought as he took his father's arm. What he was planning was the polar opposite of protection.

An hour later they sat down to a sumptuous lunch of roast beef with all the trimmings. Carson had trotted out a celebratory vintage Penfolds Shiraz worth two hundred dollars a bottle. He was doing everything he could to win his son's favour.

'I barely had that sirloin ready in time,' said Mrs Marlow, as she placed a plate of Yorkshire puddings on the table. 'Your father only gave me two hours' notice that you were coming.' She beamed fondly at Nick over her glasses.

'What happened to the live-in chef I organised for you, Dad? Clive, wasn't it?'

Carson *harrumphed* loudly. 'I fired him. All those wanky meals. Duck-leg confit and Tuscan vegetable ragout. That idiot wouldn't know a fine pork sausage if it hit him over the head.'

'What do you think about that, Mrs M? Isn't doing both the cooking and cleaning too much for you?' Nick put his phone face down on the table.

'Oh, no.' She waved a dismissive hand. 'I'm only doing it for your father. And if the truth be known, I'm just as glad that Clive's gone. He was a nice enough fellow, but he didn't fit in here at Westbrook.' She lowered her voice to a conspiratorial whisper. 'He had a boyfriend.'

Carson laughed out loud. 'The man was a pansy.' He helped himself to another serve of beef. 'Good riddance to him.'

Nick's heart hardened against Carson. It hardened against his bigotry and casual cruelty – against his arrogance and conceit. 'Would you excuse us, Mrs M? I'd like some private time with my father.'

Mrs Marlow smiled politely and left the room.

'Vince Gambino,' said Nick when they were alone. 'Why?' He surreptitiously tapped the back of his phone twice to begin recording

Carson frowned. 'The fool had no right to tell you that he worked for me.'

'I asked you why. Didn't you trust I could get the job done by myself?'

'Of course I did.' Carson put down his fork. 'Gambino was insurance, that's all. There to help you win over public opinion. That's vitally important, son.'

'Why – if you simply bribe or blackmail your way through the approval process? What does it matter what people think?'

Carson shook his head. 'You still have a lot to learn. The more people like and accept Westcorp, the less likely they are to oppose us. The aim is to neutralise any organised community opposition. Court challenges are tricky. I have to call in a lot of favours.'

Nick resisted the urge to bite his lip. Would Carson admit to corrupting a judge? 'You mean like that injunction application from the Berrimilla Progress Association. How exactly did you get that thrown out?'

'Ah, a prime example of why using Gambino was such a master-stroke,' said Carson. 'He spied on the other side. He alerted me to the fact that such an application was coming. It gave me and my legal team time to prepare.' Carson sipped his wine. 'I know you, son. You would never have agreed to me sending Gambino in.'

Nick ignored that last assertion, although he recognised the truth of it. 'And how did you prepare, Dad. Rig the court? Arrange a pet judge?'

Just then Mrs Marlow came in with coffee and dessert. Damn her timing. 'I've made your favourite, Nick,' she said. 'Baked cherry cheesecake.' She deposited the lavish dish in the centre of the table.

'None for me thanks, Rita.' Carson finished his wine and wiped his mouth with one of Natalie's favourite French linen napkins. For some reason the action made Nick see red, and his hand clenched into a fist.

Carson patted his belly and pushed back his chair. 'Watching my weight. Doctor's orders.' He walked over to Nick and placed a hand on his shoulder. 'I'm grateful we've cleared up that misunderstanding about Gambino. Now I can be frank with you, should a similar situation arise in the future. It's becoming de rigueur for corporations to use covert operatives for infiltrating opposition groups. The time will come when you'll do it yourself.'

Nick shook off his father's touch and stood up. *Over my dead body*, he thought, struggling not to respond out loud. However tempting it was, picking a fight would be counterproductive. He needed Carson onside.

'Well, I'll be in my office if anybody needs me,' said Carson, cheerfully. 'It's wonderful to have you back, son, but don't stay too long. Gambino has softened up the community for us. It's time to bring them home. We'll throw in another hundred thousand dollars of grant money to sweeten the deal. Renovate a few more change rooms. Sponsor a few more sports teams. Make Westcorp their best friend, Nick, and that bitch of an ex-girlfriend won't cause us any more problems, eh?'

Nick tried not to react to the mention of Del, but he flinched involuntarily. Just a minuscule movement, but his father didn't miss it. Carson's eyes bored into him. Nick knew that look. He felt like a bug under a microscope. Nick wanted to smash his father's smug face. Carson's radar was up and Nick should have let him go, but he was feeling reckless.

'One more thing, Dad. The Kingfisher Valley offset area – Cobbee Basin. What will happen to that?'

'Once the expansion is approved, you mean? Keep it under your hat for now, but that area's earmarked for mining.'

Nick felt sick. Carson had just confirmed Del's worst fears. 'I know I haven't been involved with this side of Westcorp's operations before, but surely that's illegal?'

'Not at all. The NSW Biodiversity Act states that mining can take place on land previously set aside as an offset under the same act. We just need to set an equivalent parcel of land aside somewhere else to compensate.'

Nick struggled to keep his temper. 'Cobbee Basin is a biodiversity hotspot, Dad. A rare, old-growth subtropical forest.' He thought of the iconic five-hundred-year-old red cedar trees that Del had told him about. 'It's unique. There *is* no equivalent parcel of land.'

Carson's eyes narrowed as his good mood evaporated. He wasn't used to being challenged. 'I won't have you talking like that, Nick. The decision's been made. The latest engineer's report puts millions of tonnes of high quality coal in Cobbee Basin. It's worth a fortune. What do you want us to do? Just leave it in the ground?'

Yes, Nick wanted to say. *Why not? How much wealth do you need?* But instead he held his tongue. There was no point arguing about it. Carson was a hoarder, but instead of hoarding junk, he hoarded money.

Mrs Marlow came in to clear the table. 'Let me help,' said Nick, glad for the excuse to leave. He gathered up a few plates, eager to get away and ring Del. When he slipped his phone back in his pocket, he noticed Carson watching him. It might have been his imagination, but as he left the room Nick seemed to feel the weight of his father's suspicions.

Nick walked down to his cottage and went into his office, intending to replay the recording he'd made at lunch. Del, experienced investigator that she was, had shown him how to activate an intriguing setting on his phone.

'It's called Back Tap,' she'd told him. 'It lets you discretely record audio simply by tapping the back of your iPhone. Go to Back Tap in the accessibility settings, choose double tap or triple tap, then choose record. Remember to turn it off when you're not using it.'

Nick had practised half a dozen times before attempting to record the conversation with his father. The setting worked well, and he felt confident that he'd activated it at lunch without detection. Carson hadn't said exactly what Nick wanted him to say. But he had admitted that Gambino worked for Westcorp. That was useful, but it wasn't enough. He hadn't admitted to bribing a judge or bringing undue pressure to bear on a public official. Carson hadn't admitted to something that would put him in jail, and right now that's where Nick wanted him.

Damn that man. Carson planned to mine Cobbee Basin. That would crush Del. Perhaps he'd spare her that part of the recording for now. But when he pressed play there was no audio at all. No admission about Gambino or anything else. When he checked the phone's settings, Nick saw he'd accidentally chosen triple tap instead of double tap. When he'd double tapped the back of the phone, it hadn't recorded a thing.

He ran a hand through his hair and groaned, angry at himself for screwing up. Winston nosed his way in the door, tail thumping, and pushed his soft muzzle into Nick's lap. 'Stop being so nice to me,' he chided, stroking the dog's soft ears. 'I'm an idiot. I don't deserve it.'

His phone rang and Nick jumped. Jesus, his nerves were shot.

'How are things?' asked Del when he answered the phone.

Nick told her of his incompetence at lunch and the failed recording.

'It's okay, Nick,' she said. 'You can try again. In the meantime, see if you can get into your father's home office. Have a scrounge around. There's bound to be something incriminating in there. And keep searching for that letter from Bobby that Natalie mentions in the diary. Odds are it doesn't exist, but it can't hurt to look.'

Nick didn't tell Del of Carson's shocking revelation about Cobbee Basin. He'd deliver that painful news in person if he ever had to, but a steely resolve was growing in his heart, along with his anger. Somehow, he would thwart his father. He would not let Carson keep rampaging through the world laying everything and everyone to waste. And he would never give up on protecting Del and the forest that she loved.

CHAPTER 42

Nick spent the rest of the afternoon looking for an opportunity to get into Carson's office. But Carson had sequestered himself in there with the door closed.

In the meantime, Nick took Winston for a long, rambling walk. He scoured the greenhouse and potting shed for a place where his mother might have hidden a letter. He tried to get into the guest suite, but it was securely boarded up. And all the while his father stayed put in his office.

At one point Nick went to see Carson on the pretext of needing a stapler. He chatted for a while, angling to see if his father was planning to leave at all. But Carson insisted that he was snowed under and would be busy all day.

'What are you working on?' asked Nick, itching to get his hands on the computer. Wishing he could rifle through the filing cabinets. 'Can I help at all?' But Carson was closed down and reluctant to talk. The excitement he'd shown when Nick first arrived seemed to have vanished. He'd never admit to anything incriminatory at this rate.

'Let me get on, will you son?' Carson's tone was abrupt. 'Haven't you got your own work to do?'

Nick was starting to suspect that his father didn't trust him.

When they sat down for dinner that night, Nick had his iPhone with him again. He'd practised several more times, confirming that the recording app was working properly and was set to double tap.

But when he put it on the table, Carson objected. 'I only have you home for a day or two. Do me the courtesy of putting that thing away.'

Okay. Would it record clearly enough in his pocket? He'd soon see.

But Carson still wasn't happy. 'Take it out of here. I've turned my phone off and left it in the next room. This dinner is meant to be our time.'

'Well said.' Mrs Marlow nodded as she put down the soup tureen. 'Phones have no place at the dining table. I saw a psychologist talking about it on TV the other day. Apparently, even having a phone nearby stops a person from being fully present for their family.'

Nick groaned inwardly. He could do without Mrs M and her psychobabble right now.

She held out her hand. 'I'll take that for you, Nick.'

He glanced at Carson who gave a slight nod. Nick handed his mobile to Mrs M and watched her walk with it from the room. Was his father suspicious of the phone? Or was he genuinely interested in having a distraction-free meal with his son?

Carson seemed happier now. He wanted to talk about Natalie. Christmas wasn't much more than three weeks away, and for a while they connected by reminiscing about how much she'd loved the holiday season when she was home. But it was getting harder and harder for Nick to keep up the pretence. He wasn't here to swap stories about Mum. Carson had no right to those happy memories, considering he'd made her life utterly miserable and caused her death.

Carson must have sensed his son's discomfort. 'It's been months since your mother died. Nobody could be more devastated by it than me. But you need to move on, son. Dwelling on the past isn't good for you.'

Nick didn't trust himself to respond, and the knot of tension in the room pulled tighter. His gut cramped and his appetite fled. This visit to Westbrook was getting him nowhere.

Nick put down his soup spoon. 'I'm not that hungry, Dad. If you'll excuse me ...'

'One week,' Carson said. 'You have one week to wind things up at Mount Morton. After what Gambino accomplished, you'll meet no more opposition.'

'I'll need longer,' said Nick. 'The assessment material isn't complete.'

'Yes, you've been dragging your feet.' Carson gave him a shrewd look. 'But I've seen what we have so far and it's close to enough. Send your team in to gather a few more testimonials from community groups for the social assessment. How Westcorp will revamp the mobile library service. How we'll save lives by upgrading the Berrim-illa Road. That sort of thing.'

'But Dad—'

'I need you back here, Nick.' Carson was using his I'll-brook-no-argument voice. 'You'll take charge of the Proton Mining takeover.'

Nick spread his arms wide. 'Sure, Dad. Whatever you say, Dad. You call and I'll jump.'

Carson frowned. 'What's got into you? I thought you'd be pleased. A major takeover is something I'd normally deal with myself.'

Nick shoved his chair back and stood up. 'I'm pleased, okay?' He turned to leave.

'When were you planning to tell me about her?'

Nick swung back around. 'Who?'

'That bitch who's been running interference. Did you think Gambino wouldn't tell me that you've been seeing her again?' Carson's face was growing red. 'How could you, son – after what she did to our family?'

Nick's first instinct was to scream that Carson was responsible for every bad thing that had happened to their family. But he didn't want to alienate him any further. His second instinct was to defend Del and throw Celia under the bus. But the editor had cooperated with them on a promise that they kept her confidence.

So, instead, Nick simply shrugged. 'Del and I ran into each other. We're friends.'

'Friends.' Carson's words dripped with sarcasm. 'You smashed Gambino in the face over a friend.'

Nick was done. Weary of the web of lies. Disgusted with himself for playing this charade. He was as bad as his father. Nick stalked from the room, retrieved his phone from Mrs M in the kitchen and escaped out the back door into the warm evening. The terrace garden was heartbreakingly familiar. The pergola's fragrant jasmine canopy. The row of potted succulents. His mother's vibrant green wall of herbs. For the first time in a long time he could feel her.

Nick knuckled away a tear. Surreal, to think that this might be the last time he'd see this dearly loved place. For it was time to draw a line under his past and let it go. The decision provoked a flood of relief. He'd pack up his things, leave tonight and not look back. If he was to stop his father, it wouldn't be like this. It wouldn't be by betraying Dad's trust in the same way that Dad had betrayed his.

There was one thing Nick wanted to do before he left, and that was to visit the guest suite. He had an unwanted vignette frozen in his mind. His mother lying peacefully with Winston curled at her feet. The quilted blue bedspread. Her hair fanned on the pillow. The image haunted him and he felt a rising anger at being excluded from that place.

Nick walked around the corner and approached the back door of the guest suite. It was sealed off as securely as the main entrance within the house. He tugged at the boards – screwed down tight. Nick aimed a savage kick at the door. Damn Carson. He walked further along and tested a window. Locked. He tested another and another. All locked.

Nick used the torch on his phone to continue down the path towards the patio's French doors. He shone the light through the glass. There was Mum's favourite reclining armchair. The graceful female nude on the mantel piece. The *Le Chat Noir* print on the textured wall that had been there for as long as he could remember.

Nick felt faint as a wave of nostalgia overwhelmed him. He wanted to pick up the nude statue and run his fingers over its smooth form. He wanted sit in the chair and gaze up at the quizzical cat in the print. But he couldn't, because the room was sealed off like a time capsule. So, Nick went into the house, avoiding his father who'd gone upstairs, and switched off the alarm system. Then he went down to the shed, found a sledgehammer and smashed in the double glass doors.

CHAPTER 43

How good it felt to walk into those rooms again. It was like coming home. His mother had spent so much time here, locked away from the world when she was ill. But even at her worst, when she wouldn't let anyone in, not even Carson, Nick was always welcome.

He wandered around the lounge room, soaking up memories. He sat in the recliner chair and pressed a button on the arm. A television popped up from a mahogany cupboard opposite. Mum wasn't a screen watcher. She loved books that she could touch and smell and turn their real pages. She wouldn't even read on the Kindle that he'd bought her. No, the television had been for Nick.

He opened the cupboard drawers. There were his cords, his Nintendo and PlayStation consoles. His dozens of games. He rummaged around and plucked out the Super Mario 64 cartridge. He used to sit in the big chair and play it for hours while Mum watched. She probably wasn't very interested in whether Mario rescued Princess Peach or not, but she never showed it. As a kid, he was convinced that she was as fascinated by the adventure as he was. Nick used to love listening to her *oohs* and *aahs* and *well dones*. He smiled to think of it. She made him feel like the cleverest boy in the world.

Nick slipped the cartridge into his pocket. Time to brave the bedroom. He tried to steel himself. But he still wasn't ready for the visceral, gut-wrenching reaction he felt when he entered the room. Nick had the absurd feeling that he'd find his mother asleep on the bed. He'd call her name, and this time she'd stretch, yawn and grace him with her dazzling smile.

But, instead, the bed was empty. He opened the big walk-in wardrobe. The top shelves where he'd found his mother's diaries were empty too, but otherwise everything was as he'd left it. Her clothes, shoes, jewellery – all there.

What about the letter – the one Mum said she'd received from his dead uncle Bobby? Nick was convinced that it didn't exist. How could it? The letter was no more than a figment of his mother's lonely imagination. But he'd promised Del he'd look for it, and here was the perfect opportunity.

Nick scoured the room, rifling through the bedclothes, checking the pillowslips and dragging out the mattress. He tipped out the drawers of the antique armoire and checked behind the Arthur Streeton painting on the wall. He turned the nightstand inside out, went through the pockets of her coats and flipped through her books. Nothing.

Nick started on the bathroom.

An hour later, and Nick couldn't think of anywhere else to search. The guest suite looked like it had been ransacked by thieves, but so what? His father could deal with it.

Nick had pocketed a few other things besides the video game: his mother's favourite emerald earrings, the ruby and opal necklace that she always wore at Christmas time, and a diamond brooch that he'd given her.

Nick was having a final look around the kitchenette when he heard footsteps approaching.

'What the hell?'

He turned to see his father standing there, wild-eyed and staring.

Carson marched around the rooms with a fist pressed against his mouth. Nick followed him into the bedroom.

'What have you done?' Carson looked around in horror at the chaos. He picked up a pillow and put it back on the bed. 'Where's the respect for your mother?'

What a hypocrite! Nick shrugged his shoulders. 'Mum won't care. She's dead, Dad, remember? You told me just a few hours ago that it's time to accept that and move on.'

Carson seemed dazed as he wandered around the room, straightening things up, closing drawers and putting books back on shelves. Then he looked in the walk-in wardrobe. He pushed aside the hanging clothes and stared at the empty shelves where the diaries used to be.

'Your mother didn't want anyone to read those diaries, even me.' Carson's voice grew louder and more commanding. 'It's time to put them back.'

Nick knew that he should leave, just walk away. But he wasn't used to seeing his father on the back foot. It tempted him to press his advantage.

'If you think I'm going to lock Mum's journals away in this mausoleum, you're crazy. They make for fascinating reading, by the way.'

'There were dozens of them, going back decades.' Carson cast him a troubled glance. 'How many have you read?'

'All of them. Every word.' Carson recoiled like he'd been hit. 'It took me weeks.' His father was wounded, but Nick kept going. 'Lots of secrets in there, Dad. About you and Mum. About Bobby—'

Carson exploded. 'Get out!' he screamed. 'You lying, treacherous snake of a son. Get out and don't come back.' His jaw jutted angrily, his face went purple and his fists clenched and unclenched in spasms. 'I don't want you in my home. I don't want you at my company. I don't want you in my life.'

'The feeling is mutual, Dad.' Nick couldn't breathe. He had to get out of there. With one last look at his raging, out-of-control father, he escaped into the night.

Fifteen minutes later Nick was packed and ready to leave. He drove out of the Westbrook gates and parked a kilometre or two down the road, fighting to draw air into his lungs. His breath came in ragged spurts, blood throbbed in his ears and tears clouded his vision. It was a long time before he was calm enough to ring Del and recount what had happened.

'Oh, Nick, how awful. Are you okay?'

'I think so.' He considered the question further. 'I think I'm more than okay. I think my life begins now.'

A muffled sound came over the phone. Was Del crying? 'I don't think you should drive back tonight,' she said at last. 'Not when you're so emotional. Find a hotel.'

She was probably right. A four-hour drive would be daunting right now, especially when he had nothing to show for his visit but failure. Nick was spent. 'I didn't get what you wanted from Dad. I'm sorry.'

'Nicholas Shaw, don't you dare say that! What you did tonight was brave and wonderful. Confronting Carson wouldn't have been easy. You might be the only person on earth who's ever found the courage.'

'Maybe. But that begs the question – what do we do now? I've burned my bridges with Dad. He'll probably never talk to me again.'

'Tell me about the moment he snapped,' said Del. 'What sent him over the edge?'

'When I told him that I'd read Mum's diaries.'

'But he already knew you'd been reading them. What exactly did you say?'

'I was taunting him, I guess. I said the diaries held secrets about him and Mum and Bobby.'

'Bobby?'

'Yeah. It was when I mentioned him that Dad went off his nut.'

'That must mean something,' mused Del. 'And you looked every-where you could think of for that letter?'

'Everywhere. I searched the house and pretty much took the guest suite apart.'

'What about somewhere around the garden?'

'Same. The greenhouse, the potting shed—' And then it struck him. As a child, Nick always missed his mother terribly when she was away at the Mayfair Clinic. So, she'd devised a game to help him cope. Whenever he was especially sad, he'd write her a secret love note and stuff it into a chink in the brick wall near the back door of the guest suite. When she came home, they'd read the notes together, and she'd spend a whole day with him for each note – doing whatever he wanted to do. It gave him something wonderful to look forward to, and it made her absences that much more bearable.

'I'm going back,' Nick told Del. 'There's one more place to look.'

When Nick arrived at Westbrook again, the front gate wouldn't open. 'Damn it, Dad.' He'd already changed the code.

Nick used his phone as a torch as he jumped up the bank and made his way to the old side gate. Pushing it open, he walked through the garden up to the house. The lights were still on in the guest suite. He could hear his father in there – swearing and screaming and throwing things. Nick paused to listen. Carson's anger was truly frightening. What was it about the diaries that had triggered such rage?

Nick moved on until he reached the back door. He shone the light slowly up the wall. It was so long since he'd played the love note game. Would he even remember where the loose brick was? He had to hurry. With the main entrance of the guest suite boarded up, the only way for Carson to return to the main house was via this door. Any moment now he could come storming out. It would be a disastrous confrontation.

Winston started barking from inside the house. Nick shushed him softly, but it only made him bark louder.

'What's wrong, boy?' Mrs Marlow's voice came from the kitchen. 'Is there something out there?'

He knew Mrs M. Soon she'd come to investigate. *Think*, Nick told himself. He closed his eyes and tried to remember. And then it came to him, as clearly as if he'd hidden a note just yesterday. He counted three bricks across from the downpipe join, and pried loose a piece of bluestone. And there, dry and safe in that small space, was a letter.

Nick extracted the envelope and ran off just as Mrs Marlow opened the back door.

'Who's there?' she called.

But Nick was long gone, sprinting down through the night garden and out the gate.

CHAPTER 44

Del had tried to grab a nap while she waited for Nick, but she was way too wound up for sleep. So, instead, she waited on tenterhooks as the hours crawled by. They seemed more like days.

Her stomach churned with excitement and hope. All Nick had told her over the phone was that he'd found a letter hidden in the wall at Westbrook. When she'd quizzed him further, he'd said that he was driving straight to Kingfisher Farm and they could talk then. Before discovering the letter, Nick had been planning to stay at a hotel. He'd sounded exhausted – emotionally spent. Now he was driving four hours in the middle of the night to show her what he'd found. It must be pretty significant to have changed his mind.

Del scrubbed her hands over her face. Right now, all she had was speculation and conjecture. She resigned herself to the state of intolerable suspense and went outside to wait. The night was balmy and clear and bright with moonshine – fragrant with the scent of wild mint and sassafras. Overhead, the Milky Way put on a show of celestial brilliance. But Del wasn't in the mood to appreciate nature's beauty.

She sat on the porch with the dogs at her feet, slapping at mosquitoes and scanning the road below for headlights. Strung tight as a drum. There were several nerve-racking false alarms, and it was after two o'clock in the morning before the beams of Nick's car turned onto the driveway. Finally she'd get some answers.

Del read the letter for the third time. It was signed *Love from your Bobby* and was dated ten years ago – more than a decade after Bobby Shaw was supposed to have died.

My darling Nat,

I have faint hope that this letter will reach you, but it comforts me to send it all the same. I'm living in a twilight zone where black is white and up is down. Sometimes I feel like Alice in Wonderland gone down the rabbit hole. I'm confined behind locked doors in some sort of gilded institutional cage where all are mad except for me.

After having suffered years of confusion, nobody believes that I've finally remembered who I am. Doctors called me Brian O'Rourke, and for a long time I believed that I was indeed that person. But not any more. My memories of you and Carson are as clear now as if we saw each other yesterday. Yet they insist that I'm delusional and a danger to myself and others. I'm not allowed to have a phone, nor any way to communicate with the outside world. I don't even know where I am.

My only solace is my books, my music and my beautiful garden that I've tended for many years. I send out dozens of letters, but I don't believe that the nurses post them. I've given this one to a brand-new girl who might not yet know that she should bin it. Fingers crossed. I've never been one for conspiracy theories until now, but there IS a conspiracy to steal my life and keep me from my family. I'm begging you and Carson for help.

Love from your Bobby xx

Del stared at Nick. 'Fuuuck!'

Nick stared back, grim-faced. 'Fuck indeed.'

They sat speechless for a while at the kitchen table, trying to digest what they'd read and what it meant. Del picked up the envelope. It was addressed in the same hand as the letter. 'Natalie Shaw,' she said. 'Westbrook, Winga.' No postcode. She turned it over. On the back was scribbled *sender: Robert Henry Shaw, address: Unknown.*

'Is this even possible?' she asked.

'It could be a hoax,' said Nick. 'But by who and to what end?'

'Carson?' said Del. 'To gaslight Natalie and convince her that she was mad.'

Nick's mouth became a hard line. He got up to boil the kettle. 'Yesterday, I'd have said Carson would never be so cruel. Now?' He shrugged. 'Now I don't know.'

Del found two clear plastic ziplock bags and carefully slipped the letter into one and the envelope into the other. 'Don't touch these,' she said. 'They're evidence. We'll work off copies.'

Del was switching into investigative mode. Partly to help her function through her shock. And partly because if the letter was genuine, it would be the biggest news story of the year.

'Do you have samples of your uncle's handwriting?'

'I've been thinking about that,' said Nick. 'Mum kept some postcards from Bobby in the back of one her diaries.'

She was about to say 'Great, let's go get them', when she noticed Nick's drawn face. He was making them mugs of instant coffee and he looked bone weary, emotionally wrung out. 'Lie down in the spare room,' she said. 'Catch some sleep.'

Nick shook his head and stirred another teaspoon of coffee in his mug. 'The diaries are back at my McClellan Vale chalet and Carson knows I have them.' He checked his phone. 'It's almost three o'clock now. I guarantee that by seven o'clock this morning I'll be locked out and the diaries will be gone.'

'Okay.' Del went to stand beside him and briefly squeezed his hand. 'The chalet is only an hour away. We'll go fetch them together. Now give me another spoonful of that coffee, and some extra sugar. I'll drive.'

During the trip to McClellan Vale, they explored what the letter might mean.

'Let's play the what-if game,' said Del. 'We know that Bobby was in a prolonged coma after the car crash. What if doctors tell Carson that he could hang on for years, but he'll never recover. While Bobby lives, he remains the heir to Westcorp.'

'Right, but Carson was granted power of attorney. He was effectively in control of Westcorp anyway.'

'Stay with me,' said Del. She took a bend in the dark road too fast, wrestling with the wheel to straighten up. 'What if that's not enough for Carson? What if he's impatient to run the company in his own right? You know better than anybody what a control freak he is.'

'Damn straight. That's why Dad refuses to list Westcorp on the stock exchange. He can't bear the thought of being publicly answerable to shareholders.'

'Right. So, what if he gets so desperate that he somehow has Bobby declared dead, and then spirits him away to another hospital. Gives him a new identity, this Brian O'Rourke character. Carson rationalises his wickedness away. He's not doing anything very wrong. Bobby will pass soon anyway.'

'There was a funeral,' said Nick. 'They cremated Bobby's body and scattered the ashes.'

'Mum supposedly scattered my dad's ashes too. They held a public ceremony to lay a memorial plaque.' Del slammed the brakes and swerved to the verge to avoid a large wombat trundling across their path.

'And?' said Nick, after the car was back on the dark road.

'They were a dog's ashes – my father's kelpie. Who was to know?'

'Okay, that's weird,' said Nick. 'But the funeral home didn't cremate a dog. There must have been a body.'

'I haven't thought it through that far,' admitted Del. 'It could have been anybody, though. Someone who died in the same hospital, maybe a homeless man. With Westcorp's millions at his disposal, Carson could bribe almost anyone. We know he's bribed judges and politicians. Maybe it was a doctor, a mortician—'

'Keep going,' said Nick.

'What if after a long time, years maybe, Bobby wakes up. But he doesn't know who he is. Your father looks after him, pays for his care. As long as Bobby thinks he's Brian, there's no real problem. Carson may even have convinced himself that he was doing his brother a favour – saving him from a life and job he never wanted.'

'But then Bobby remembers,' said Nick.

'That's right. Carson faces a dilemma. If he sets Bobby free, he loses Westcorp and goes to jail. That's a powerful incentive to keep Bobby locked away.'

'Shit,' said Nick. 'Carson has no idea what sort of incriminating evidence might be in those diaries. No wonder he's acting like a cornered rat.' He put a hand on her knee. 'We'd better hurry.'

When they reached McClellan Vale, all was quiet. They drove in slowly with their headlights off and pulled up beside the chalet. Thank heavens for the bright moon. They stole over to the front door by moonlight, afraid to use the torches on their phones. Nick tried the keycard. Del held her breath, half-expecting that it wouldn't work. But the welcome green light flashed and they were in.

Now they could use their torches. 'I'll get your things from the bedroom,' said Del. 'You get the diaries.'

'Forget my things,' said Nick, urgently. 'I can buy more clothes. You'd better help me.'

They began ferrying the diaries out to the car. How many were there? It seemed to take forever.

'Quick,' said Nick. A light had come on in the manor house, and they saw headlights approaching. 'It's probably security. Let's go.'

Del threw the last of the diaries onto the back seat of the car, flung open the front passenger door and jumped in. Nick leaped behind the wheel and they took off, wheels spinning on gravel. The security car flashed its headlights and headed straight for them.

'Hang on to your hat.' Nick wrenched the wheel sideways. They veered onto the grass and shot past the other car with centimetres to spare.

'Yes!' yelled Del as they tore towards the gates. Another car appeared to their left but it was too late. 'Woo hoo!' They were home free.

Del leaned over and kissed Nick's cheek before she could stop herself. 'Thank you, honey,' she whispered. 'Thank you.'

CHAPTER 45

The sun was rising by the time they arrived at Kingfisher Farm. With the adrenaline wearing off, Del's eyes were involuntarily drifting shut. Nick was driving, but he must have been struggling to stay alert as well. Neither of them had had any sleep.

Tiny and the collies greeted them, all wagging tails and excited whines. Despite their exhaustion, Del and Nick were determined to get the diaries safely stowed away before getting any rest.

Darby emerged from her bedroom in a dressing gown, bleary-eyed and yawning. She stopped short when she encountered Nick in the hallway with an armful of books.

'What's going on here?'

'It's okay, Mum,' called Del, who was right behind him. 'I'll explain later. But in the meantime, Nick needs to stay here for a day or two. Can he have the spare room?'

'Well, yes, I suppose so ... '

Del gave her astonished mother a swift peck on the cheek as she hurried past.

Nick fished out a few diaries from the pile on the spare room's dressing table and flipped through them. 'This one.' He turned to the back. 'Get the letter.'

They compared the old postcard from Bobby with the letter that Nick had found hidden in the wall. 'Shit!' they whispered in unison, staring at each other. The handwriting matched.

'No wonder Carson never liked me,' said Del. 'You dating an investigative reporter must have scared him witless'

'Time for the police,' said Nick.

Del put a hand on his arm. 'Let me call Frank Walker from the *Sydney Morning Herald* first. You know, the man who'd have been my boss had I taken that job? I guarantee he'll get to the bottom of this quicker than the cops will. If Bobby is alive and Carson gets wind of an official investigation, he'll move him for sure. And for all we know, the police commissioner is another public official beholden to your father.'

'Now there's a scary thought.' Nick put the diary back on the dressing table stack and yawned.

The yawn was contagious, and Del could fight her weariness no longer. 'Let's get some sleep. We'll need all our wits about us tomorrow.'

She woke hours later with the sun streaming in the window. The day had well and truly begun, and Del wondered what it might bring. She crept into the spare room, where Nick lay fast asleep. On impulse Del lay down beside him. She shut her eyes, breathed in his warm smell and a powerful sense of déjà vu took over. It was the morning after Nick proposed. That faraway morning when her hopes and dreams had all still been possible, before her world fell apart.

Del didn't want to move for fear of losing the moment. She lay there for the longest time, almost dozing off, but yesterday's events were knocking at her consciousness, demanding attention.

Del got up, careful not to wake Nick, and gently pulled his blanket higher. What he'd achieved amazed her. He'd faced the demons of his past with courage and determination. He'd exposed his father's wrongdoings at tremendous personal cost, and he was truly on her side. They'd both changed so much in these past months.

Del checked the time, then grabbed her laptop plus a folder of copied documents. She took one last look at Nick. Let him sleep. Del tiptoed from the room.

She found a worried Darby hovering in the hallway, demanding an explanation.

'You'll get one,' said Del. 'And soon. Just let me do one thing first.'

Del set up the laptop in the lounge room, organised her documents and made the phone call. It took some time to get through to Frank Walker, editor-in-chief of the *Sydney Morning Herald*.

'Well, this is a surprise. Changed your mind, have you, Del?' he asked. 'My job offer still stands.'

'I have something big,' she whispered, as if someone might over-hear. 'Tell me what you think.'

Frank listened in silence while Del told her story. 'Good God, Del. What do I think? I think that you and Nick Shaw need to jump in a car and get here ASAP.'

Del felt a rush of relief and gratitude. The onerous responsibility of stopping Carson no longer fell on her and Nick alone. Kingfisher Valley suddenly had a powerful champion. 'We're on our way.'

Del showered, dressed and threw a few clothes in a bag. Then she woke Nick.

'We're going to Sydney,' she said. 'We have an urgent meeting with Frank Walker.'

While Nick got ready, Del scanned Bobby's letter, its envelope, the postcards and the relevant diary entries. With a few clicks of her finger, all that incriminating evidence was safely in the hands of the most widely read masthead in the country. Frank would have a crack team of investigators on it already: tracing the postmark, engaging handwriting experts, leaving no stone unturned to find Brian O'Rourke AKA Robert Henry Shaw AKA Uncle Bobby. Of course, if he was still alive, Carson might try moving him. *Good luck with that*, thought Del. She knew Frank Walker. Nothing could shake him once he sank his teeth into a story.

When Nick emerged from the bathroom, Del finally took pity on her mother. Darby was cooking up a farmhouse breakfast. Over bacon, eggs and mugs of sweet tea, Del brought her up to speed.

Darby took her time digesting what she'd been told. 'So ... ' she said at last. 'If this is true, it means that Carson Shaw doesn't own Westcorp. His brother does. He can't extend the Mount Morton mine. He can't make any decisions on behalf of the corporation at all.'

Del smiled. Darby had a way of clarifying things. 'That's it in a nutshell, Mum. We're going to Sydney for a few days to see if we can help with the investigation.'

'Well, what are you waiting for?' Darby grasped Del's hand with both of her own. 'Thank you, darling. This is so marvellous. If there's anything I can do ... '

'Look after Tiny and the Babydolls. And ask Ken to come and stay, will you? I don't like you being here on your own.'

She realised instantly how ridiculous that final comment must sound. For eight years her mother had lived alone, and Del hadn't given a toss. She suddenly appreciated how lonely Darby must have been when her husband died and her daughter abandoned her all in the space of a few days.

Darby let go of her daughter's hand. 'I thought you didn't like Ken staying over? You said it was disrespectful to your father.'

She hugged her mother's stiff shoulders, feeling the sting of tears. 'This is your home and I have no right to dictate to you. Ken has been nothing but kind and helpful towards me, and he didn't deserve my hostility.'

'Ken is a good man,' Darby said. 'Loving him doesn't mean that I didn't love your father.'

'You love him?' Del hadn't expected that. The old resentment reared its head, and Del struggled to push it down. How could Darby have loved Dad and yet helped him die? Until Del could answer that question, she couldn't truly resolve her relationship with her mother. But that would have to wait.

'Call Ken,' said Del, shoving her feelings aside. 'And I'll ring you from Sydney once I have some news.'

Nick came into the kitchen. 'We're ready to go.'

Del hugged the dogs and said goodbye to her mother. She and Nick got in the car and exchanged glances. The nervous excitement she saw in his eyes mirrored her own. So much was at stake. Protecting Cobbee Basin, exposing Carson's crimes, righting a terrible, historic wrong – all these things depended on the success of their mission. And Del could think of no finer, more trustworthy ally than man who sat beside her.

CHAPTER 46

Del looked out the curved full-length windows of the streamlined top floor office. The harbour's sparkling blue waters stretched out below, fringed by golden beaches, green fore- shores and dotted with colourful sailboats. The vibrant city of Sydney lay at her feet.

This imposing building was where she would have worked if her life had turned out differently. She might have gazed daily upon the Opera House and the Harbour Bridge from her desk. There was a time when she would have done anything to make that happen. Yet Del had no regrets. She was a different person now.

Frank Walker magically emerged from a door that was seamlessly set in the timber panelling of the rear wall. He was a big, balding man, with a belly too wide for his belt. He might have been nondescript, someone who'd disappear in a crowd, if not for the aura of energy that surrounded him.

'Hello, you two.' His eyes shone with excitement, and his arms spread wide in an expansive gesture of welcome. 'Have we got a story on our hands or haven't we, eh?'

Del and Nick were both amazed at how much progress Frank had already made. In the space of a few hours, his team had verified Bobby's handwriting on the letter and traced the envelope's postmark to the Wisemans Ferry Post Office.

'And get this,' said Frank. 'The Mayfair Clinic operates a secure psychiatric facility at Wisemans Ferry. It's called the Priory.'

'Carson donates millions each year to Mayfair,' said Nick.

'Exactly. He'll have a ton of influence there. But don't you worry. If a patient named Brian O'Rourke is, or has ever been, at the Priory, we'll find him.'

'How?' asked Nick.

'We have our ways.' Frank winked at Del. 'Us newshounds don't reveal our secrets, eh?'

Del grinned. There was nothing mysterious about it. She guessed it would take less than a day to find a staff member who could be persuaded to spill the beans.

'What if Bobby's dead?' asked Nick. 'Or what if Carson has him stashed somewhere else? He might not be at this Priory.'

Frank shrugged. 'Well, I guess we'll soon find out.'

Del put a soothing hand on Nick's arm. He was getting more and more agitated. This was clearly harder for him than he'd imagined.

'What if Bobby's there now, but my father moves him?'

'We have the place under surveillance,' said Frank. 'Nobody could smuggle a shop's dummy out of the Priory without us knowing about it.'

But Nick did not seem reassured. 'What if Dad's already moved him?'

'Then we'll look for him,' said Del. 'Let's not lose our nerve now.'

Nick frowned and shook his head. 'I think we should alert the authorities.' He stood up and went to the window, gazing out at the harbour.

Frank glanced at Del with raised brows. She nodded and went to stand beside Nick.

'Are you sure the authorities will act quickly enough? Carson is a highly respected man. At the very least they'll take the time to hear his side of the story. He'll lawyer up and paint you as the vindictive son with an axe to grind about being fired. It could be days before they even decide to investigate.'

'She's right.' Frank joined them at the window. 'But me? I have Commissioner Fowler on speed dial.'

Nick ran a hand over his head. He still stared out the window, but she could tell he was listening.

'Let Frank do his thing for a day or two,' she urged. 'He'll bring the police in the moment he has something concrete. Right, Frank?'

Frank clapped a hand on Nick's shoulder. 'You have my word.'

Nick looked from Frank to Del and seemed to make up his mind. 'All right,' he murmured. 'We'll do it your way.'

They went back to their hotel. It seemed that Frank had mistaken the nature of their relationship, as he'd only booked them a single suite. But it was large and luxurious, and Nick had offered to take the couch. Del ordered room service – a late lunch of hamburgers and chips – and they grabbed a couple of beers from the minibar. When the food arrived, they sat wearily back in the sumptuous Chesterfield armchairs to eat, each lost in private thought. And they were both asleep before they finished their meals.

Hours later, Del's phone woke her. She answered it sleepily, unaware at first where she was, wondering why she was dozing during the day on a chair.

'Del, are you there?' asked Frank.

Del sat up, suddenly alert.

'We found two nurses who are prepared to swear statements about a patient named Brian O'Rourke and who he claims to be. I had to pull some strings of course, but time was of the essence. On the basis of the nurses' testimony, the police raided the Priory.'

Del held her breath.

'The DNA proves it. We have him.'

'Oh my God!' she screamed. 'Nick.' Del shook him properly awake. 'They've found Bobby.'

CHAPTER 47

Two days later, they met a ghost. Uncle Bobby greeted them at the door of an executive suite that Frank had arranged for him at the Double Bay InterContinental Hotel. Frank had also guaranteed no cameras, although it had taken an argument for him to agree. They'd appeased him with the promise of an exclusive, sit-down interview later on. The other media outlets would be green with envy. Bobby's return from the dead was the hottest news story around, both at home and internationally. It was ironic that Del had helped break the biggest scoop of the year only after she'd quit journalism.

Bobby was a tall man, much taller than his brother, but otherwise the resemblance was uncanny. It was like looking at an older, softer version of Carson. He was classically handsome, with the same hawkish nose, prominent jaw and full head of hair, although Bobby's was a natural steel grey. Altogether, a compelling presence. But the difference lay in his gentle, dignified smile and thoughtful blue eyes – eyes that currently shone with a kind of childlike wonder.

'Nicky?' Bobby stared at Nick with disbelief, and then his face broke into a broad grin. 'You were five years old when I last saw you. A lifetime ago.'

Nick opened his arms and stepped forward to embrace his uncle in a long heartfelt hug. The pair clung to each other as if they'd never let go. Del's heart was breaking for them both. The reality of Nick's adult self, a grown man, brought home the harrowing truth of their lost years.

At last Bobby turned to Del. 'And who is this delightful young lady?'

Nick introduced her. 'If it wasn't for Del here, we would never have found you.'

Bobby took her hand and kissed it. 'Then I'm eternally grateful. Please,' he gestured towards the open plan living area. 'Come in.'

Once Nick and his uncle started talking, there was no stopping them. Bobby seemed intent on retrieving twenty-five years of stolen memories in one day. And Nick seemed intent on helping him.

Del felt like a third wheel. 'I'll make us a morning coffee, shall I?'

Neither of them heard her. She wandered into the designer kitchen with its stunning bayside views and tried to puzzle out the coffee machine. Del was in no hurry. Those two didn't need to be interrupted. She'd give them some privacy – well, a limited privacy, anyway. Nothing would stop her from eavesdropping. So, she settled down on a sunny corner couch, tucked her legs up under her, and listened.

Bobby and Nick were talking quickly and urgently in the other room, behaving as if there was some sort of time limit on their chat. It was so good to know that the pair actually had the rest of their lives to reconnect.

It shocked Bobby to hear of Natalie's death. For a minute or two, all Del could hear were low, choked voices and sobbing. She had to stop herself from running in to comfort Nick. The men spent a long while talking about Natalie, hungry to hear each other's stories. Their memories of Nick's mother did not overlap.

The conversation turned to Carson. He was in police custody, along with the founder and managing director of the Mayfair Clinic. More arrests were surely in the offing. Nick confided Carson's years of sexual exploitation to his uncle, who was profoundly ashamed to hear about it.

'I hate my father.' Nick's voice brimmed with pain and anger. 'He's dead to me.'

'Dead to you? That sounds like the sort of thing Carson would say.'

'You must hate him too, Bobby. After what he did – stealing your life? How could you not?'

There was a long pause before Bobby's voice came, speaking with quiet emphasis. 'When I woke from my coma, I had amnesia. They told me that my name was Brian and I believed them. Why would my doctors lie? So, for years I struggled to recall a life that didn't exist.

'Ten years ago, my memories started returning. My doctors were wrong. I knew without doubt who I was. I spent the next decade fighting and pleading and raging. Begging for someone to listen. I've been pitied, gaslighted, ignored, drugged, laughed at – everything but believed.

'And now I learn that my own brother put me through that hell. Carson is a deeply flawed person and I make no excuses for him. He must pay for his crimes, but what's the point of hating him? I've spent enough time living with anger. I want to know Carson again, for we loved each other once. I miss him, and I've no doubt that he missed me after our parents died. Missed me terribly. He might have had Westcorp all to himself, but that would have been a poor substitute for losing an entire family, even for my brother.'

Bobby's voice rang louder and clearer. 'I want to talk to Carson – to ask if the prize was worth having that terrible secret eating away at him. Knowing that one day his house of cards could topple, and he'd lose everything. And now his worst fears have come true. His downfall was the cost of my freedom. We've swapped places, Carson and I. He showed me no mercy for all of those years, Nicky. I don't intend to repeat the mistake. This must be a time of healing for our family – a time for understanding and forgiveness.'

The hairs on the back of Del's neck stood up. Bobby's compassion and dignity in the face of such suffering stunned her. But it was exactly what Nick needed to hear. And if Del was honest with herself, she needed to hear it too. Bobby had given Nick permission to love his father, in spite of everything. That was a precious gift. There'd been enough hatred and blame and recrimination in the Shaw family to last a lifetime. In the Fisher family too. A time of healing had begun.

CHAPTER 48

Three hours later they returned to their hotel, both charged with emotions that had nowhere to go. Gobsmacked by their meeting with Bobby – a man back from the dead. Astounded by his grace and wisdom, and staggered by the ordeal he'd endured for twenty-five long years.

'I need a drink.' Nick guided Del to the lobby bar with a firm hand on the small of her back and ordered himself a whisky.

'Champagne cocktail?' he asked.

'Please.'

She watched Nick down his drink. It barely touched the sides of his mouth. He ordered them both another one, then another one. Del couldn't keep up. Nick's gaze was fixed on a large landscape painting on the wall. It showed a creek meandering through a rainforest, and it reminded Del of Kingfisher Valley. But she doubted that Nick really saw it. He seemed lost in a world of his own.

Del sat quietly beside him, content to let him process his emotions in whatever way suited him. After a while, Nick noticed the drinks lined up before her on the table.

'Come on, join me,' he urged. 'Carson is defeated, Uncle Bobby is free and Cobbee Basin is safe. This is a celebration. Don't let me drink alone.'

Del finished her first glass and raised her second. 'To Bobby.' The sweet bubbles slipped down her throat with delicious ease.

'To Bobby.' Nick grinned and downed another whisky.

They spent the next two hours laughing and toasting anyone who'd contributed to their triumph. Nick's mother, Natalie, was top of the list, followed by Frank Walker. They toasted Del's father, and Darby, and the people of Kingfisher Valley who'd fought so hard against the mine. They toasted the brave women who'd come forward with their stories of Carson's abuse. Their testimonials were with Frank now.

They toasted the Priory nurses who'd made statements, and the police who'd acted on them so promptly. They toasted each other, and Tiny, and Cobbee Basin itself. They even toasted Celia, who had unwittingly been the key to their success.

Two middle-aged women entered the bar and smiled to see Del and Nick in such obvious high spirits. 'Join us,' called Nick, expansively. 'We're celebrating.' Soon the newcomers were toasting Cobbee Basin too, listening to the story of its protection with rapt attention.

It was an afternoon of pure joy. Del and Nick worked their way through the cocktail menu, as giddy with the excitement of victory as they were with alcohol. When they finally went up to their room, Nick couldn't find his key card.

'Here, use mine,' said Del, but then couldn't find hers either. For some reason they found this hilarious. Del leaned against the wall, giggling, while Nick went down to reception for a replacement. What an astonishing day it had been! She and Nick had shared such a powerful experience, and Del suddenly wanted to share something even more powerful.

When Nick returned with the key card, she gazed into his deep green eyes as if seeing them for the first time. Had those interesting flecks of amber always been there?

Nick took a step sideways. 'All that drinking on an empty stomach,' he said as he opened the door. 'How about I order room service?'

They sat on the couch eating pizza, drinking coffee and talking about Bobby.

'I wonder what he's doing tonight,' said Del. 'His first night of freedom in so many years. Should you have stayed with him, do you think?'

'Bobby didn't want me to. He said he needed to be by himself for a while, to grieve for my mother and come to terms with his new life.'

'All that lost time.' Del struggled to imagine what Bobby was going through. Now that the champagne buzz was wearing off a little, the gravity of what he'd suffered was hitting home in a painful way. She moved closer to Nick, letting her thigh rest against his, and toyed with the idea of raiding the minibar.

'I lost a few weeks after my accident,' said Nick. 'It was terrible, not being able to remember. I can't imagine the nightmare of having amnesia for years and years like Bobby.'

'Carson has a lot to answer for.'

'Enough of this gloomy talk,' said Nick. 'What do you want to do tonight?'

Del ran a finger along the fabric of his trouser leg. 'Let's watch a movie and fool around.'

Nick leaned in and she shut her eyes, anticipating the press of his lips on hers. But he suddenly pulled away. 'It's been a long day. Why not rest for a bit while I have a shower?' He helped Del to her feet and guided her to the bed. 'Won't be long.'

Del lay down, fluffed up her pillow and stifled a yawn. She'd wait here for Nick, then make love to him. Was it weak to give in to a moment of reckless passion? Maybe, but it didn't matter, because this might be their last night together. Who knew what the future held for them? Del closed her eyes. Why was Nick taking so long? And as Del pondered this last question, she fell asleep.

Next morning, Del woke with a dry mouth and a thumping headache. What wouldn't she do for some strong coffee and a bacon and egg sandwich? She wandered from her bedroom to find Nick softly snoring in the main room, the TV remote still clutched in his hand.

Last night came back to her in an embarrassing rush. God, she'd just about thrown herself at him. But Nick hadn't taken up her drunken offer. He hadn't made passionate love to her, then held her all night in his arms. He hadn't gone to sleep murmuring sweet words in her ear. Instead, he'd claimed the couch and watched television. Well, she'd certainly misjudged that situation. It wouldn't happen again.

Del showered, dressed, took some Panadol, then quietly let herself out of the suite and went downstairs for a quick breakfast.

When she returned, Nick was beginning to stir. 'You're an angel,' he said, eagerly accepting her offer of coffee and croissants. 'Do you feel as crook as I do?'

Del nodded and couldn't help smiling. She might have made a fool of herself with Nick last night, but one thing was certain. They would be friends forever.

A few minutes later, Nick received a phone call. He swallowed the last of his pastry before answering. 'Tell him the answer is no.'

'Who was that?' Del asked, although she could guess.

'Silverwater Remand Centre,' said Nick. 'Dad wants to see me.' He put his phone down. 'I'm not ready.'

He stood and went to the window, staring out at the sparkling harbour. Del followed him and took hold of his hand. Nick gently squeezed her fingers. 'I might never be ready.'

They'd intended to stay in Sydney for one more night. But for Del, the Emerald City no longer held its old allure. She felt suffocated by the anonymous throng of people and the relentless roar of traffic. She longed to see birds other than pigeons, starlings and mynahs. And she pitied the poor street trees in their individual concrete collars, isolated from their companions.

In these last few months Darby had taught her about forests. About how the trees shared nutrients through their roots, forming a complex support system known as the 'wood wide web'. Del had researched the concept and found it had a solid scientific basis. Trees communicated via a vast network of latticed fungi buried in the soil – in other words, they talked to each other.

When Del was a child, her grandmother used to read her *The Magic Faraway Tree* books by Enid Blyton. The stories took place in an enchanted wood where a magical tree grew – a tree so tall that its topmost branches reached the clouds. Del had always loved hearing about how the trees of the enchanted wood whispered to each other. She had no idea that it was true for trees in real life, too. But not for these city trees. They had no one to talk to. They must feel as sad and lonely as Bobby had felt for all those years trapped at the Priory.

Del closed her eyes and imagined she was back in Cobbee Basin – back by the river where she and Darby had scattered Dad's ashes. The vibrant forest, redolent with wild mint and eucalyptus, alive with kingfishers. Fallen logs clothed with moss. Orchids and ferns bursting high on branches and treetops ringing with birdsong. Paradise on earth. A sudden longing for Kingfisher Farm overwhelmed her.

'Nick,' she said. 'Take me home.'

CHAPTER 49

Del unloaded the box of streamers from her car and carried it into the Berrimilla Hall.

Darby sang out from the hall's kitchen. 'Give those to Ken, will you? And ask Nick to load the champers into these ice boxes.' She beamed at Del from the doorway. 'Can you believe he's donated two cases of French champagne for tonight?'

'What can I say,' laughed Del. 'He's a generous guy.'

It had been two weeks since she and Nick had returned from Sydney. Tonight's party would celebrate the victory of the Progress Association's mission to stop the mine. For such an emotional and hard-fought campaign, success had been ridiculously simple.

Bobby had swiftly stepped up to his rightful role as head of Westcorp, and then just as swiftly stepped back down again. He'd called an emergency board meeting, giving an emotional address about what had happened to him over the past twenty years. It brought a room full of hard-headed mining executives to tears. Then he made an impassioned speech in praise of Nick and the fine work he'd accomplished for Westcorp. Nick was unanimously voted CEO, while Bobby maintained his own connection as a silent corporate partner.

'I never wanted the damn company in the first place,' he'd told

Nick after the meeting. 'You run it. Just let me explore some pet projects.'

'What sort of projects?'

'I had plenty of time on my hands during those years at the Priory. Towards the end, I even had limited access to the internet. Wasn't that a revelation? A one-way street for me, of course – no way to communicate with anybody. But I could research to my heart's content, and the nurses ordered any book or journal I wanted.' He chuckled. 'They had to give me a whole extra room for my library. Anyway, as far as I can see, fossil fuels are on the way out. Westcorp needs to diversify.'

'So?'

'So – two words. Geothermal energy. The earth's crust is made of stone and water, and a layer of molten rock below called magma. It's a limitless source of energy that can be converted into reliable, pollution-free electricity. You can drill deep wells and magma heats the water, which turns into steam. The steam spins a turbine to make electricity for the grid. We can even repurpose obsolete coal-fired power plants to do it.'

'I've read about geothermal energy,' said Nick. 'Doesn't ultra-deep drilling have its challenges? The intense heat melts the equipment.'

'True,' Bobby said. 'But combining conventional drilling with gyrotron-powered millimetre-waves solves the problem. MIT is already experimenting with the technology. I want Westcorp to get in on the ground floor.'

'I have no idea what you just said,' laughed Nick.

Bobby grinned, his handsome face lighting up with excitement. 'I won't bend your ear any further. Just leave me to pursue my research, and I'll leave you to run Westcorp. Deal?'

'Deal.' And they'd shaken hands.

Today, Nick had officially cancelled the Mount Morton Optimisation Project, and the whole of Berrimilla was gathering to celebrate their victory.

Del looked out the window. Two cars were arriving, filled with more helpers. Nick came in the double doors with a case of Moët & Chandon.

'Mum says to put those in the kitchen.'

'Yes, ma'am. There's more booze in my car, along with some soft drinks and orange juice. But after that's stowed away, I want to talk to you.'

Nick beckoned her outside.

'This better not take long.' Del checked her phone. 'It's already four o'clock. The party starts in three hours.'

Another truck full of people arrived, cheering and dangling balloons out the window.

'We have more than enough helpers,' said Nick, guiding her to his car and opening the passenger door for her. 'And this is important.' Tiny chased after them. 'Okay,' said Nick with a grin. 'You can come too.'

'Where are we going?' asked Del as Nick started the car.

'On a picnic.'

'A picnic? Hundreds of people will be descending on the hall in a few hours' time, and you decide it's time for a picnic?'

'That's right.'

They turned down Rakali Road. Nick parked by the twin-trunked sassafras tree that marked the track down to the Kingfisher cascades. Del had taken Nick fishing there one glorious sun-drenched afternoon last week. He'd promised that they'd come back. Del hadn't expected that it would be quite so soon.

Nick grabbed the picnic things and they followed the narrow path through the forest, with Tiny bounding on ahead. They skirted the ancient black booyong with its tangle of buttressed roots and towering canopy. Del could have sworn she heard the trees whispering to each other.

They emerged onto the riverbank where the four waterfalls cascaded from the cliff face as they'd always done. It was a comfort that this corner of the river looked the same as it had when she was little. It represented a link to her past. And as Del watched Nick spread the picnic blanket under a tree, she wondered if it might also be a link to her future.

'Sit,' he said. Tiny responded enthusiastically to the invitation, depositing his bony rump on the rug. 'Not you,' laughed Nick.

Del pushed the dog away and sat down. A kingfisher flashed past like a flying jewel, and Del gave a small cry of delight. 'This is lovely, Nick,' she sighed, 'although for once your timing's a little off. They'll be waiting for us back at the hall.'

'Who cares?' He pulled a bottle of champagne from the esky and poured them both a glass.

'What are we celebrating this time?' asked Del. 'And what's that piece of paper wrapped round the bottle?'

'You mean this?' Nick unfastened the document and handed it over.

Del's hand flew to her mouth as she read it, and a soft cry sounded in the back of her throat. 'Does this mean what I think it means?'

'It does,' said Nick, solemnly. 'Cobbee Basin is safe forever. Bobby began the process of having the area gazetted as a national park.'

Del stared at him in disbelief. Cobbee Basin protected in perpetuity. This was what she'd dreamed of. Goosebumps rose along the back of her neck. How she loved – would always love – this man.

'I'll never be able to thank you enough for all you've done,' she managed, stumbling over her words.

'I can think of a way.' Nick leant across and pressed his lips against hers, gently covering her mouth with his own. The kiss sang through her veins, and for a delicious moment the world went away. She wished they could stay like that forever.

When they finally parted, Nick's eyes held hers. 'Tell me, sweetheart. Are we good?'

'Yes,' whispered Del, in a daze. 'We're so much more than good.'

They clinked glasses and Del took a sip. 'Ever since I met you again, I seem to do nothing but drink champagne.'

'Are you complaining?'

Del grinned. 'Now, what else do you have in that esky?'

He offered a Tupperware container with a flourish. 'Your favourite, madame. Lobster salad.'

Del shook her head in bemusement. 'When did you get the chance to make this?'

Nick had been staying in the spare room at Kingfisher Farm since they returned from Sydney. He must have sneaked out to the kitchen in the middle of the night.

When they finished the salad, Nick took out a container of mascarpone cream and chocolate-dipped strawberries. And what was that? The sweet music of Beethoven's Moonlight Sonata sounded over the river.

'Wait a minute,' said Del, mouth full of strawberry. 'This is beginning to seem awfully familiar.'

'Hello, what's this?' Nick raised his eyebrows in mock surprise as he lifted a translucent crystal tulip from the picnic basket and presented it to her. 'For you.'

Del looked inside. Her engagement ring nestled within the flower's azure heart. The beautiful ring that she'd been so proud to wear just a few short months ago. Months? More like a lifetime.

'After that hit on the head, it took me a while to remember the first time. This is take two.' Nick's face shone with love. He'd never looked more handsome. 'Will you marry me?'

Del plucked the ring from its nest of crystal petals and slipped it back onto her finger with a satisfied sigh. Back where it belonged.

'Will I marry you?' she said. 'Try and stop me.' Del reached over to pull him close.

Time seemed to stand still. Slowly, they undressed each other, almost shyly exploring their bodies, which were so familiar, and yet somehow strange. Del drank in Nick's smell – the faint musk of his body, the scent of his aftershave. And the world disappeared again. She forgot everything but the warm tingle of feeling that flowed from his fingers.

Nick kissed the pulsing hollow of her throat. He tasted her lips and throat and breasts as if he'd never tasted them before. He stroked the tender skin of her inner thigh until she gasped with pleasure. Her arms, draped around his neck, tugged him closer. She felt the strength of his shoulders under her palms, the strength of his back and the wild thudding of his heart. Del felt his eager erection, and desire left her dizzy. She urged him home.

'Not so fast,' he whispered, nibbling her ear. 'Let's make out some more.'

'Make out?' She smiled. 'What are we – kids?'

'Maybe. Because being here with you right now? I'm reborn.' His mouth captured hers before she could speak. The kiss carried her away, making her giddy with a new kind of wanting. And she suddenly knew why he'd waited. He needed her to truly understand that he'd changed – that he wasn't that same person. Well, neither was she. And they made love through that long afternoon with all the wonder and passion of lovers discovering each other for the very first time.

CHAPTER 50

S hadows were lengthening by the time Nick and Del arrived back at the Berrimilla Hall. Their monumental reconnection had left them both smiling. It seemed to Del that they'd shed the burden of these last few months, and could go lightly into their future with a fresh vision. The cloudless December day was melding into a perfect mountain evening; it was warm but not too warm, with the hint of a breeze.

A familiar car pulled up beside them. 'It's Kim and Taj,' Del told Nick excitedly. 'I can't wait for you to meet them.'

Kim's husband, Taj, was a tall man with penetrating, coffee-coloured eyes and a dark complexion. He had a swathe of jet hair falling over his forehead and a scar running down one cheek. He looked a little wild.

'Taj came to Australia as an Afghan refugee,' said Del. 'Now he's one of the country's foremost experts on dingoes.'

Del and Kim were talking nineteen to the dozen as the four of them went inside. The party had already started. Trellis tables groaned with platters of sandwiches, sausage rolls and party pies. Paper plates held a profusion of homemade slices, rum balls and other sweet treats. Children ran around with balloons and streamers, stuffing their faces with lollies. Someone had brought along a huge rectangular cake with *Victory to Berrimilla* piped across its iced surface.

Ken and Darby were holding court in one corner, with folk lined up to toast them. When Del and Nick came in, people turned to cheer. This was a far cry from the reception she was used to back at Winga, where half the community viewed her with suspicion or outright hostility. It filled Del with a warm glow.

Her mother rushed over. 'Where have you two been?' she chided.

Del held out her hand and spread her fingers, just as she'd done on that fateful morning back at the *Gazette* office. The ring, with its brilliant central diamond and halo of bead-set sapphires, exploded with light just as it had done before. But this time she wasn't shunned and ignored.

'Oh my God!' screamed Darby. 'Is that what I think it is?'

People crowded around, admiring the magnificent antique band and congratulating Del and Nick on their engagement. For Nick was no longer the villain of the piece. He was the hero.

Two men began clearing the middle of the hall, as Ken took to the small stage. 'I'm Ken,' he said, 'and I'll be your DJ for tonight.'

Applause and raised glasses. It seemed that tonight people were ready to applaud anything.

'We have a double celebration on our hands. You all know that, thanks to our mate Nick here,' he pointed to Nick, who was standing by the door with Del, helping himself to a second vanilla slice, 'Westcorp has cancelled its planned mine expansion into Kingfisher Valley. But on top of that, we have some more fantastic news. This afternoon Nick Shaw and our very own Del Fisher got engaged.'

This provoked the biggest reaction of all. People clapped and hooted and cheered. They crowded around to admire the ring and congratulate the happy couple. The amount of love in the room overwhelmed Del, and she burst into happy tears. Taj brought her a chair. April, from the post office, brought her tissues. Ken offered her a glass of water, and Pam, the vet, made her a cup of coffee. People were falling over each other to help. It had always been like that in Berrimilla, for as long as she could remember.

Del thought about Sydney, a place where she'd once longed to live. Sure, you could see a fabulous show every night or shop until you dropped. You could work with a view of the Opera House or eat delicious food in five-star restaurants. But its hurrying citizens didn't look at each other on the street. They averted their eyes and rarely knew their neighbours. In a city with a population of five million, people died of loneliness.

'Now, I have a treat for you all,' said Ken. 'I've curated a playlist of personal favourites for your listening pleasure.' Some laughter, along with plenty of groans. 'So, let's kick the night off with Luke Combs and "Beer Never Broke My Heart".'

An upbeat country song blared from portable speakers on either side of the stage and people began to dance. Nick grabbed Del's hand. 'Let's go, sweetheart.' He pulled her to the floor and spun her round until she was breathless. And so they danced into the night, giddy with happiness and hope.

Next morning, Del and Nick lay in late, loath to leave the shelter of each other's arms. They made love, bodies moving together so closely that it was impossible for Del to tell where her skin started, and Nick's stopped.

A knock came at the door. 'Wake up, sleepyheads. Breakfast's ready.'

Darby always cooked a big breakfast, but today she'd pulled out all the stops. There were hardly enough burners on the stove to juggle the pans: eggs, mushrooms and spinach, bacon and sausages. Ken was cooking thick tomato slices under the grill and toasting bread.

It was a full house at Kingfisher Farm that morning. Kim and Taj had also stayed overnight. Del couldn't wait to fill Kim in on everything that had happened since her last visit.

For a while nobody talked. They were busy with the serious business of eating. Everyone had drunk too much the night before and were famished. The hearty meal was going a long way to revive them.

When they were full, Del took Kim down to see the Maremma puppies. She'd housed them with half a dozen of her quietest ewes.

'Mum sold her crossbred Merinos to raise money for the shearing-shed roof,' said Del. 'The only sheep at Kingfisher Farm from now on will be heritage Babydoll Southdowns. So no more lamb for every meal, thank heavens. Babydolls are far too valuable to put in the freezer, even the wethers.'

'They're beautiful,' said Kim, while she fed them handfuls of oats.

Kimba and King, the male pup, were playing hide-and-seek, wriggling beneath the bellies of the sheep, then pouncing out at each other. The ewes seemed entirely unfussed by their antics. The pups interrupted their game to greet their visitors, all wagging tails, bright eyes and licking tongues. King touched noses with Tiny through the wire netting. 'They look great,' said Kim. 'Is your mum resisting the urge to bring them up to the house?'

'Mostly,' laughed Del. 'Although I did need to rescue them from under her bed once. She'd smuggled them inside and they got themselves stuck behind a box of books.' They gave the pups one last pat. 'Come on,' said Del. 'I'll show you the vineyard.'

They walked up the track and sat on the log bench beneath the old blue gum, admiring the low hill of sweeping vines. Cottonwool sheep dotted the emerald strips of grass lying between rows of darker green grapevines. The distant ridges of Yenga National Park rose into a sky of vivid blue, providing the perfect backdrop to the picturesque post-card scene.

Kim took a photo. 'You'll be picking in a month or two, right? Last time we talked you hadn't sold your harvest. Any luck yet with the local wineries?'

'It turns out that won't be a problem,' said Del, looking sheepish. 'Nick's uncle now owns the McClellan Vale Wine Estate. Says he'll give me a good price.'

Kim's eyes widened and she burst out laughing. 'Nothing like having friends in high places. I thought Nick's uncle might have been at the party last night.'

'He's still adjusting to life on the outside.' Del plucked a dandelion stem and rolled it between her fingers. 'Bobby doesn't like crowds.'

'Join the club,' said Kim.

'He's not letting the grass grow, though,' said Del. 'Bobby became a self-taught scientist while he was at the Priory. Sort of like those convicted criminals who emerge from jail with law degrees. It's all the time they have on their hands, I suppose. Anyway, he's heading up the company's research and development division. He has grand plans, our Bobby. Wants to put Westcorp at the forefront of renewable energy technology.'

'Sounds awesome,' said Kim. 'And what about Carson?'

'He didn't get bail. The judge ruled that with his resources he was too much of a flight risk.'

'And Nick?'

Del shrugged. 'Nick won't see him.'

'Who could blame him?' said Kim. 'After everything his father did.'

'I don't know,' mused Del. 'Bobby says it would be good for Nick to see Carson. The pair of them could have an honest conversation for the first time in their lives. Bobby's been visiting him, you know. Says he's forgiven his brother – that it's the only way he can move on with his life.'

Kim shook her head in wonder. 'The man is a saint.'

At midmorning Kim and Taj said goodbye, after first extracting a promise from Del that she and Nick would visit Journey's End soon.

Nobody was hungry when Darby served up a light lunch in the kitchen. And Del had been wrong about the menu. Roast lamb and salad rolls. It seemed that Ken still had some carcasses in his coolroom.

After the meal, Darby called them all to attention by banging a spoon on the china teapot. She touched Ken's shoulder and he stood beside her. 'We have an announcement to make. This will come as a surprise, but Ken and I intend to live together at his farm.' She fixed Del with anxious eyes. 'The decision isn't up for debate.' Ken took hold of her hand. 'I was hoping … ' She glanced at Ken, who gave her an encouraging smile. 'I was hoping that you and Nick might be prepared to stay on here part-time at Kingfisher Farm. I know the house isn't much chop, but—'

'No,' Del said. 'The answer is no.'

Darby's face fell. 'Oh. That's all right, love. Ken and I will find a way to manage.'

'Mum, I meant *no* to part-time. We want to live here full-time.'

Darby looked confused. 'How can you say that without asking Nick first?'

'Because I've already asked him. We were getting ready to talk to you about it, weren't we, Nick?'

'That's right. I've done a great deal of soul-searching lately,' he said, 'and my priorities have changed. I've been groomed, since birth, really, to take over the reins of Westcorp. I always thought it was what I wanted. But it wasn't. It was what my father wanted. So, I'm appointing someone to act for me as CEO in what is effectively a permanent capacity.'

Darby's eyes widened. 'But this is marvellous.'

'There's more,' said Del. 'We're buying back the land next door. Restoring Kingfisher Farm's original boundaries. Those river flats will be perfect for grapes. What do you think, Mum?'

The look of joy on Darby's face said it all.

'The truth is that I've always been interested in winemaking,' said Nick. 'Dad discouraged me. For him, mining was the main game. But I'd like to try something new, something for me this time.'

'Nick wants to put more land under vines and build a proper winery here,' said Del. 'It's so exciting, Mum. That Bluebird Shiraz label that Dad always dreamed of? It's going to happen, along with dozens of other varieties. And they won't simply be made by another winemaker with our grapes. They'll be made right here, Mum – right here at Kingfisher Farm.'

Darby came around the table to embrace Nick. 'Christmas may still be a week away, but it feels like it's already here.'

As twilight fell, Del and Darby sat side by side on the cane porch chairs that Dad had loved. She could feel him here more strongly than ever, and she knew that he approved of what she was ready to say. 'I'm sorry, Mum.'

'What about? Oh, you mean about Ken.' Darby waved her hand in dismissal. 'Don't give it another thought. I always knew you'd come round.'

'No, Mum. I mean about Dad. Blaming you for all these years.'

Although Darby didn't speak, Del could sense the protective shield rising around her.

'I thought that you'd given up fighting for him,' Del said. 'That if not for you, he might still be here.'

'I know, love.' Darby's voice was barely a whisper. 'But you're wrong. When I helped Allan get those drugs, I *was* fighting for him. I'd never fought so hard in my life.'

'Tell me about it. Help me understand.'

Darby heaved a shuddering sigh. 'His kidney transplant failed. Of course, you know that.'

'Go on.'

'What you don't know is that Allan became friends with some of the other transplant candidates during his long dialysis sessions. He was particularly devastated by the death of one woman who didn't get a kidney in time. She was barely forty years old, with a young family. Your father was overcome with guilt when he got his kidney. But that was nothing compared to the guilt he felt when his new kidney failed. Allan was dying. His only chance of recovery was another transplant, and even then, the doctors said the prospect of success was small.

'He was so sick, Del. You saw him. Sick and weary and suffering. He didn't want to take a kidney from someone who might have a better chance. I couldn't make him. So, when he asked me to help him get the drugs to end his life, I had two choices. I could break his heart and watch him suffer against his will: the bone aches, the constant nausea and vomiting, the agonising cramps and rashes and grossly swollen legs. The incontinence. He couldn't sleep or eat. There was no respite for him, no hope.'

Darby was sobbing softly now, her head bent in her hands.

'Or I could help him die with dignity, like he wanted,' she managed through her tears. 'And I'd do the same thing again, even if it meant losing you.'

Del was weeping too, now. She knelt before her mother's chair and laid her head on her lap, letting Darby stroke her hair like when she was little. She'd been holding on to Dad for selfish reasons. Until that very moment, she hadn't truly seen things from his point of view. And she knew in a heartbeat that if she'd been in Dad's position, she'd have wanted an easier death too.

'Will you forgive me, Mum?'

'Shush, my darling. There's nothing to forgive. I'm just blessed to have you back.'

Nick and Ken emerged from the house with beers in hand. They stopped short when they saw the weeping women clinging together.

'Funny way to celebrate,' said Ken, scratching his head.

That night Darby went home with Ken. The moon rode high in the star-spangled sky when Del walked with Nick to the vineyard. Tiny and the collies trotted at their heels. They sat on the log bench and breathed in the fresh scent of earth and grapes and eucalyptus.

'It wouldn't have worked the first time we tried this,' said Nick. 'Not with me under my father's thumb and you off in Sydney chasing headlines. What were we thinking?'

'What were we thinking?' she echoed.

Del closed her eyes and relaxed into Nick's arms. This was, without doubt, the happiest moment she'd ever known. A bright future lay ahead of them, a future filled with joy and love. Life didn't get any better than this.

ACKNOWLEDGEMENTS

Many thanks go to the team at Pilyara Press. They have given me endless encouragement in my writing. I'm grateful to my proof-readers Desney King and Heather Sherwell for their eagle-eyed reading.

Thanks go to my agent, Clare Forster, and also to Benjamin Paz – both of the Curtis Brown literary agency. They have provided invaluable help towards furthering my career. I'm also eternally grateful to dear friend and fellow author Kathryn Ledson, who read the first draft for me and offered such stellar editorial suggestions.

Appreciation goes to the Bulga-Milbrodale Progress Association whose courageous battle to protect their town inspired this story. Thanks go to Jennie Curtis of Babydoll Sheep Breeders Australia who, by mentoring me in my own Babydoll sheep breeding journey, has indirectly assisted in the writing of *Paradise Valley*.

I'm grateful to my family for their loving support and to my writing friends for their companionship and encouragement. And finally, deepest thanks go to my generous and enthusiastic readers who have supported me throughout my writing journey and made the publishing of *Paradise Valley*, my eleventh novel, possible.

ABOUT THE AUTHOR

Bestselling Aussie author Jennifer Scoullar writes page-turning fiction about the land, people and wildlife that she loves.

Scoullar is a lapsed lawyer who harbours a deep appreciation and respect for the natural world. She lives on a farm in Australia's southern Victorian ranges, and has ridden and bred horses all her life. Her passion for animals and the bush is the catalyst for her bestselling books.

If you enjoyed this book and have a moment or two, please leave a rating or review. Reviews are of great help to authors.

www.jenniferscoullar.com